Also by Terry Spear

WOLF
ON THE
WILD SIDE

TERRY
SPEAR

sourcebooks
casablanca

Published by Sourcebooks Casablanca, an imprint of Sourcebooks
P.O. Box 4410, Naperville, Illinois 60567-4410
(630) 961-3900
sourcebooks.com

Printed and bound in the United States of America.
OPM 10 9 8 7 6 5 4 3 2 1

Dedicated to Thomas Richardson, who has such a fun sense of humor and always gives me a smile while he shares who the alpha of his fur babies is. Hint—it's not Tom. Thanks for brightening my day with your entertaining comments and for loving my books and my bears!

Chapter 1

EARLY THAT SUMMER MORNING BEFORE HEAD-ing into work, Kayla Wolff and her quadruplet sister, Roxie, were running as gray wolves on their wooded acreage, not expecting any trouble. Except for a cougar they had to chase off once and a black bear another time, they usually didn't have any wildlife difficulties. They'd had to sic Sheriff Peter Jorgenson on hunters last fall though.

Kayla was excited about getting together for dinner tonight with Nate Grayson, the only wolf she'd dated since moving to Silver Town, Colorado, a wolf-run town. Nate's sister, Nicole, had actually mated their brother Blake.

Kayla loved it here, and she was planning to mate Nate on the Fourth of July in a little over two weeks if he didn't ask her beforehand.

Along with their two brothers, she and Roxie owned and managed the Timberline Ski Lodge nearby. She had been busy serving as the catering manager for a wedding yesterday, so she was glad to get back to working on promotional stuff today.

As wolves, she and Roxie had been playing with each other when they heard the sound of two men speaking on their property. Other wolves in the pack were welcome to run here anytime, but the others usually ran in the pack territory. And their brother Landon had property with his mate, Gabrielle, around her veterinary clinic, so they often ran as wolves there rather than at the lodge.

Kayla didn't recognize the men's voices. She and Roxie drew nearer, circling around and keeping low so the men wouldn't see them, trying to get a whiff of the men's scents before they alerted the sheriff that they had human trespassers. They could be just wolf guests from somewhere else, and Kayla and Roxie certainly didn't want to alienate wolf visitors to the area. Unless they were causing trouble.

The hot summer breeze kept shifting, and they had to keep circling when they normally would avoid humans at all costs. Though Kayla did have the notion of just chasing them off as wolves. That was definitely her wilder wolf side coming to play.

She listened to the men's conversation in the meantime, and finally, a black-haired man with a curly beard and reddish sideburns came into view. He was a stocky figure wearing a T-shirt that stretched tautly over muscled arms and chest, jeans tight on bulky thighs, a black cap shadowing his features, mirrored glasses, and hiking boots. It was early morning and there was no need to wear sunglasses at this time. The woods were shaded and dark and the sun still just dawning. The other man was tall, not as muscled, with short blond hair; he looked about the same age as the bulky guy—mid-to-late twenties—and was wearing a blue-jean ball cap, a gray T-shirt, jeans, sneakers, and polarized aviator sunglasses.

"I told you. With your experience, it's a piece of cake. He'll pay us good money to do it," the blond guy said. "His uncle is good for his word."

"You're sure you can trust the others?" The muscled guy sounded dubious.

"Hell, yeah. We grew up together. We're all friends. They're eager to do it and to follow your lead since you're experienced at this kind of thing. It's copacetic."

"It better be. You know what happened the last time."

"Yeah, and you didn't know those guys. This time it'll be different."

"I'll talk it over with his nephew first."

The blond guy didn't say anything more, but he looked annoyed, his mouth pursed, as if he expected the bulky guy to go along with the program based on his words. "Yeah, sounds like a good idea," he finally said, as if he had no choice in the matter.

Roxie was on the move again, trying to get closer. Kayla wanted to woof at her sister to stay with her. She didn't want them to move any closer to the men, afraid that if the two of them did, the men might spy them more easily. Sure, she and

Roxie hadn't been able to smell them to see if they were human, but she was all for circling them further. If they were wolves, no problem, unless they were up to mischief. But humans? They could be unpredictable.

"All right, but it better work out." The muscled guy turned around and saw Roxie.

For a moment, everyone froze. Kayla ran at the men to give Roxie time to move, then turned quickly and bolted out of there, hoping her sister was gaining on her and the men were running in the opposite direction and not planning to shoot them if they were armed with guns. Kayla heard movement in the woods behind her and glanced over her shoulder to see Roxie catching up to her, her eyes filled with excitement.

Relieved it was just her sister and there was no sign of the men, Kayla thought she could use less excitement in her life. When she had to serve as a wedding caterer and deal with a bridezilla like she'd had to a couple of weeks ago, that was enough of a "thrill" for her. She and Roxie both managed the brides, but Roxie could get growly with an unreasonable one, so Kayla often just took care of them to avoid problems.

Roxie nipped at her in fun. Kayla nipped back at her, glad everything had turned out fine. Though she was going to lecture her when they returned to their home next to the lodge. She was glad their sister-in-law Nicole hadn't been with them because she was pregnant. She and their brother Blake would run with Roxie and Kayla most mornings, but Nicole had been under the weather with morning sickness of late.

After Kayla and Roxie reached the house and ran in through the wolf door, squeezing in at the same time—their usual routine—they raced up the stairs to their respective bedrooms to shift and dress for work.

Once Kayla had shifted, she called out to her sister, "You shouldn't have gotten so close to the men!"

"You shouldn't have tried to grab their attention so I could get away."

"What if they'd been armed?" Kayla pulled on her panties.

"They weren't. They didn't have anywhere to hide a gun, holster, nothing."

Kayla sighed, glad to learn that. She had really worried about it. She fastened her bra. "All right, but you shouldn't have gotten so close. I was going to circle around them further to catch the breeze headed in a different direction. So did you smell their scents?"

"Human. But since they seemed to be there having a private meeting and then saw a couple of wolves, I figure they won't be hanging around, so no sense in calling Peter to try to locate them and fine them for trespassing."

"Okay." Kayla buttoned up her blouse.

"Hey, you've got to admit that was an interesting aside to our normal morning jaunt through the woods."

"Yeah." Kayla laughed. "It was memorable, all right. But don't tell our brothers. If we do, they'll leave their pregnant wives home to run with us to ensure we stay safe. Even if the guys wanted to stay home with them to make sure they were fine, Nicole and Gabrielle would make them go with us." She finished dressing.

"Absolutely. Mum's the word."

Kayla wondered how long that would last! Within a pack and with them working so closely with their brothers at the lodge, she suspected the word would get out one way or another.

Eager to take Kayla Wolff for a night out on the town in Green Valley, Colorado, Nate Grayson drove to her and her sister Roxie's house next to the Timberline Ski Lodge. He and Kayla liked to get out of Silver Town on a date on occasion when they both could manage. His private investigator cases had stacked up, and she had been so busy with marketing strategies for her family-run ski lodge and restaurant, not to mention handling several catering venues for different celebrations—weddings, birthdays, anniversaries, retirements, you name it—that they often couldn't get away.

As soon as she came to the front door of her home, Kayla was all smiles, wearing a red dress and high heels, the fragrance of peaches and cream enveloping her. "Hey, you look lovely," Nate said, hugging and kissing her, and she hugged and kissed him right back. He enjoyed having her scent on him, claiming him as he was claiming her. Once he'd met her, he'd never been interested in anyone else.

"You look pretty dapper yourself. I'm glad we could both get away for this." Kayla looked just as eager to enjoy the night with him.

He'd dressed up for the occasion too, though a jacket and tie were required for the restaurant. It was a warm June night as he walked her to his car. "Yeah, me too. Even though we know some of the wolves of the Green Valley wolf pack and they know us, there aren't as many of them living there, and they don't run the whole town. *Everyone* knows us in Silver Town."

She laughed. "Are you afraid to be seen out with me too much?"

He smiled. "Not me." He was more concerned that *Kayla* wanted more anonymity because she tended to be shy about things like this. But he was eager to show she was all his and no other wolf better think she was available.

When they finally arrived at the Great Gatsby

restaurant in Green Valley, it was still light out at seven in the evening. The restaurant was all lit up, and it really set the stage for a nice romantic dinner. Nate parked and walked Kayla inside, and they were seated at their reserved table right away. A gold-and-black theme ran throughout the restaurant: gold chandeliers, black tablecloths, black-and-gold wallpaper, and gold candles on each of the tables. The women on the waitstaff were wearing gold flapper-era fringe dresses, and the men were dressed in black-and-white-striped double-breasted jackets and trousers.

"This is so nice. Thanks for taking me here. I've never been here, and it's really a lovely restaurant, great atmosphere. Everything's so elegant," Kayla said.

"It is. I wanted to make this extra special tonight since we haven't been able to get together lately what with your work and mine. And we're always having meals at your house or mine, so I wanted to do something different. I haven't been here either, and I was waiting to take you here. I'm sure glad to be here with you."

"Oh, me too with you."

One of the waitresses jiggled the gold fringe on her dress at Nate when she came over to take their orders, and he smiled, amused. "And what would you like to have for dinner?" she asked Nate first, as if she was coming on to him, but he figured it was part of the Great Gatsby show.

Kayla and Nate ordered T-bone steaks, mashed potatoes, slivered carrots, and glasses of merlot.

"Are you celebrating anything special?" the waitress asked.

Nate said, "Just being in love."

"Aww, now that's special."

Kayla blushed. Nate reached over and took her hand and squeezed. They'd been seeing each other since they'd both moved here a year and a half ago, which was a long time for *lupus garous* to date before they decided on mating. He just felt she hadn't been ready for it yet. But he sure was. Everything about her made him want to be with her day and night.

One of the men served them their glasses of wine and made sure to show Kayla extra-special attention. She was blushing furiously, and when the wine steward left their table, she smiled at Nate. "You were looking a little growly."

"I knew it was just an act, but, uh, yeah, I might have not hidden my growly side enough." He smiled. He had to admit he had been feeling a little growly despite his best intention of seeing it as it was.

"That's okay." Kayla clinked her wine glass against his. "If that flapper had wiggled her dress fringe at you one more time, she would have heard *me* growl."

Nate laughed. He just couldn't see Kayla doing that.

Kayla licked the wine off her lips, and he wanted

to groan at the sight. He needed to spend more intimate time with her. He wanted to get on one knee, pull her onto his lap, kiss her, and ask her to mate him. But he was determined to stick to his plan to do it at the cabin he'd reserved for her birthday in eight days. He and his sister and parents were planning a surprise birthday bash at the lodge for the quadruplets the night before, though Kayla was actually born after midnight on the following day. They'd celebrate her birthday the next day too, according to Roxie.

Then their meals were finally served.

Kayla cut into her medium-rare steak, took a bite, and practically purred.

He smiled. "Good, huh?" He took another bite of his. Man, the food was the greatest. He couldn't have planned this outing any better.

"Yeah, this is delicious." She reached over and squeezed his hand. "Thanks for bringing me here for such a special night."

"I'm having the best time too."

They enjoyed the music playing in the background, drinking their wine, eating their dinners, and pausing to kiss each other—which felt so right.

"This was truly delightful," Kayla said, finishing up her dinner.

"Being with you, it sure has been." He was so glad they had been able to get away for the evening. He finished eating the last of his steak and paid the bill.

"Do you want to come home with me tonight?" he asked.

She sighed.

He knew that was a no. He sighed. She smiled, and they stood up, clasping hands. She kissed him before they left the restaurant, then they headed out.

"I don't want to be with anyone else, you know," she said. "I just have so much on my plate. I'm in charge of a wedding reception coming up and also a fiftieth wedding anniversary party for a couple."

"Yeah. I know." Which was why he wanted to propose to her right after her birthday celebration at the cabin, as long as she'd come with him there. They would have an uninterrupted week of fun. He wanted to mate her and be with her every night, no matter how busy their days were. He wanted to be there with her, for her so she could tell him all about her rough day and he'd help her to chill out, just as he knew she would be there for him during rough times.

"You are the best thing that ever happened to me, Nate. Truly. Don't give up on me."

"There's no chance of that, honey." He kissed her and then hugged her close. "Being with you has been life-changing."

"For me too. We'll be there soon for sure."

"We will be."

They left the restaurant, ready to head home. He removed his jacket and was putting it in the back seat when he heard gunfire down the street and breaking glass. What the hell?

He grabbed Kayla and got down between the cars for protection, holding her tight.

"Gunfire," she whispered as if whoever was shooting might hear her words and would come for them next if she didn't speak quietly.

"Yeah, at a business a couple of blocks down the street." As a retired Army Ranger, he knew just what gunfire sounded like. And of course with their wolf's hearing, he could place where it was coming from. "Come on, let's go. I want to get you out of here." He didn't hear anyone headed their way that could be trouble. He got her car door, and she climbed in, and he shut the door. Then he hurried to climb into the car, started the engine, and pulled out of the parking lot and onto the street.

"I bet you want to check it out, being a private investigator." Kayla glanced behind her.

"No. I don't want to run into someone who's shooting up a store. And certainly not when I worry about your safety."

They were just getting ready to turn onto the highway that would take them back to Silver Town when he saw a black pickup truck racing up behind them like it was going to run right over them. Nate didn't have anywhere to pull off, and he wasn't about to tear off at reckless speeds through town to avoid getting rear-ended.

A car was approaching them from the opposite direction, and that's when the jerk behind him tried to pass them.

"What's wrong with him?" Kayla asked, seeing the truck approaching in the sideview mirror. "He's passing."

"Yeah. I don't have anywhere to go, and he's not going to make it before the other car gets here." Nate slowed way down so the truck could safely pass them.

The racing truck pulled around them, but he wasn't going to have enough time to pass them before colliding with the oncoming vehicle. The truck was going, hell or high water. Nate slammed on his brakes. To avoid being rear-ended, he hadn't done that earlier, but now he was trying to give the pickup time to get around them.

As if the driver was experiencing road rage, the truck cut Nate off, nearly hitting his front bumper. Nate swerved to avoid getting hit, and his tire struck the curb so hard it exploded. Instinctively, he threw his arm across Kayla to protect her from hitting the dash, even though she was seat-belted in and the seat belt caught her.

"Ohmigod!" she cried out, sounding a little rattled.

The oncoming car managed to move over enough that he avoided getting struck by the racing truck, thank God. The truck continued on its way, tearing down the road.

"Our tire just blew. No one was shooting at us." Which had concerned him at first when he heard the tire blow. He turned off the engine and pulled her into a hug. "Are you okay?" He'd worried more than anything about Kayla getting hurt if the truck bashed into them.

"Yeah, you?" Kayla embraced him hard.

"Yeah. I've got to change the tire. Be back in a minute and we'll get on our way."

"Bastards," Kayla said, getting out of the car at the same time he did.

He unbuttoned his shirt, and she smiled appreciatively as he bared his chest. He smiled and flexed his muscles a little. He shouldn't have, considering the situation they were in, but she chuckled, and it seemed to lighten the mood.

He opened his trunk and pulled out his spare tire and moved it around to the side of the car. Before he could grab the car's jack, she brought it out for him.

"Thanks, but you really didn't have to do that. I don't want you to get dirty." He appreciated her help. He wasn't so macho that he didn't want her assistance, but he didn't want her to get any grease on her pretty dress.

"That's okay. I'm being careful, and I'm used to changing a tire when I need to."

As soon as he removed the lug nuts, she held on to them for him. Once he had changed out the tire, she handed him the lug nuts. "I should have gotten their license plate number for reckless—" she said but abruptly stopped speaking when two police cars tore down the road past them, blue lights flashing, heading in the direction of the initial gunfire and shattered glass.

They both turned to look at the police cars.

"Too bad they weren't after the guys speeding down the road," Kayla said.

Which made Nate wonder… "You don't mind if we go the way the police cars went and see what's going on, do you?"

"Always the PI."

"Yeah, sorry. I wouldn't have done it when the gunshots were going off." He sighed. "This is our special date. I really shouldn't have mentioned it." He put the jack back in the car, closed the trunk, and pulled a bottle of hand sanitizer out of his console. He gave it to Kayla first so she could clean her hands. Then he washed his and pulled on his shirt.

Kayla began buttoning it for him. "No, I really want to know what's going on too. Ending a date on an investigative errand works for me."

"Are you sure?" He was dying to learn what was going on, particularly if the truck that had forced them off the road had been involved in a crime—a hit-and-run or something. He wanted to report it to the police. But he didn't want it to take away from their date. Still, when they had first met,

Kayla was eager to help him solve a situation of theft at her lodge, so he knew she had an interest in investigations.

She finished buttoning the top buttons on his shirt while he buttoned the lower ones. "Yeah, you know me. I would think about it the rest of the night otherwise, imagining all kinds of different scenarios."

"All right. I feel the same way." He tucked in his shirt, and they returned to the car. Then he drove off in the direction the police cars had gone.

When they reached where the police cars were parked at a jewelry store, the lights from police cars were flashing all over the place. Some people standing there seemed curious about what was going on, and the whole place was being taped off as a crime scene. Store window glass was broken all over the sidewalk so a couple of policemen kept onlookers from going past the crime scene tape.

"A jewelry store robbery," Kayla said.

"Yeah. What if the truck that ran us off the road was involved in the robbery, and that's why they were racing down the road, trying to get away? That would explain why they risked everyone's lives to pass us."

"That makes sense. Now I really wish we had their license plate number. At least we know it was a black pickup," she said.

"Exactly. It was a double-wide cab, Chevy Silverado."

"You know your vehicles."

"Yeah. It's a hazard of the work I do. Now if only we knew their license plate number, the police could nail them." He parked near the store. It was closed for the night, but someone had turned the lights on inside to conduct their investigation.

He and Kayla both got out of the car and approached the officers protecting the crime scene. "I'm Nate Grayson, a PI out of Silver Town. Could we speak with the detective in charge of the investigation?"

"Is it something that's important to the case of robbery?" the officer asked.

"Possibly. We were run off the road by a black pickup that was racing away from the direction of the jewelry store. The truck forced my car up onto the curb, and I blew a tire. They possibly could have been involved in the robbery and that was why they were in such a hurry to get away. I want to give the detective a description of the truck in case it was involved in the robbery," Nate said.

"I'll go get the detective," one of the officers said, and hurried into the store.

Nate wrapped his arm around Kayla's shoulder and leaned down and kissed her. "Sorry. I shouldn't have dragged you into this."

"Don't be." She wrapped her arm around his waist and hugged him, reassuring him she was fine with all this. "This is exciting, and the best thing is that if they do find the truck and learn the driver was involved, we helped to catch him, especially after he ruined your tire. If they were involved, they were the ones who dragged us into this. And you know if it does pertain to the case, we both would have wished we had done our civic duty and said something to the police about it. I don't see any ambulances, so it appears no one was injured, but what if the next time these guys do it, someone is hurt or killed? If they get away with this one, they most likely won't stop doing it."

"Exactly. It could escalate into something much worse. And this might not have been the first time they committed a robbery either."

The detective came out, and Nate explained what had happened to them. "I don't know if it's related to the robbery, but the fact that the truck forced me off the road and they were coming from the direction of the robbery makes it possible that they were involved."

"Thank you for the information. You…didn't happen to see the license plate number, did you?" Detective Houston asked.

"No, sorry. I saw two men were in the front seat of the truck. The truck had darkly tinted windows, so I couldn't make out their faces." Nate had only been able to make that much out because of his wolf's night vision, and the streetlights helped too.

"Could there have been more than that?"

"Yes," Kayla said. "I think I saw two or three men in the back seat when they sailed on past. Nate was busy trying to control the car when they practically hit us."

"Okay, thanks. That's a big help."

Nate gave the detective his PI business card, and the detective handed him his card.

"If I have any questions, I'll be in touch," the detective said.

Afterward, Kayla and Nate walked back to his car, and they drove to Silver Town.

"Dinner was delightful. We'll have to get together again as soon as we can," Nate said, hoping it would be really soon. Even though he wanted to be with her tonight, he was working like crazy every spare minute he had on finishing up a hope chest for Kayla for her birthday. He hoped she would love it. He was almost done hand-carving a wolf on the front of it. But he knew Kayla had to work on the final promotional touches for the Fourth of July celebration. And he had cases to work on too.

Then he got a call on Bluetooth from his sister, Nicole, his partner at the PI agency. "Hey, I just wanted to remind you I won't be in to the office early."

"Uh, yeah, you're going for your prenatal checkup. I remembered. But probably when you don't show up at the office in the morning, I'll wonder where you are." Nate smiled at Kayla.

Nicole did the same thing to him if he had something he had to do and she'd forget why he wasn't at the office, so it wasn't just him.

Nicole laughed.

"I'm just taking Kayla home from a date," he reminded Nicole, hoping she wouldn't say anything about the cabin trip and spoil the surprise for Kayla.

"Oh, hi, Kayla. Sorry for the interruption. I forgot you were on a date with Kayla tonight. Hope you had a great time." Nicole sounded guilty for interrupting them. She was hoping he'd mate Kayla soon.

"We did, thanks, Nicole. We might have witnessed the getaway vehicle that was involved in a jewelry store robbery," Nate said.

"Oh, wow. In Green Valley? Don't tell me that you were investigating a robbery case on your date, Nate," Nicole said, her tone scolding.

Nate knew his sister would learn about it soon enough… No hiding anything from his twin.

"Yes, in Green Valley." Kayla told Nicole what had happened after they had left the restaurant.

"Oh, no. At least they didn't wreck your car, but you need to replace that tire," Nicole said.

"Yeah." He swore Nicole thought she was his second mother.

"Okay, well, I'll let you go and talk to you in the morning," Nicole said. "After my doctor's appointment."

"Good luck with your exam," Kayla said.

"Thanks. I'm ready to have these babies, but they're not due for another few months," Nicole said.

"I hear the same from Gabrielle too," Kayla said.

Nate couldn't believe both Kayla's brothers' mates were due with twins at the same time.

"Night, Nicole," both Kayla and Nate said.

And she wished them a good night.

Nate finally reached Kayla and Roxie's place and walked Kayla to her front door. "I know you're swamped right now, so when you have time, we'll get together again." He really wished they were already together—spending every night with each other.

As wolves, they didn't wear jewelry—too easy to lose if they had to shift—so he couldn't do a traditional human engagement party with a ring or anything. And once they were mated, it was for life, so no having to get married to make them partners forever unless they wanted to. But he was all for having a wedding, and he knew his family and hers would want that too—if Kayla did.

He just hoped she didn't turn him down or want to delay a mating until later. He was past ready for this.

Chapter 2

KAYLA HAD HAD SUCH A WONDERFUL TIME WITH Nate last night that she was practically bouncing on her toes as she entered the kitchen after taking Rosco, their Saint Bernard, for his morning walk.

Roxie finally joined her, wiped the sleep from her eyes, and yawned. "You are up even earlier than I am this morning. And you even took Rosco out for his morning walk before I could go with you. See?" She motioned to the tea Kayla had made and the apple-and-maple baked oatmeal she had just dished out for the two of them. "You so need Nate in your life."

"I do."

"Then what are you waiting for? You know he wants you too."

"I know. It's going to happen. Okay, so don't you dare tell him, but I'm planning to ask him the day of the Fourth of July celebration. I just want to make this really special."

Smiling, Roxie raised a brow. "Unless he asks you first. Then what?"

"Well, it will be a different kind of celebration. An already mated one." Kayla carried her bowl of oatmeal and tea to the table. Then she frowned at Roxie as she joined her. "Is there something you know that I don't?"

They both took their seats at the table, and Kayla drank some of her tea.

Roxie sighed. "That the two of you should have been mated eons ago. You need to prioritize things better. Mating with a hot wolf first and then enjoying the time with him while you both do your jobs." She reached over and patted Kayla's hand. "I know you're cautious about things. Especially about taking a mate. It's for life, and we live such long lives, but I know you've never felt anything for another wolf like you have for Nate." Then she frowned. "You're both all right in the physical department, aren't you?"

"You mean attracted to him physically? Sexually? Do we have unconsummated sex?" Kayla blushed. She couldn't help herself. Normally, she could talk to her quadruplet sister about anything. But *that*, she realized.

"Yep, on all counts." Roxie sipped some of her tea.

Kayla tilted her chin up and raised her cup off the table. "I don't kiss and tell."

Roxie laughed and spooned up some of her oatmeal. "Then I take that as a big yes. This looks yummy."

"Tastes yummy too. I wanted to try out something different."

Roxie took a bite of hers and smiled. "You're absolutely right. I thought maybe the two of you would sneak into the guest room last night or that you might not be coming home and stay at his place."

"Nah, we both had too much—"

"Work to do. You will always have too much work to do, Kayla. Prioritize."

"I am. Fourth of July—lots of fireworks." Kayla smiled.

Smiling, Roxie shook her head.

"Oh, I meant to tell you about last night. You were already asleep when I came home, but we were pushed off the road by a pickup truck and blew a tire. We thought it was a case of road rage until we saw police going to the scene of a shooting. I should have mentioned that first," Kayla said when she saw Roxie's eyes grow big. "The shooting took place at a jewelry store." She explained the rest of what had happened. "Nicole already knows since she called us when we were driving home."

"Wow. It's good you both weren't hurt, but you should have told me that last night."

"I didn't want to wake you. You're a grouch when that happens, you know."

Roxie laughed. "Yeah, sometimes. Hurry up and eat. We need to take a wolf run before it gets light out and we have to go to work."

Kayla laughed. "You're the one who got up so late

this morning." They usually got up much earlier so they could get in a wolf run in the mornings. Once the full moon was here, it was an iffy proposition. They had wolf staff who handled the day-to-day operations whenever the siblings had issues with shifting. It was a good thing their pack had a lot of royals— wolves that didn't have any issues with shifting no matter what the moon phase was because they had so few strictly human roots diluting their genes.

"Hopefully, we won't run into those two men again or any others on our wolf jaunts. We were both so busy with work yesterday, I forgot to tell you that I had smelled that the black-bearded guy we had seen in the woods had been at the lodge," Roxie said.

"And the other? The blond guy?"

"No, not him." Roxie took another bite of her oatmeal.

Kayla drank some more of her tea. "Okay, so the black-haired guy's a guest and just needed to find a place to talk privately with a friend."

"That's what I figured."

Kayla sighed. Good. They didn't need any trouble this morning on their wolf run.

They quickly finished up breakfast and cleaned the dishes, then stripped off their clothes in their bedrooms—the heat filling their muscles, stretching, feeling glorious as she turned into her wolf. She and Roxie left their bedrooms and bumped into each other on the way down the hall—standard sibling rivalry for both of them—trying to beat each other to the wolf door. It was definitely their ritual, and when their brothers had lived with them at the house, they had waited until the sisters had had their fun. It never ceased to amuse their brothers. Or the sisters. Kayla realized when she and Nate mated, she would miss that with her sister.

Both Kayla and Roxie were just as fast as each other, but they weren't about to give leeway to the other. They got stuck in the wolf door trying to get out and barked happily at each other as they finally squeezed the rest of the way out. They would have been laughing their heads off if they'd been in their human form. Kayla just hoped they'd never get stuck in the wolf door like that again. She could just imagine she and her sister having to howl for their brother Blake to come and rescue them since he lived right next door.

They ran past Blake and Nicole's house, but it was still dark, so they knew the two weren't up and about yet and wouldn't go for a run with them. Since Nicole had gotten pregnant, she hadn't managed to run with them most mornings. Blake stayed home with her because of it, but she would run at night with them because she was always feeling better by then.

Kayla and Roxie scared a couple of rabbits, not meaning to, and the bunnies ducked into a burrow underneath a fallen tree. Now if Rosco had been with them, he would have chased the bunnies.

This land was all private property owned by the Wolff siblings, and whoever needed a home next would build on the property on the other side of Blake and Nicole's place. It was all wooded, perfect for running as wolves and safe from visitors to the area. Even other wolves in the pack didn't normally come out here since their pack leaders, Darien and Lelandi Silver, had so much land available for the pack members to run on that normally was safe. Kayla's family had signs posted here and there that said the land was private property, but some didn't pay attention to that.

Still, Kayla couldn't imagine building a house here or even what she wanted. She was afraid that when she mated, she would be absolutely overwhelmed by it all. But for now, she was having a blast. She realized if she was living here with Nate, she'd be able to do this with him early in the morning before work and with Roxie too. And when Nicole had her babies, how much fun would it be to supervise the little ones while running with Kayla's very own mate? She took a deep breath of the fresh air. She'd love it.

That's what she had to think of more. About all the good things she could do with Nate around their work schedules. She just hoped Roxie wouldn't feel like a third wheel when Nate and Kayla went with her for runs in the morning and at night.

Though there was another situation she hadn't discussed with Nate—and that was the business of her not being a royal. His sister was fine with Blake not being one, but that didn't mean Nate was totally comfortable with it. They had to be on the same page concerning that for sure.

After a couple of miles through the woods, Kayla and Roxie turned around and raced each other back. The two of them were so equal in speed that she knew they'd end up at the wolf door at the very same time and be struggling to get inside like they'd done trying to get outside. Did they care? It was part of the fun.

Kayla nipped at her sister's ear, and Roxie turned to get her back, which gave Kayla the time to get a little bit ahead of her.

Roxie barked in a playful way and immediately caught up to her. When they reached the door, they dove through it at the same time. Once they finally wriggled through it, they raced through the house and up the stairs. In their own bedrooms, they shifted and began getting dressed.

"You know one of these times we're going to get stuck," Roxie said.

"That's why you need to eat more veggies, not so much chocolate."

Roxie laughed. "Says you. I saw you eat that extra chocolate bar after lunch yesterday."

"That was stress food."

"Yeah, that catering venue you had for the birthday party was annoying. What was it? Three people changed their minds about their meal orders and then complained that you had messed them up and were mad they were not eating at the same time as everyone else?"

Kayla buttoned her blouse. "Exactly. Blake said he was glad he hadn't had to deal with it. For once, it would be nice if someone like that admitted they had made the mistake. We don't mind changing out the meal, but I do mind being blamed for them changing their minds. At least as far as our wolf run, I had a blast as usual. I always think that it's going to take too much time, but running helps me to focus and work out any stress I might be feeling before we tackle the day's work."

Roxie poked her head into Kayla's bedroom while she was pulling on her shoes. "Yeah. Every time I feel lazy about it, especially at night, I just need to push myself out the door."

"So we're running tonight," Kayla said.

"Naturally."

———

At the PI office that morning, Nate had actually remembered Nicole had her doctor's appointment and asked her about it right away to learn how it went.

Nicole smiled at him. "You remembered."

"I had it on my calendar."

She laughed. "Everything's good." Then she got a call and took it. When she got off the phone, she said, "Hey, we have a case to look into in Green Valley. A twenty-four-year-old man who lives in a farmhouse on his parents' property has gone missing."

"They have a couple of PI agencies in Green Valley." Not that he and Nicole would turn down cases from there, but Nate was just curious why the parents would hire someone from out of town to search for the missing son when they had local PIs who could do it.

"Yeah, but his parents wanted someone who wasn't from there because they're afraid that someone who might be responsible could be in league with the police in Green Valley. Anyway, we need to begin working on it."

"Oh?" He was surprised about that because the Green Valley wolf pack leader was also the mayor and had developed good relations with the police force, so he wondered what that was all about.

He was trying to concentrate on his work, but he sure couldn't quit thinking about Kayla—about her sweet smiles and the teasing light in her pretty brown eyes. The way she always slid her tongue over her lips after she'd eaten, making him want to lick them for her. The way she laughed at his jokes like he really tickled her. Even the manner in which she swept her hair off her cheek in such a sexy way when the wind blew the strands over her eyes.

He really wanted to run with her as a wolf too. He knew she and her sister ran early in the morning before work, but he never could get up early enough to catch them before they left. He needed her to stay the night with him so they could run on the pack leaders' territory, morning and night.

For the entire week, Nate had been working on numerous cases, and he was having dinner with his sister tonight to do some follow-up stuff about the missing guy from Green Valley. While Nicole was fixing dinner, she said, "Why don't you call up Ryan and see if he's learned anything about the jewelry-store robbery case?"

Ryan McKinley was the pack leader and mayor of Green Valley and had his own private investigation agency there. Nate called him, put it on speakerphone so Nicole could learn what was going on too, and told him about having been there when the robbery went down.

"If you hear anything, I'd love to know about it," Nate said. So far as he knew, the police had never caught the four men who were involved in the actual armed robbery and the getaway driver.

Thankfully, the robbers hadn't hurt anyone during the robbery, but they'd gotten away with a ton of jewelry in black plastic bags, the news had said.

"They hit three more jewelry stores in various cities south of us," Ryan told Nate.

"Hell. The same people?"

"They were armed, wearing black ski masks and all black clothes, and carrying black plastic bags. They shot out the store windows and got away within minutes of stealing the jewelry. It sounds like the same MO as the ones who committed the robbery in Green Valley, according to news sources."

"Sounds like it. Have you heard what they were driving? A black truck possibly? Do they have any viable suspects yet in those cases?"

"The police are questioning everyone about the crimes, but no one's been charged or jailed yet. If we hear anything, we'll let you know. And about helping Nicole out while you're gone on vacation for a week, we'll have you covered."

"Thanks, Ryan," Nate said, and Nicole echoed his response. He just had to ask Kayla if she'd like to do that with him for her birthday. He was afraid she might reject him because of the shifting issues she might have during that time when the moon was full, but he wanted to prove to her he was fine with them.

"No problem. I've got several PIs who are willing to aid you, Nicole. And let us know if you need any help in the case of the missing guy in Green Valley. Phil Peterson, right? Even though his parents don't trust some of the authorities here, we know more people living in the area than you do, and if we can assist you, just let us know."

"Yeah, Phil Peterson, and we'll do that."

Then they ended the call.

The wolf pack that ran the PI agency there were great at helping the Silver Town wolves with their jobs, like one extended happy family. So they didn't mind that Nate had a PI job he was taking care of in their territory.

Nate had the case file open on his sister's dining room table that evening after work, glad Nicole was also a former army officer. Both of them owned the PI agency that they'd started in Denver and moved to Silver Town, so they worked together on cases when they needed each other's help.

"You know," Nicole said, "you were supposed to be having dinner with Kayla tonight."

"I know. But this case is eating at me," Nate said. His sister pulled the roasted chicken out of the oven for the two of them, while her mate, Blake Wolff, was at the ski lodge working late.

"You told Kayla you were working on this case?" Nicole asked.

"Yeah." He was rereading police interviews and needed to reinterview some of the witnesses. Sometimes witnesses were less nervous around a private investigator since he couldn't arrest them. But if he learned any of them had had anything to do with the disappearance of the missing man, he'd turn the information over to the police.

"Kayla could have come over here and had dinner with us, you know." Nicole served up their meal on plates.

Nate looked up at his sister. "She would have felt left out. She would be here just for dinner, then she would have to leave so we could look this over together. Besides, you know how I am when I'm working on a case like this."

"I know. Focused. Nothing else exists or matters. But Kayla's such a sweetheart. She doesn't see anyone else. She's shy and reserved—avoiding meeting other people when she doesn't have to—but I suspect she had her heart set on having dinner with you."

"She didn't seem to mind when I canceled on her." He wanted to get as much work as possible done before he took a week off to be with Kayla and not leave it all for his sister to handle.

"Right. That's how she reacts when she's disappointed but doesn't want you to know how she feels." Nicole set their plates on the table. "You better have told her you're going to make it up to her."

Nate adored Kayla and had wanted to date her from the moment he'd seen her at the lodge and she'd helped him on a prior case. For the past six months he'd been working on a cedar-lined hope chest for her birthday. His mother and sister had made a quilted pillow seat cushion for it in Kayla's favorite shades of blue and white, with wolves and the mountains in the background. He'd just finished carving the front of the chest with a wolf howling in front of a backdrop of mountains—Kayla, a wolf with a voice—last night, wanting to finish it ahead of her birthday. He didn't want her feeling bad about their missed date, though he had thought his reasoning for canceling on Kayla was perfectly sound until his twin sister made him doubt himself.

"I will."

"Nate." Nicole frowned at him as she sat across from him. "Unless you don't want to date her, make this right."

"I will." Nate felt guilty then. He hadn't realized Kayla had been disappointed at all.

Nicole rubbed her belly, and he glanced at her. She was now six months along with twins, and he sighed. "How are the babies?"

Nicole smiled at him. "Good way to change the subject and be human for a moment."

He chuckled. "I do care."

"I know. You just need to show it more." She began eating her chicken. "To answer your question, I'm fine. So what have we got on the case?"

"Phil's parents suspect he's in trouble. He was reluctant to tell them what he was bothered about before he vanished, and the police couldn't find any evidence of foul play, so they believe he has just taken off on his own as he's known to do." Nate buttered his baked potato and broccoli.

"And at his age, it's reasonable that he is just doing his own thing and that nothing's wrong, if he does this often," Nicole said.

"Which is why the police aren't really working on the case. They have a lot of cases they know need to be solved. So the parents hired us to see if we could find him and ensure he's all right."

"Did you interview witnesses who saw him last yet?"

"Some. But others are next on my list. I've spoken to his parents, of course. You…wouldn't want to come with me and do that, would you?" He figured she would unless her pregnancy was bothering her too much.

"Yeah, sure. I'm pregnant with twins, but it doesn't mean I can't do any more investigations. In fact, I'll be taking up the slack while you go to the cabin with Kayla."

Nate opened his mouth to speak, then closed his mouth.

"Don't tell me you're even considering canceling on staying at one of the pack's wolf cabins with her for a week. I thought you were planning something really special for her birthday—I mean, beyond giving her the beautifully hand-carved wooden hope chest."

"Yeah, no, I mean, I hadn't planned to cancel the reservation, but this case—"

"Can wait. Have you... You haven't even asked her if she can go, have you? I swear, dear brother, if you don't ask her soon, I'll do it."

He ran his hands through his hair. "Yeah, I'm telling her, but I wanted it to be a surprise."

Nicole sighed with relief. "I'll keep after the case the whole time if we don't solve it before you leave with her, but I'm not going to update you on it. Not while you're with Kayla at the cabin."

He smiled at Nicole and set the file aside and started eating his chicken. "Yeah. Kayla and I need this time together alone." Especially because he was going to ask her to mate him and he wanted it to be a pre-honeymoon for the week. He finished his dinner and called Kayla. "Hey, it's me. Listen, about tonight, I'm sorry."

"Oh, don't be," Kayla said. "Roxie and I just finished eating rib eye steaks. They were delicious."

He glanced at his empty plate. Steaks sounded good. "Well, it won't happen again."

"Yeah, it will. You have a job to do, and it's no big deal."

Nicole raised her brows at him, expecting him to say more.

"I've got to go. Roxie is pouring more bubbly," Kayla said to Nate.

"Oh, girls' night out." At least he was glad they

seemed to be having a good time of it, but he hoped it wasn't to cheer Kayla up because he'd let her down.

"It is. Unexpected too. Roxie was going to be at the lodge late, so we just switched things up so she could be here with me instead."

Sure. That's why Blake wasn't here with Nicole. All because of Nate.

He rubbed his whiskery chin. "Hey, can I come over for breakfast?"

As soon as he said it, he knew he was in hot water with Nicole, who was shaking her head and looked perturbed. Yeah, he probably should have offered to take Kayla to breakfast, but if they ate at the lodge's restaurant, he wouldn't be paying for it since she co-owned the restaurant with her siblings. And he was certain she wouldn't want to go into Silver Town to have breakfast because it would take too much time away from her work. He knew she would have turned him down, though he should have at least made the gesture. He was probably in trouble with Kayla. Maybe with her whole family.

There was a lengthy pause, and Nate got the impression his sister was right. Kayla wasn't happy with him.

Kayla knew she had to expect that Nate would be busy with cases sometimes, but she still felt hurt that his cancellation had been such a last-minute thing, and, like usual, she just acted like it was no big deal. She was glad Blake took over for Roxie at the lodge and then their sister had been here for her instead.

"Breakfast," Kayla said to Nate. "Yeah, I eat breakfast, so if you're here when I'm eating it, you can have some too." She wasn't going to make a special breakfast date with him just so he could tell her he wasn't coming. She understood that his cases could take priority. She just didn't want to get excited about seeing him and be let down again.

Smiling, Roxie shook her head.

"Okay, it's, um, a plan then. See you at eight?" Nate asked, sounding like he was in hot water with Kayla.

"Sure, see you then." She didn't want to make him feel bad, but he'd made her feel that way! After they hung up, she poked at her cauliflower. "Well, he wants to have breakfast with me, but who knows if that's for sure or not."

"Hmm, well, just in case, I'll have breakfast at the lodge," Roxie said.

Kayla looked up from forking up some more cauliflower. "No. Way. You were here for me tonight. He wasn't. We're not going to rearrange things every time he's supposed to see me when he could just cancel on another date with hardly any warning."

"What about your cabin trip?" Roxie asked, sounding concerned.

Kayla finished her meal and began to clear away the dishes. "*What* cabin trip?" She turned and frowned at Roxie.

"Oh, uh, sorry. I wasn't supposed to say anything."

Kayla's mouth dropped. Now she really felt bad for making Nate feel that way.

"It's, uh, a birthday surprise, and well, I thought Nate would have told you by now. Anyway, Nicole wanted to make sure we had everything covered at work because she didn't want Nate to learn you couldn't do it. I don't know why he hasn't asked you yet." Roxie got busy wiping down the counters as if she felt bad that she had given away the surprise.

Kayla tucked a curl of hair behind her ear. "Maybe he's having second thoughts about it."

"No." Then Roxie frowned at her. "You're not doing anything that would make him reluctant to ask you, are you?"

"No. Of course not. I don't think so anyway. I wish you hadn't told me. What if he doesn't ask me?"

"I'll tell you what. If he doesn't, I'll go with you and make sure Jake knows we're renting the cabin in lieu of Nate doing it."

"You don't want to."

"Yeah, I do. Ever since Nicole mentioned it, I've been jealous of the two of you for getting to do that. So if he can't make it—for a perfectly good reason—we'll drive out there instead. Who knows? Maybe he'll make it to the cabin later, and you and he can spend some quality time together and I'll return home."

"No. If you come with me, then we're there together. If he comes later, he can be there—with the two of us."

Roxie smiled. "I think I'm rubbing off on you. That's not a good thing."

"Ha. I've always wanted to be more like you. Surer of myself. More…outgoing."

"Everyone loves you just the way you are. Especially Nate."

A week at a cabin? Kayla smiled. She couldn't believe it, but she was thrilled. Maybe she'd just skip her Fourth of July plans to ask him to mate her and do it at the cabin instead. Then they'd have their whole week to celebrate their new life together. Unless that's what he planned to do with her. She just hoped he didn't cancel on her!

―――――――――

The next morning, Kayla—worried Nate might not show up—forced herself not to be excited about him coming to breakfast, though she'd had a devil of a time trying to figure out what to wear today. If it had been a "normal" day, she wouldn't have been so indecisive. And she'd straightened up the house three times already. She was trying not to let Roxie see her fussing so much over things, but her sister knew. As wolves, they really couldn't get away with much without the other knowing, especially when they were also quadruplets. She was just glad Blake and Landon weren't living here any longer or she figured they'd give Nate a talking-to.

She was still fixing a special omelet for her and Roxie—buttery mushrooms and crumbly feta cheese—and one for Nate, whether he could make it or not. Hmm, this was going to be good.

But then Nate arrived early, and she was so thrilled to see him. She couldn't help it. He just brightened her day. Before she could throw herself at him—which she was really trying hard to hold back from doing—he took her in his arms and hugged her soundly. "I'm so sorry about dinner last night. Nicole gave me hell over it."

Kayla chuckled. "I love your sister." She hugged him back, and they kissed—tenderly, then open-mouthed, tongues caressing.

Then she heard Roxie dishing up the omelets.

"Are you ready to eat?" Kayla asked Nate as she got him a cup of coffee.

"Yeah. Thanks so much for having me over for breakfast."

"I'm glad you're here. So what's the case you're working on?" Kayla asked as they took their seats at the kitchen table.

Nate told Kayla and Roxie about the missing person's case he was still looking into.

"Do you think he's really in trouble?" Kayla hadn't thought Nate had cases that could be that dangerous. She could see why he had been focused on the job and had canceled on her for dinner.

"He could be. His parents never called the police when he disappeared before, for one thing. And for another, they were concerned enough to hire me. I believe their gut instinct is that he's in trouble. I've got to interview a bunch of people who knew Phil today to learn what they know about his going missing."

"What do you think happened?" Roxie asked.

"I don't know for sure. He's not a young kid, and no one's come forward to say they saw something related to him that would indicate he was in trouble. I'm hoping I can learn something about his last movements—like who saw him before he vanished—and get to the truth."

"I hope you find him safe and sound," Kayla said.

"Yeah, I sure do too."

After they finished breakfast, Nate was going to help with the dishes, but Kayla said, "No, you have to locate the missing guy."

Nate smiled at her but didn't make a move to leave the house. He looked determined to stay and help.

Roxie said, "Thanks for helping, Nate." She handed him the frying pan. "Meet you at the lodge,

Kayla." And then she hurried to take Rosco and their year-old short-haired orange cat, Princess Buttercup, to the lodge and leave the two of them alone.

Kayla laughed. "I guess you're helping me with the dishes."

"I'm glad to. That's why I offered." He began scrubbing the pan with gusto.

Kayla was so glad he was here with her. "I'm sorry if I might have sounded annoyed with you last night." She finished putting the last of the dirty dishes in the dishwasher.

"Oh, you were fine. I knew I was in trouble."

She laughed. She wasn't about to deny it.

"Okay, I'm going to be working on this case all day and probably a little late, but I want to see you too, so let's just leave it open as to when we can get together but know that I want to see you as soon as I can." He set the frying pan on the drying pad.

"Absolutely. What you have to do is really important. Anytime is fine with me." She wrapped her arms around his neck, and they kissed. He was always so tender toward her, but their kisses always morphed into something passionate and filled with longing.

He kissed her jaw, her neck, sucked hard, and she knew he'd left a hickey there! As if he was trying to prove to everyone that she was the one for him. But she wasn't about to leave it at that and branded him with a kiss mark on his neck too. He smiled at her, seeming well pleased. He pressed his burgeoning arousal against her, and she figured he was going to feel uncomfortable on the way to work this morning.

"I'll see you as soon as we're able," she said, and then they said goodbye and she headed off to the lodge while he drove back into Silver Town. And she frowned.

He didn't ask her to go with him to the cabin!

Chapter 3

NATE WAS SO GLAD HE HAD BREAKFAST WITH Kayla, making him realize how he should never cancel on her unless there was a real emergency and he had no other choice. She made his morning so much brighter that he was ready to get after this missing person's case and any other that might need his immediate attention with renewed zeal.

"How was breakfast?" Nicole asked at the office. She raised her brows at him, as if she knew just how it had been once he was with Kayla.

"It was great, and, yes, you're right. I shouldn't skip out on dates with her."

Nicole smiled. He knew his sister loved it when she was right about something regarding him.

Not long after getting to the office, Nate and Nicole drove first to Phil Peterson's parents' farm outside Green Valley to speak to them again. He believed Phil's parents might have some more ideas about where Phil could have gone after giving it some further thought.

"Did you speak with any of Phil's friends about him disappearing?" Nate asked Phil's parents. Sometimes family could learn more from the missing family member's friends than an outsider they didn't know could.

"Not really," his mother said. "I mean, we *did* talk to them, but none of them expected him to just take off like that. I told the police that too. Phil was looking forward to working a new job as a journalist at the paper. He wasn't planning on running off. We think his friends know more than they are telling us though."

"What makes you think they're hiding the truth from you?" Nate asked.

"They clammed up. They always talk to us, and they were casting each other looks like they had to keep a secret. Maybe we're reading too much into this, but it really seemed as though there was more going on than they wanted us to know," the mother said.

"We learned from them that they'd all been at the Red Dog Pub the night he went missing," the dad said. "We asked if Phil had said anything to them about taking off, and they said no. But I swear they looked sheepish about it."

"Of all his friends who were with him at the Red Dog Pub, who do you believe might be the weak link in the group who might break under pressure and tell us more about the situation if he or she knows something?" Nicole asked.

"Sarah. At nineteen, she's the youngest, and she's also the most easily manipulated. If you can get her away from Everest, her boyfriend, she might talk," the mother said.

"Maybe Gerald will talk. He really liked Phil and took his disappearance the hardest, even though Everest was supposed to be Phil's best friend. But Everest said Phil would show up when he felt like it and didn't seem to care in the least that he was gone," Phil's dad said. "Most likely their friend Randy won't tell you anything. And his girlfriend, Ann, does everything Randy says."

"Do you think there was a falling-out between Everest and Phil?" Nate asked.

"Yeah. The night of the pub outing, but no one will say if anything happened. I even went there," the dad said, "and asked other people who frequent the joint if anyone saw anything. No one admitted to seeing anyone."

"What about your daughter?" Nate asked.

"She wouldn't go to the pub. The arts and theater are her thing. Rowdy pubs are not," the mother said.

But Nate believed Phil's sister might know or suspect something and didn't want to tell her parents about it. Then Nate saw her watching them surreptitiously from the hall.

Nicole saw her too and smiled at her. "I'm going to step outside for a moment." She stood up from the couch and walked outside the house to the front patio.

Phil's sister disappeared from the hallway, and

he heard a door open and shut out of his view. Nate hoped Nicole was going to speak to the sister and hadn't left the house because she wasn't feeling well.

"Can you think of anyone else who might have been involved in Phil's disappearance?" Nate asked. Even though family and friends were the first to consider as suspects, he had to look into other possibilities—if Phil hadn't vanished on his own.

"I know he wasn't involved in drugs," his mother said.

"Ruby watches a lot of crime shows. Once a homicide detective learns drugs are involved, that gets into a whole slew of new suspects—drug dealers, drug users. But she's right. He wasn't dealing, and he wasn't using," the dad said.

"And no girlfriend?" Nate asked, thinking that just because Phil's parents were adamant that he hadn't been involved in drugs didn't mean he wasn't.

"No," the mother said.

"I know we talked about this before, but have you had time to think about any enemies he might have had?" Nate asked.

"We've talked about nothing else since he didn't return home," the mother said. "There's no one else we can think of."

"But Phil really didn't tell us about everything that was going on in his life," the dad added. "I'm sure he had secrets."

"Sure, everyone does. It's just natural that

children don't tell their parents everything that's going on in their lives. Then again, if something seemed unusual that might have something to do with this, we'd like to know," Nate said.

"Since Phil stays at the secondary farmhouse on the property, he can come and go as he likes. He and his friends were always arriving at all hours at his place. It seemed odd, we thought. Sure, after work, if they all got together for a party or something, but the hours were strange," the dad said. "And it wasn't for long. Like for less than an hour. It's a bit of a drive out here for someone to come here and just stay for a few minutes."

The mother sighed. "I'm sure there was nothing to it."

Yet since they had mentioned it, Nate figured they felt that something wasn't quite right.

"We both have restless nights, so one or the other of us would see all the goings-on," she said. "We don't want you to think we watch out the windows day and night. We'd hear the cars rolling in on the gravel road and go check to see what was going on. It's remote out here, and we wanted to make sure someone wasn't coming to rob us or something."

"Did you ever ask him about it?" It seemed odd. Nate wondered if Phil and his friends *were* involved in the drug trade, and the parents had really figured that out but couldn't admit it to themselves.

"We sort of joked about it," the dad said, sounding

serious, like he was afraid the son would move off the property or something if they pressed him about what he was up to.

But he was their son, and he had a pretty sweet deal here. Free home, according to his parents. He could do what he wanted.

"We didn't want to make him mad. He might move somewhere else," the mother admitted.

Just as Nate suspected.

"He apologized that he'd woken us up. And then they all stopped coming over. At least we thought they had. You know actions speak louder than words, so we were thrilled they were being so considerate. But then we realized they were all using the old dirt road on the back of the property to get to his place," the dad said. "At least we didn't hear the vehicles any longer on the gravel road. But whenever we got up in the middle of the night, we'd take a peek, just as a matter of habit to see if they were there, and sure enough, half the time, they would be. Then they'd take off."

"So they weren't staying overnight," Nate said.

"No, they'd get together for an hour or less. Then we suspected they'd all head for their own places. So we don't know what that was all about," the dad said. "But when we asked his friends about his vanishing—where they thought he might have gone or why he might have left—none had a clue. So they said."

"All right. Well, if you think of anything else, just call us," Nate said, wanting to see to Nicole and make sure she was okay.

"Thanks, we will." The dad shook his hand, and Nate walked out the door.

Nicole was alone on the front porch, and Nate hoped she'd been able to speak with Phil's sister. Or maybe Nicole had just felt nauseous and had needed some fresh air.

"How are you doing?" he asked as he walked her down the steps to the walkway and out to the car parked in front of the farmhouse.

"Oh, I'm good."

"Okay, that's good. Where to now?" he asked her as they got into his car, and he started driving on the gravel road. He could see how the sound would wake people if they were light sleepers. Of course as wolves, they'd hear it even if it was an asphalt or cement drive.

"His sister said Everest and her brother had a big fight at the Red Dog Pub."

"So she *did* talk to you." He switched direction and headed for the pub.

"Yep. We need to speak with the weak link. *Sarah*. Apparently, she was drunk, like they all were, and she sat on Phil's lap. Everest was furious and physically slugged Phil, but Phil laughed it off, which infuriated Everest even more."

"How does his sister know about this?" Nate

asked, surprised. "I thought she didn't frequent the pub like her brother and his friends did."

"Phil's sister, Vicki, went with a girlfriend to the pub after seeing a play just to learn what Phil and his friends saw in the place, since they went there all the time. Everest saw Vicki, grabbed her, and made her sit on *his* lap in retaliation to see how Phil liked it. Phil punched Everest in the face. They brawled, the bouncer threw them out of the pub, and Vicki said that was the last time she'd seen her brother."

"Does Vicki think Everest killed Phil?"

"Yeah, but she's scared to say so. Everest's daddy's a prosecutor, and she said Everest has been in trouble before—drunk driving, hit-and-run—and the lawyers keep getting him off of any charges. So if Everest did kill her brother, he might never be charged with a crime, and he might even go after Vicki for saying anything about it."

"Okay, she could be in danger too. I guess that's why Phil's parents didn't want a PI agency in Green Valley to look into this. Maybe they thought Everest's daddy would shut them down." Then Nate explained the business of Phil's friends going to his house at all hours of the night and everything else that Nicole hadn't learned while she was outside on the porch.

"Did you ever look in his house to see if there were any drugs or anything else that could clue us in to his whereabouts?" Nicole asked.

"Yeah, the first time I spoke with his parents, but the place was clean. And you know, with our wolf's enhanced sense of smell, I would have smelled drugs if there had been any, but there hadn't been. Still, it makes you wonder what was up. They could have been just handing the money over there but keeping the drugs away from his house."

"I think it sounds pretty suspicious," Nicole agreed. "His parents' gut instincts say the same thing. They're suspicious. Especially since he hasn't returned home and they haven't had any word from him."

Chapter 4

AT THE SKI LODGE, KAYLA WAS SERVING AS THE catering manager for a wedding where a bridezilla was having a major meltdown about the banquet room being too small. But Kayla had set it up with her nearly twelve months ago, told her the seating arrangements and the occupancy size, and asked the bride if she was sure she didn't want to reserve two banquet rooms at the time. Bridezilla had said no, it was too much of a cost. So what did she think? She could pay for one room and get two now when it was actually the big day? Their other banquet rooms had been completely booked two weeks after the bride's was reserved.

Roxie had planned to be the catering manager for this wedding, but she was dealing with a registered couple whose charge card had been declined. The siblings often flip-flopped roles depending on who was involved with some crisis at the time. Kayla would rather have handled the credit card issue, but Roxie had already been trying to cope with the couple, who were in the wedding party and having their own meltdown.

Blake was dealing with a complaint that someone

staying in the room next to theirs had a couple of barking dogs. He usually helped as a catering manager or a banquet manager of any function that didn't have to do with weddings. As to a guest having dogs in one of the rooms, pets weren't allowed at the lodge. Only Rosco was because he was the owners' and because he was an avalanche rescue dog. They'd also used him on searches for missing hikers in the summer, though the wolves used their own heightened sense of smell to search for lost visitors. Their cat Princess Buttercup stayed in their office until she went home at night.

So Blake had gone up to see about the barking dog issue.

Landon was helping set up the banquet room next to the bridezilla's where a party was ready to get underway for a sixty-year-old man's birthday celebration.

Kayla swore the bride was giving the guests attending the birthday party the evil eye for daring to take up the room she should have had. Kayla was trying to arrange things in the room in a better way to accommodate the bride's guests and wedding party. When things were running smoothly, Kayla loved wedding parties that were held here. They were great moneymakers for the lodge. But when they had to deal with a bridezilla, no amount of money was worth it, she felt. She was ready to return to their office and crawl into her shell to work on promotions like she loved doing. Dealing with confrontations was not her thing.

Kayla loved her siblings. She knew if Roxie hadn't been busy with the credit card issue with the one couple, she would have taken Bridezilla off Kayla's hands. Her brothers were another story. They didn't want to say something to an out-of-control bride they could regret later.

Come to think of it, Roxie tended to speak her mind too. So if someone was being a royal pain in the ass, she'd probably say something about it.

The bride frowned, flipped her blond hair over her shoulders for the millionth time, and stalked across the floor to speak to one of her bridesmaids who had just arrived. "I told you to dye your hair brown so I would be the *only* blond in the wedding party. I have to stand out in the photos."

Kayla raised her brows. Talk about a prima donna. If Kayla had a good friend who had said that to her, she would have straightened her out.

Scowling, Bridezilla pointed at her bridesmaid. "You're dismissed."

"What?" The blond bridesmaid sounded shocked.

Kayla parted her lips in surprise. She couldn't believe the bride would go that far and do that to her friend!

Bridezilla shrugged and folded her arms across her waist. "I made it *very* clear to you yesterday that you had to change your hair color to brown. But you *didn't* do it. So *fine*. You can't be at the wedding."

The bridesmaid's jaw dropped. Her eyes were filled with tears. Her mouth was quivering. Kayla wanted to give her a hug and tell the bride off, but her parents were paying for the venue.

"Go!" Bridezilla waved her hand at the door. "Next time maybe you'll listen to my rules."

"Don't worry," the bridesmaid said. "There won't be a next time." Then she hurried across the floor and out of the room.

The other bridesmaids were staring at the departing bridesmaid, looking dumbfounded, but they held their tongues, probably worried their heads would be on the chopping block next.

"I'll be right back," Kayla told the bride's wedding coordinator. She headed out of the banquet room and found Roxie dealing with the bridesmaid, who was all in tears. Kayla joined them at the front desk and learned the girl was checking out. Kayla gave her a hug. "I love your hair, and I don't blame you for not changing it. I wouldn't have either. If she'd been a real friend, she wouldn't have insisted on it." Then she said to Roxie, "Give her the room for free last night. And no charge for checking out late today."

Roxie smiled at Kayla. Her sister always said Kayla had too soft a heart, and they wouldn't let her handle billing issues because of it. Any sob story would convince her to allow someone to stay the night for free.

The girl gave her a heartfelt hug back. "Thanks so much."

"You're welcome. My sister would have given you a refund if she'd seen what the bride had said to you." Kayla didn't want the woman to think she was the only one with a heart.

Roxie was smiling at Kayla like she wasn't sure about that.

"Do you want me to take over for you, Kayla?" Roxie asked her as the bridesmaid rolled her bags out of the lodge.

"No." Kayla didn't want Roxie to have to deal with Bridezilla just because she was ready to turn into a wolf and bite her. "Hey, when I get married, if I ever act like that, slap me so I can wake up and realize how important everyone is to me."

"You?" Roxie laughed. "No way. I would be shocked if you were mean to anyone over anything. You're never a drama queen, ever."

"Well, just make sure I'm not. I would never want to treat anyone bad like that after all they've done to make my day special. Okay, I'm going back to the banquet hall."

"Just text me if you need me to take over. Seriously." Roxie gave her a hug.

"Okay, I will." But once Kayla set her mind to do something, she did it. No matter how unpleasant.

Blake called Roxie, and she said, putting it on speaker, "Yeah, Blake?"

"Help me chase down two miniature schnauzers that have wrecked a guest room and got out as soon as I opened the guest room door." Blake sounded frantic, out of breath, like he was running down the stairs.

"Ohmigod, there they are!" Kayla saw them dashing down the stairs and across the lobby. Rosco stood up, looking unsure what he should do.

"The two schnauzers are headed for the banquet room hosting the wedding!" Kayla said, tearing off to try to stop the disaster about to unfold.

Roxie was right behind her, calling Landon to drop whatever he was doing to help them catch a couple of runaway dogs. Kayla gave Rosco a hand signal to stay where he was near his dog bed so he wouldn't chase after the schnauzers since the siblings were running after them and she was afraid he might think he needed to join the race. They sure didn't need him in the banquet room adding to the havoc. She could just imagine what the bride would say about that.

———

Nate and Nicole parked at the Red Dog Pub. The place was open for lunch and was crowded with patrons. They started talking to the bartender who had been on duty the night Phil had vanished. The pretty, dark-haired woman leaned on the counter and said, "Okay, the police have already been here, and I've talked to them."

"Right, but we're here as private investigators looking into the case for the family. We've heard there was an argument between Phil and a friend of his," Nate said.

"Uh-huh."

"There were words," Nate said.

"And a scuffle," the bartender said. "I had the bouncer throw them out of here."

"Do you know what it was about, exactly?" Nate asked.

"A girl with them sat on Phil's lap, and that's when the other guy got angry. Then Everest grabbed a different girl that I'd never seen in the pub before and forced her onto his lap. That's when Phil threw a punch at Everest. I called security to break things up and send them out of here."

Which confirmed just what Phil's sister had said.

"And you told the police this?" Nate asked.

"Yep."

"Anything else?" Nicole asked.

The bartender shook her head. "I've never seen them fighting in here before. They're in here a lot. And they drink a lot. They were drunk that night."

"Did Phil seem...despondent at all during the whole session?"

"No. He was cheerful, even when his friend got mad at him. He was laughing, wasn't taking anything seriously. Not until Everest grabbed that other girl and forced her to sit on his lap. Then Phil got angry. Oh, I think Phil said something about the girl being his sister? I might have been mistaken about that. It was noisy in here. That's all I know."

"Okay, thanks," Nicole said. "Is there anyone else we can talk to about the case?"

"Just his friends. They would know more about what went on than I would. It was a busy night, and except for the fight, I hadn't really been watching them."

"All right, thanks," Nate said.

Then they left and decided to see Gerald, the friend who was so nervous about Phil going missing, and drove over to his apartment.

They soon arrived at Gerald's apartment complex, parked, and headed for the door. At Nate's knock, Gerald opened the door. As soon as Nate told him that Phil's parents had hired the private investigators to search for the truth behind Phil's disappearance, Gerald nearly closed the door in their faces.

"You know what happened," Nate said, smelling the fear wafting from the man.

Gerald ran his hands over his long, red hair pulled back into a ponytail. His mustache was a little lighter red than his hair, and he had a full red beard. His green eyes shifted from Nate to Nicole and down to the patio. "He... He, uh, just needed to get away. He has to sometimes. We all know it. His parents know it. And the police say there's not a reason that raises any red flags concerning his, uh, disappearance."

"But you know where he is, don't you?" Nate bet Gerald knew more than he was letting on.

Gerald looked like he desperately wanted to close the door in their faces again, as though he knew Nate and Nicole were a couple of alpha wolves and he couldn't get anything past them.

"We know about the fight at the bar," Nicole said.

That was a great way of telling Gerald he didn't have to squeal on his friends about it because they already knew.

"And we know Everest does whatever he wants to," Nicole said. "And gets away with it."

"Exactly, so I have nothing to say." Yet Gerald still didn't shut the door.

"If you didn't have anything to do with Phil's disappearance, there's no reason for you not to tell us the truth," Nicole said.

"I–I could be an accessory, couldn't I?"

Okay, so that didn't sound good—like Gerald *was* involved in Phil's disappearance. Which meant Phil most likely wasn't just taking a break from everyone. Who else was involved? His other friends?

"If you were a witness to a crime but are willing

to tell the truth now, you have a much better chance at getting immunity from prosecution." That was if Gerald had nothing to do with actually killing Phil.

"Everest's dad's a prosecutor, and he's got a lot of powerful friends, and some are on the police force."

"Can we go inside and talk to you?" Nicole asked, rubbing her back. Nate assumed it was bothering her.

"Uh. Yeah, sure." Gerald let them inside and locked the door behind them.

"Tell us what you know," Nate said as Gerald ushered them into his messy bachelor pad: empty beer cans on tables, the odor of pot lingering in the air, a computer on a desk nearby, the monitor showing a game paused, and a flat-screen TV on one wall that was on too, featuring a werewolf movie.

Nate had no clue what the name of it was. He never watched werewolf shows. They were just too unreal for him.

He and Nicole sat down together on the saggy brown sofa while Gerald sat down on an equally saggy blue recliner. A man began howling in pain as he tore off his clothes and turned into a hideous werewolf on the screen.

Gerald grabbed the TV controller and paused the movie. "Great movie, by the way. If you haven't seen it, you ought to. Okay, so we all went to the Red Dog Pub the night Phil went missing. Everest's girlfriend, Sarah, was mad at him, so she sat on

Phil's lap and was kissing him. Everest slugged Phil over it, but then when Phil just laughed, Everest headed over to where Phil's sister, Vicki, was watching, grabbed her arm, and forced her to sit on *his* lap. Sarah was incensed Everest would do that. Not because she cared anything about Vicki, but Sarah felt Everest had slighted her all night. And she felt it was all Phil's fault for pulling her onto his lap in the first place and riling Everest up. But the thing of it was, she'd encouraged Phil to do it. She was jealous because Everest was talking to some other girl at the pub, so Sarah wanted to get Everest's attention. She got it all right."

"You all left together, right?" Nicole asked.

"We were in two separate vehicles. Phil, Randy, and Ann were in one car, and I was with Sarah and Everest in the other. Everest was fuming that Sarah sat on Phil's lap, and she was griping at him about the cute black-haired girl he'd been talking it up with at the bar earlier. Anyway, Randy dropped Phil off at his farm, and that was it."

"As far as what you've told us," Nate said. "What really happened?"

Gerald shifted in his chair. "Everest wouldn't let it go. He accused Sarah of sneaking around his back to be with Phil, and she said she wasn't. Though it did make me wonder. Then Everest said, 'You wouldn't care if he committed suicide tonight, would you?' Well, if it could get her out of hot water with Everest, she would go along with about anything." Gerald didn't say anything after that.

"What was your role in all this?" Nate asked.

"I didn't want to go along with any of it. I mean, if they planned to carry something like that out."

"But you didn't put a stop to it either." Nate was afraid Gerald was just as culpable.

"You don't know Everest. Once he decides something, it's a done deal. But for some reason, he"—Gerald shrugged—"must have changed his mind." But Gerald wasn't looking at them now, his gaze turned down, focusing on his feet as if he realized he'd said too much.

"Are you sure?" Nicole asked. "I mean, now Phil's gone."

"Okay, go over the scenario again," Nate said, ready to look for holes in Gerald's story. Why would Gerald be worried he could be guilty of anything if he really hadn't known anything about what had happened to Phil?

But Gerald didn't say anything differently, like the whole business had been rehearsed. He held his hands up, palms up. "That's all I got."

When he didn't have anything further to say, Nicole said, "If you think of anything else that might be helpful, please let us know." She handed him their business card, and then they left.

"Did you get all that recorded?" Nate asked Nicole. That was what she liked to do.

"You bet. You know that's what I always do."

Nate was glad she did. "Yeah. So now we hold on to this until we can speak to the others involved in this. If Gerald had anything to do with Phil's disappearance, it'll come out. We'll learn something from the others, or we'll turn this over to the police and let them work on this bunch."

"Yeah, if the police think there's anything to it."

"True. They might believe Phil just took off because he was mad at Everest and there's nothing more to it." Which meant they needed to gather more information to really have a case against Everest and the others. Like finding Phil's body, if he was no longer among the living.

Nicole leaned back against the car seat.

"Is your back bothering you?" Nate asked, ready to return her home so she could lie down for a while. She'd been taking an afternoon rest, and he certainly didn't want her feeling like she had to go with him on any more interviews.

"Yeah, the hazard of being pregnant and carrying two babies at the same time."

"Are you okay with continuing the witness interviews, or do you want to take a break? I can take you home." Nate was certainly leaning in that direction.

"No, I don't want to return to Silver Town when we're here already and can get this done and maybe learn something. I'm good. Really."

"Well, just let me know if you need to stop. I'm

serious, Nicole. I know you tend to tough it out when you're not feeling well, but I don't want you hurting when you don't need to." Beside the fact he didn't want to injure the babies in any way by having her work too long or hard.

"I'm good."

He hoped so, not only because he was her brother and cared about her but also because his parents and her mate would surely have words with him if he didn't ensure she was fine.

Chapter 5

AT THE LODGE, KAYLA WISHED THE DOORS TO the banquet room had been closed before the two runaway schnauzers reached it, but the florist was still hauling wedding flowers into the venue. Kayla could just imagine what a disaster this could be if the two miniature schnauzers raced into the room and tore into everything, knocking over ceramic vases, sending the roses flying everywhere, bashing into the chairs that she had just rearranged for better seating.

If she'd been a wolf, she could have caught up with them much faster than as a human in heels. She just hoped she didn't break her neck as she chased after them. The dogs ran straight into the banquet room, and Kayla expected to hear screeches and screams and see Bridezilla rush out, shouting for Kayla to take care of it. Blake caught up to Kayla before they reached the room, Landon rushing to help them out, Roxie right behind them. When they ran into the room, Kayla expected the worst, but then she saw the bride crouched down and hugging the dogs, getting kisses and kissing them back.

Kayla couldn't have been more shocked. She glanced at Blake to see what he had to say, hoping he was going to continue to deal with the dogs.

"They tore up the bedspread and a roll of toilet paper. Not to mention the room will have to be disinfected," he said.

"You're going to take the dogs out of here and find the owner, right?" Kayla asked Blake.

Roxie smiled at Kayla.

"Uh, yeah. Of course." Blake looked like he absolutely didn't want to take on the bride, but Kayla's job was to handle the banquet details, and Blake was supposed to be taking care of the dog situation. He moved in to take charge of them. "Do you know who the dogs belong to?" he asked the bride, since they seemed to know her so well.

"Yeah, my cousin. Why?" the bride said, frowning at him, like he better not say anything negative about them.

"We don't allow pets at the lodge. All guests sign the paperwork spelling out the rules from the outset. No pets except for service dogs are allowed," Blake said.

"So what do we do now? My cousin is one of my bridesmaids," the bride haughtily said, as if being queen for the day changed the rules for the lodge.

"Your cousin will have to pay for the damages and the cost of cleaning the room. She can't stay here any longer. The dogs can be boarded, but she'll have to find other accommodations." Blake was being a lot sterner than Kayla would have been.

Sure, normally that was how this worked for sneaking in pets and causing so much trouble, but Kayla still had to handle things for the bride until she and her groom married and took off.

Kayla would have said everything that Blake had except that the bride's cousin couldn't stay here any longer. Not in that room because they had to clean it up and she had to pay for the damages and such. But if the bridesmaid wanted to stay with another guest—then so be it. Though Kayla had to say that it was the first time she thought the bride looked human—when she was loving on the dogs.

Then a woman came into the banquet room and her eyes widened to see the dogs. Kayla figured she was the owner. Sure enough, they whipped around to greet her with just as much enthusiasm as they had with the bride.

"I take it you're the dogs' owner. You can either take them to the Silver Town Animal Clinic where they can be boarded, or you can pay to have them transported there," Blake said.

One of the men in the wedding party came over and petted the dogs. "I'll take the dogs to the clinic. You got their leashes?" he asked the bridesmaid.

"In the room." She sounded mad and upset that she'd been found out. What did she expect? That her dogs would just quietly sleep in the room all day? She gave him the room key.

"You'll need to pack up your things also, miss," Blake said. "I'll go with you." He glanced back at the others in the wedding party who were petting or talking to the dogs. "Just make sure the dogs don't leave the banquet room until they have their leashes and are leaving the lodge."

Though Kayla knew Blake didn't like seeing the dogs in the banquet room either. Well, neither did she, unless they were service dogs.

"Do you need me to do anything else here?" Landon asked Kayla.

She shook her head.

"Okay, I'm returning to the sixty-year-old's birthday party that I'm handling then." Landon left after that.

"Unless you need me, I'm going to take care of the bridesmaid and her extra charges," Roxie said. "Blake can have someone clean up the room and change the linens."

"Sounds good." Kayla was glad *she* didn't have to charge the bridesmaid for all those expenses. The bridesmaid wouldn't like it, but she shouldn't have sneaked her dogs into the lodge like that when she knew pets weren't allowed.

"You have a dog in the lobby," the bride told Kayla as Roxie left, her voice cutting.

"He's a rescue dog." Kayla explained what he did.

Surprisingly, the bride smiled. "Wow, that's really cool."

But as soon as Blake returned with the man who had the leashes in hand and he escorted him and the dogs out of the banquet room, the bride turned into Bridezilla again and was snapping at her bridesmaids to get everything set up pronto. And to do it right.

Kayla shook her head.

In Green Valley, Nate and Nicole went to speak with Sarah next, thinking she might shed some light on what had happened to Phil. But when they arrived at her apartment, Everest opened the door to their knock. They should have expected that might be the case. "We don't want any," Everest said, not waiting for them to explain why they were there. Then Everest frowned at them. "Hell, don't I know you?" he said to Nicole.

"We're private investigators hired by Phil's family to learn what we can about where he has gone to." Nate felt like he knew Everest too. From somewhere. He frowned. "Were you in the army?"

Everest frowned. "I told you; we don't want any." He shut the door in their faces.

"Hmm, so he's guilty of foul play and doesn't want to say anything or he'll incriminate himself?" Nicole asked Nate as they got into his car.

"Yeah, I'd say so. And he sure looks like someone I've seen before. Maybe in the army."

Nicole snapped her fingers. "He was the one who crashed into my car while driving a government van. I broke my leg and suffered a concussion. He went on the run, and when he was caught, they found he'd been drinking whiskey in the van and was DUI. He was kicked out of the service."

"Oh, yeah… I remember him at the post at some time when I was stationed there. He ran through a stop sign in the hospital zone and one of the military police stopped him. He did it right in front of the officer too."

Nicole pulled her hair back into a clip. "He sounds like bad news. The accident happened ten years ago, so I just didn't connect the name with the soldier. They always called him Corporal Johnson. I didn't know his first name was Everest or that he lived in Green Valley. I don't know, but a man who would screw up his service career so bad over drinking and driving a military vehicle, who knows what else he could get himself into. Particularly with a powerful father who can fix things for him."

Nate rubbed his chin. "I agree, and I knew him as Corporal Johnson too."

"He ended up with a dishonorable discharge. At least while Everest was in the military, his parents couldn't get him off. I wonder if they ever fought to get that changed so that he had an honorable discharge.

But it indicates the guy isn't totally honorable." Nicole looked at the list of names and addresses of the potential witnesses they needed to talk to. "Okay, so we go talk to Randy and his girlfriend next?"

"Ann first. Maybe she'll break. If she knows anything." But Nate couldn't quit thinking about Everest and if he was involved in some criminal activity, especially if it led to making Phil disappear.

"Right." Nicole directed Nate to Ann's apartment, and when they arrived there, they left the car and went to the door.

"Watch Randy be at her place, and he keeps Ann from talking to us like Everest did with Sarah." Nate felt they were coming up with nothing but dead ends and the friends would all stick together and stonewall them.

Ann answered the door with a beer bottle in her hand and took a swig. "Yeah? What do you want?"

"We're private investigators hired by Phil's parents to look for him," Nate said. "Can we talk to you about the last time you saw him?"

"Oh, that's easy. We were at the Red Dog Pub. And then we dropped him off at his house on his parents' farm." Ann wiped a strand of black hair away from her face.

"And the business with the fight at the pub?" Nicole asked.

Ann's lips parted, and he figured she was surprised that they knew about the fight there.

"Oh, it was no big deal," Ann said, trying to brush it off as though it was nothing important.

"Witnesses who saw the confrontation said it was. And then the bouncer threw Everest and Phil out of the pub. That's not nothing," Nicole said.

"All right, sure, they had a fight. I'm not sure what it was about exactly. I had to run to the little girls' room, and when I got back, I saw Phil and Everest being escorted out of the pub by one big bouncer dude. And we all left then too. No reason to hang around, not to mention we had to take Phil home."

"No one said anything to you about what had happened during the fight while you were driving Phil home?" Nate imagined it would have been the sole topic of conversation.

"Not that I can recall." She flipped her black hair over her shoulder. "I'd had a lot to drink."

Which could be true, but it was also convenient that she didn't know anything. "What about your boyfriend? Randy? Did he see what had happened?" Nicole asked.

"Oh, he went to the bathroom at the same time I did."

How very convenient.

"When we talked to the bartender, she said you all were there." Nate figured it was time to make up a lie of his own and see how Ann dealt with it.

"Well, that's just her word against ours, now isn't it?" Ann closed the door in their faces.

Now that was telling. So she had been there and witnessed the whole thing.

"You'd think Phil's friends would want to know what happened to him, wouldn't you?" Nicole said, as she got back into Nate's car.

"I'd think so. Unless they are covering up for someone else who's a friend *or* they were involved and are covering up for their own role in Phil's disappearance. We have one last stop—to see Randy."

They found where Randy was living and parked at his house. He was just pulling up into the driveway. "What do you want?" he asked, getting out of his car. Blond-haired, blue-eyed, and with a scruffy blond beard, he was the fairest of the friends.

Nate explained who they were and that they wanted to ask him about the last time he had seen Phil. "Did he seem distraught about anything?"

"Oh, you mean like he might have wanted to commit suicide?" Randy asked, his expression brightening as if he thought that was a way to deal with the fallout from this.

"No, for having left without saying anything to anybody and worrying his parents," Nate said, trying not to sound annoyed. "I was just wondering about his frame of mind after the fight at the bar."

"He was mad. Everest was mad. They get that way sometimes. Everest thinks Phil had some feelings toward Sarah, but Phil drinks and then pulls Everest's strings. Anyway, so we all got thrown out of the pub and went home. That was the last of it. I was with Ann the rest of the night. I don't know what the others were doing. All I know is Phil went into his house and shut the door. I don't have a clue where Phil went after that. He was as drunk as us. I just figured he'd slept it off."

"Was Ann there when Everest and Phil started throwing punches at each other at the pub?" Nicole asked.

"Yeah. Sure, where else would she have been? She doesn't like seeing any of us fight. Not that she stepped in to stop it either. She doesn't like confrontation. But she didn't want to get hurt either. I didn't bother trying to stop them. When they get like that, they just need to work it out between them. But we did take them home in separate cars."

"What about Phil's sister?"

"Oh, she shouted for Everest and Phil to stop it. She tried to pull Phil's arm, and he shoved her aside. Then she got mad and just watched until the bouncer threw us all outside. She and her friend got in their car and headed for home. We were behind them all the way to the farmhouse. Vicki got out of the car and headed into her parents' home, and then her friend took off. We pulled up and let Phil out at his house, and then we left. That's all there was to it. We told the police Phil sulks like that when he gets mad. And getting thrown out of the pub before he was finished drinking made him mad."

"You don't have a clue as to where he might have gone?" Nate asked.

"Nope. Not in the least."

So that told them Ann had lied about seeing the confrontation at the pub. No wonder Phil's parents were concerned something more was wrong.

Nate straightened. "What do all of you do at Phil's house in the middle of the night? His parents said you would land in on him at all hours. And stay for just a short time."

Randy's expression darkened. "I don't know what you're talking about. That's all I have to say." Then he went inside his house and shut the door and locked it.

"Wow, I hadn't expected you to hit him up with that," Nicole said.

"He was thrown off his game, wasn't he?" Nate said.

"Yeah, he sure was, which is why he shut us down right away. So they were involved in something illegal. Have you checked on court records to learn if they were involved in any criminal activities?"

"I have, but I haven't been able to run anything down on any of them except that Ann had a couple of speeding tickets. Randy had one, but that was it."

"Do you think if Everest has done anything more, his parents have gotten him out of the trouble?" Nicole asked.

"Yeah, possibly, if what the others told us was true."

Once they were done, they headed back to Silver Town. Whether Nicole wanted to lie down or not, Nate drove her to her home next to the lodge. It was time for lunch, so he'd make her some, and then she could rest. "You're having a nap after I fix you some lunch."

She laughed. "Okay. I never expected to have my brother take care of me while I'm pregnant."

"Well, someone's got to do it. Blake's at the lodge. If you want, I can call him and have him take care of you, but you have to take a nap. I don't want those babies to come too early." Nate really was worried about her, which was another reason why they wanted to reduce their caseload before he was with Kayla for a week and before Nicole was much further along.

"Thanks, Nate. How about if we call Blake to have him return home, and we can all have lunch together. Kayla too. And then I'll lie down. I promise. But I'll be back into the office later to help with the caseload."

"Only if Blake says you can."

"All right. I agree." Then Nicole called Blake to invite him to have lunch with her.

At the same time, Nate called Kayla. "Hey, I'm bringing Nicole home to have lunch with Blake and take a rest. Do you want to join us?"

"Yeah, sure, let me tell Roxie she's got to hold the fort down. She can go to lunch after I return." Kayla sounded really relieved, like he'd rescued her from a pit of snakes.

He wondered what she was doing, but she probably couldn't talk about it while she was at the lodge. "Okay, great. See you soon." Then he ended the call and smiled at Nicole. "See? Kayla and I are fine together."

Nicole sighed. "Yeah, but you have to keep after it or someone else is going to start asking her out because the two of you aren't mating."

"We'll get there." He was certain Nicole realized he was going to ask Kayla to mate him at the cabin but was dying to know for sure. He wasn't planning to tell anyone before he asked Kayla though. What if she said no? Or she wanted to wait a while longer? He adored her, and he was afraid she'd never want to mate him. He knew she was afraid of change, maybe of commitment. What if she just wanted to remain good friends? It would kill him. Besides, he knew she was afraid of shifting if she stayed overnight with him during the full moon, and he wanted to prove to her that he would be just fine with it. Yet he was afraid that she'd reject his plan to stay with her at the cabin because of the moon issue.

"That's what I want to hear."

When they arrived home, Blake and Kayla were

already fixing chili for everyone. Nate loved seeing the siblings working together on the meal.

Nicole did look worn out. Blake quickly gave her a hug and gently ran his hand over her belly. Then he kissed her, and they all sat down to eat and talked about their day.

Nate couldn't wait to be with Kayla like that. Kayla and her siblings treated him like he was family, but it would be different if they were mated. When Kayla started to tell him about the bride from hell, he wished he'd been there to straighten out the woman.

"I was just glad Kayla was dealing with it and not me." Blake served up bowls of chili for everyone. "I had to take care of a situation where a guest had sneaked two schnauzers into their room. The dogs were barking their heads off in there. I thought their owners were off hiking or something. Who knew when they would return? The dogs had torn up the bedspread in their room and the toilet paper roll."

"Yeah, but you didn't tell them the best part." Kayla topped everyone's chili with sour cream and shredded cheese. "Blake accidentally let them loose, and they went straight to the banquet room where the wedding and reception were going to take place."

"Oh, no," Nicole said.

Kayla explained how the bride's cousin, who was also a bridesmaid, owned them.

"So what happened?" Nicole asked.

"We charged her for damages and a cleaning fee and kicked her out of the lodge," Blake said.

"No," Nicole said, sounding shocked.

Kayla smiled.

Nicole frowned at her. "He's just teasing me, right?"

"Nope." Kayla ate some more of her chili.

"Then what? I know there are no rooms available anywhere during the height of the summer rental season," Nicole said.

"She's probably staying with someone else in their guest room," Kayla said.

Nicole glanced at Blake. He smiled and shrugged. "What I don't know can't hurt anything."

They all laughed.

"But if I learn she moved those dogs from the kennel to someone's room—" Blake said.

"I'll bodily throw her out myself," Kayla said, sounding serious about it.

Everyone smiled at her.

"I would."

Nate squeezed her hand. He didn't think so, but she could sure surprise him sometimes, and he loved it.

After eating lunch, Blake stayed with Nicole while Nate walked Kayla back to the lodge. Before she went in through the staff door, he kissed her and gave her a hug. "I'll call you as soon as I can so we can get together. And if the bride gives you any more grief, I'll come over and give you some support."

She smiled. "Thanks. I know you'll be busy, so whenever is fine with me. I've got to relieve Roxie so she can eat lunch and then get back to the wedding venue. They all are eating at the restaurant right now, and Landon's in charge of making sure that goes smoothly." She kissed Nate again, and he swore she didn't want to go anywhere if it wasn't with him.

"Yeah." He didn't want to give her up either.

Chapter 6

KAYLA AND NATE DIDN'T HAVE A CHANCE TO GET together that night because Nate was tied up with cases all afternoon and worked late. Kayla worked late, too, to finalize the wedding and send the married couple off on their honeymoon—and Kayla hoped the bride didn't give her husband as much grief as she'd given everyone else. Some of the guests had left, while others were hanging around to enjoy the resort. The cousin with the dogs left too.

Kayla had stayed later than usual because Nate wasn't able to do anything with her anyway, so she figured she'd put in the time so the others could go home and be with their pregnant mates. Well, all except for Roxie. She went home to do laundry.

The next morning, Kayla made omelets for her and her sister. Their Saint Bernard and tabby cat were curled up in his dog bed together, having already eaten and taken a walk, and were getting in some more sleep before their busy day at the lodge.

"You need to get laid," Roxie said to Kayla, carrying their mugs of maple-black-tea espresso to the dining room table while Kayla served up their curried omelets with broccoli and sun-dried tomatoes.

She was always testing out new omelet recipes, and this one looked like it was going to be a winner.

"You're always saying that." Kayla sat down to enjoy breakfast before they ran as wolves, then headed over to the lodge to work. She often worked at home when she didn't have a banquet venue to manage, but now with her brothers helping out their mates—who were both pregnant with twins—Kayla was heading into the office every day. After that, she needed…time to decompress. "I just want to make sure everything's covered." Getting laid hadn't been a priority for her, though she would love to spend the night with Nate again. They hadn't done that in some time.

Roxie sighed. "We all know you. You do a great job on the promotions, and we'll all pitch in to help you with whatever needs to be done. You're not alone in this, but you've always, well, put relationships on a back burner since you called it quits with your ex-boyfriend."

"Our brothers have other pressing issues, and we've had to step up to take on more managerial problems with the lodge."

Roxie couldn't argue with her about that. "If you don't hurry up and mate Nate, I'm going to have to start dating him."

Kayla rolled her eyes. "You're too outgoing for him."

"I could tone it down."

Kayla smiled. "No. You couldn't. You are you, and I am—"

"A total workaholic. So what's the excuse for not asking him to have dinner with you last night? Or breakfast with you this morning? Or lunch this afternoon? Dinner tonight? You're retreating from the dating world into your shell."

"We both worked late last night." Kayla let out her breath. Her brothers and sister had been born the night of the twentieth of June, so they were Geminis. And Kayla had been born after midnight—so a Cancer. The hermit crab reference always seemed to come up at times like these. So what if Kayla liked her solitude after a day of being out in the public and having to deal with so much?

"As a private investigator, Nate has always got cases he's working on. The one he told us about is probably not the only one he has to prioritize. And his sister has been experiencing so much morning sickness of late, and yesterday, she was so worn out she didn't make it back to work for about four hours. Nate has been taking up the slack in their PI agency. Our brothers' are not the only ones affecting someone's workload with their absenteeism. Nicole's time off is affecting Nate's workload too. And another thing, he never asked me about going to the cabin. I think he might have changed his mind because this case he's working on needs to be resolved pronto," Kayla continued.

Roxie gave up trying to convince Kayla and finished off her omelet. "Now I really love that version of the omelet. The vegetables added color, fiber, and taste."

"Yeah, I really enjoyed it too." Kayla was glad her sister wasn't giving her any further grief about Nate. Her backup plan—if they didn't go to the cabin—was to propose a mating to him on the Fourth of July. She wasn't about to give up on that. By the Fourth, they were going to be mated wolves. *Guaranteed*, she thought. Unless he was holding back because he was unsure of things with her.

"Well," Roxie said, gathering up their plates to take into the kitchen, "our brothers took care of the ski lodge all on their own before we finished what we had to do in Vermont to move here. So now it's our turn to run things."

"But they didn't do any promo for the new ski lodge here. So it wasn't like they handled *all* that needed to be done." That was the thing: promotions took a whole lot of work, which was mainly why Kayla handled it almost full-time.

"That's true. But we have enough staff to cover the mundane stuff, and you need to take a break before you crash and burn." Roxie cleaned up the kitchen while Kayla made them thermoses of hot maple-tea espresso to go. "He'll ask you to go to the cabin. Just plan for it."

"As soon as we get all the stuff done for the Fourth of July—"

"Then you'll be getting stuff ready for the new ski season. And our brothers will be taking paternity leave to help out with the new babies when they're born."

Which was the problem with each brother having a pair of twins at the same time. Though their brothers and their mates were glad they weren't expecting quadruplets like the Wolff family had. Even Dr. Mitchell, the retired veterinarian, was returning to work full-time to take over Gabrielle's workload for about four months after the babies were born. Probably sooner if she ended up on bed rest before the babies were due. Even though the wolves had an easier time of it than humans did, they could still run into trouble during a pregnancy. They were all eager to see the babies, and they'd all be helping out with them after they were born, serving in the capacity of a bunch of wolf nannies.

Roxie set the frying pan on the drying pad. "If it were me, I'd be seeing him every night and every morning and—" Roxie paused. "Wait. You're not holding out until I find a mate first so you can have the house for yourself, are you?"

Kayla smiled. "Why is it that you aren't dating anyone seriously? You wouldn't be waiting for me to marry, then leave you the house, would you?"

That was the agreement they'd all had, though

nothing was written in stone. The idea was that whoever found a mate would move out and live with their mate. Blake and Nicole had built their own home a short distance from this one, and therefore it was also nice and close to the lodge. Landon had moved into the vet's home behind Gabrielle's clinic. So it was true that if Kayla mated Nate, the notion was that she'd be moving into his apartment and they'd want to build a home of their own on the land next to Nicole and Blake's home. She was practically getting hives from the thought of having to deal with all that stress.

Roxie laughed at the suggestion she was waiting on dating anyone. "I'm just casually dating some wolves. None seriously right now. Come on. We need to get in our wolf run before work." But she was texting someone, and Kayla hoped it wasn't Nate. Roxie was known to get involved if she felt she could help her siblings get together with the wolves she thought were right for them. It had worked in Blake's and Landon's cases, but it wouldn't necessarily work in Kayla's.

Then the two of them went for their morning wolf run. Though Rosco always wanted to go with them, he couldn't be depended on to stick with them. He'd run off, chasing the wildlife instead. They didn't want the distraction when they ran as wolves.

When they returned to the house, shifted, and dressed, ready for work, Roxie strapped Buttercup in her stroller to take her to the lodge. From the time they took her home from one of the hotel rooms as a kitten, she'd been going to the lodge every day with Rosco.

"Are you going to try a leash on her again?" Kayla didn't have the patience or fortitude to struggle with an uncooperative cat, but Buttercup had loved the stroller walks when they took Rosco for walks on his leash. Talk about Buttercup being a princess. When she was smaller, whoever took Rosco out would put Buttercup in their pocket. But she was too big for that now.

"Yeah, sure, sometime. It would be fun, though she loves the stroller."

Kayla walked Rosco to the lodge on the walkway from their home to the two-story building while Roxie pushed the little pink stroller.

They were halfway there when Roxie frowned at her and said, "About the birthday parties coming up—"

"About the party… I think it's high time we celebrate the birthdays together." Kayla always had mixed feelings about it. Yeah, it was fun to have her own party separate from her brothers and sister, but on the other hand, it seemed kind of silly when it was just the next day and they had to have another one just for her. "I know I should have talked to you about this sooner since it's in just a few days."

"No. Way. You're special. Our poor mom didn't

think you would ever come. It took until the next day for you to arrive."

"Half an hour later—after midnight. Sheesh. It's just that with all the babies coming and changes—"

"No. I mean if you really want to do it, sure, but not because you're afraid it will be too much for everyone else to handle. We love having the two birthday parties. If you want, we can celebrate mine with yours if you're feeling lonely. The guys can have theirs the day before." Roxie cast a glance in Kayla's direction. "This better not be about Nate."

"This isn't about Nate!"

Roxie stared at her.

Whoops! Kayla figured that's where this conversation was headed…again. That she didn't deserve a second chance of finding a mate so she was self-sabotaging herself with excuses why she wasn't just asking him to mate her. She didn't want to think in those terms. But maybe she was…a little bit. But she was also afraid he wouldn't be able to handle the business of her shifting in the middle of the night during the full moon. What if they were in the middle of making love?

"Fine! I'll invite him over for dinner tonight. All right?" That was another of Kayla's downfalls. She absolutely hated confrontations and would agree to practically anything to end them.

"Yes! Perfect. I'll visit with one of our brothers and his mate. Or if they're busy, I might finagle a date with someone so you won't think I'm waiting for you to mate Nate and leave the house to me."

Kayla smiled, then went in through the main entrance where guests took pictures of the two of them walking the dog and cat into the lodge. Everyone loved Rosco and Buttercup. But seeing the cat in the stroller was an extra treat.

"Don't forget to call him. I know you. You'll get wrapped up in work and forget about calling until it's too late," Roxie said.

Kayla released Rosco so he could greet everyone at the lodge—a group of kids out of school was eager to pet him—and then settle by the fireplace. Buttercup always stayed in their office after a swarm of kids had to see her too. Kayla pulled out her phone. "Calling him now." She thought of texting him, but she felt she needed to speak with him so she could tell if he really was free to do this or if he was feeling obligated.

"Okay, checking with the front desk to see if we're having any issues," Roxie said.

"Okay, good." Kayla called Nate while Buttercup settled on her fluffy pink cat bed next to the desk. "Hey, you might be busy with that case you were telling us about, but I thought you might like to have dinner at our place tonight. Roxie plans to go to one of our brothers' homes for dinner."

"Are you sure you are okay with it?" Nate sounded like he really wasn't certain she wanted to do this. Like she was feeling guilty about not getting together with him or she'd been coerced.

She wanted to groan out loud. She wanted to just chill out with Roxie and their dog and cat. And do some more promo stuff tonight. But she knew in her heart of hearts she would have a great time with him too.

"Yeah, I'm sure." Kayla had to get out of her darn shell. Life was long for them, but she wanted to enjoy it. She could always find work to fill her time.

"All right. I'd love to. What time?" Nate asked, sounding eager, which made her feel guilty all over again.

"Seven? Would that give you enough time to do your work and come over?"

"Sure. Look forward to it. Or you could come over here and have dinner with me. I'll fix burgers on the grill."

"Uh, yeah, that would be nice." She loved grilled burgers, and it would be nice to have someone else cook for her. She loved to cook, but this would be great too.

"All right. See you at seven."

She smiled. Maybe Roxie was right. She felt really good about this, and it sounded like Nate wasn't up to his eyebrows in work. Then Roxie poked her head into the office.

"Good news. Nate and I are on for tonight at his place, so that means you can stay home and have dinner there if you prefer," Kayla said before Roxie could ask.

"What? Me? Stay home alone? No way. I'm going out for dinner. But great on the date. Um, I need you to go with me to open a guest safe that's still locked. The guest who now has the room wanted to place something in the safe, and he can't open it. So we need to do it and see if the previous guest left anything in there."

"Okay, so are we going to find a million dollars? A bag of uncut diamonds? A cache of passports? An incriminating photo?" Kayla asked, hoping it would be something exciting and mysterious as she grabbed the master key to get into the room safe.

Roxie laughed. "Probably someone's cell phone like the last time."

At the PI agency, Nate was so glad that Kayla was coming over for dinner. He'd been trying to let her deal with all the issues she'd had, what with the summer promotional business, banquet managerial tasks, and having to take on more managerial duties while her brothers were out of the office, but also just to have time to decompress after work. And he'd been busy with Nicole being out of the office so much too.

He'd even fantasized about Kayla and him

being together in a place of their own, grilling burgers, talking over their days. But he hadn't wanted her to feel pressured about having to see him if she was feeling too overwhelmed about things. No matter what happened on the missing guy case, he planned to ask her tonight to go with him to the cabin after her siblings' birthday party to make it an extra special weeklong birthday celebration for her.

All settled down to work, he was surprised when Nicole showed up at the agency early. "I thought you weren't coming in until this afternoon. Are you feeling all right?"

"Oh, yes, just great. Just some morning sickness earlier. Blake went into the lodge to help out, and I'm here to work on pending PI cases."

"Okay, good. I haven't learned anything new on the case with Phil. His parents haven't heard from him. I keep in touch all the time, just in case. And I let them know where we're at on this."

"At least they know we're spending a lot of time on it." She began looking at the cases that were stacking up. "Do you want to have dinner with us tonight?" Nicole asked.

Nate smiled. "I have a dinner date with Kayla tonight."

"Oh, wow, yes! I'm so glad you asked her out."

"She called me and wanted to have a dinner date."

"Oh," Nicole said, smiling. "Even better. We'll

see if Roxie wants to have dinner with us then. So where are you taking Kayla?"

"I'm grilling burgers. I figured she'd like that best. She's really a homebody, you know, and after working at the lodge all day, she'll want some time to chill."

"Okay, perfect. Roxie just told me that Kayla and her boyfriend back in Vermont called it quits when he was inebriated and totaled his car when they were together. Did Kayla tell you about that?"

"Roxie did. She said Kayla and her boyfriend were out celebrating her birthday."

"Right. Well, Roxie said Kayla gets kind of upset during that time. We're supposed to go to her birthday party the day after the other siblings' surprise party. You know theirs are in just a couple of days. But I wanted to warn you she might be less than… cheerful for her own birthday party."

"I believe that's why Roxie told me, worried I'd be offended or something." He'd noticed how stressed Kayla was on other occasions when they'd gotten together for meals and she seemed lost in her thoughts, worried about work, which was why he figured she hadn't really needed his company at the time. He was glad she wanted to be with him tonight.

"Did you ask her about going with you to the cabin?"

"I will tonight."

Nicole let out her breath in a frustrated sigh. "You are procrastinating, Brother. If she doesn't want to go because she's worried about work commitments, at least you'll know right up front. I know you're worried she'll say no and you're putting off asking her. If she can't make it, then Blake and I can go with you to the cabin to lift your spirits. So what are we working on?" Nicole asked, setting the other cases aside.

No way did he want to be at the cabin with his sister and her mate. They could take the cabin over instead if they wanted. Besides, someone needed to take care of the cases they were working on.

"We don't have anything too rigorous." Though if they did, he was handling it.

Nicole laughed. "For now, I can manage. When I've had nights of very little sleep after the babies are born, that will be another story. I may not make a whole lot of sense or be a whole lot of help."

Chapter 7

When Kayla and Roxie arrived at the guest's room at the lodge to check the safe, they opened it and found a set of keys with a metal skull hanging from the ring. "Well, the person will be missing his car keys, so whoever had the room couldn't have gotten far if his car is in the parking lot," Kayla said, looking them over.

Roxie had checked on the guest and gave her a rundown. "He didn't officially check out this morning. The housekeeping service cleaned the room for the next guest, and the guest's bags were all gone, so we assume he just let the charges on his card stand. Looks like he has a house key on the ring," Roxie said, eyeing them. "Those with the numbers on them look like safe deposit box keys."

"Well, he will want them back or he'll have to pay the bank to have the lock replaced on the safe deposit box, which gets expensive. Also it looks like a mailbox key, don't you think? Do you want me to check for the car in the parking lot while you look up the room reservation to see if you can find a way to notify him?" Kayla asked.

"Yeah, let's do this. See? Sometimes management issues can be intriguing."

"But not for the poor person who left his keys behind."

"True," Roxie said. "I'll tell the guest staying in that room his safe is ready to use."

"Okay." Kayla headed outside and began using the key fob all over the parking lot, targeting one row after another, but it appeared the owner's vehicle wasn't parked there. Maybe he got a ride to the airport then? She returned to the lodge and met up with Roxie at the front desk. "No vehicle in our lot. What if a couple of people were staying in the room and they both had a set of car keys? So they left, but the one forgot about his keys in the safe?"

"Sounds possible. If he didn't have a car here, it seems strange that the person would lock up his keys in the safe. If it was because of the safe deposit keys, who would know where he banked, and how would they get access to the safe deposit boxes anyway? I checked for the person who registered for the room and called the phone number he had given us, but it went to voicemail." Then her phone rang, and she looked at the ID and smiled.

"Hi, this is Roxie Wolff, manager at the Timberline Ski Lodge, and we found your keys in the safe this morning." She smiled at Kayla but then frowned. "They're not yours? You didn't use the safe at all. Ohh-kay. It must have been the previous guest then. Sorry for troubling you." She smiled. "I'm so glad you had an enjoyable stay and hope to see you again soon." Then they ended the call. "Not his keys." She looked through the registrations online. "Okay, the guy who reserved the room before him used one of those third-party registrations. It can take forever to track the guest down then. He didn't register a vehicle in the lot either. Not that we have in the system."

"Tonight at dinner, I can ask if Nate could look into it," Kayla said. "If not him, then Nicole."

"That's what I was thinking too. Maybe, in the meantime, the guest will realize he left his set of keys behind and contact us to see if we have them."

"That would work too." Kayla saw Blake was working on management issues, checking out security tapes. She took a breath of relief. "If you're here for the time being, Blake, do I have time to work on promo stuff?"

Blake smiled at her. "Yes, to your heart's content. Landon is here too."

Now *that's* what Kayla loved to hear.

The rest of the morning and afternoon, Kayla was busy working on what she loved doing most, though she loved a good mystery and had tried her hand at locating the owner of the keys, just like each of her siblings had done—without success.

"Have a great dinner," Roxie said to her as Kayla was getting ready to go. "Enjoy a wolf run with

Nate. You know, anytime he wants to run with you at our house, you two can do it."

"Thanks. I love our wolf runs, and I don't expect him to want to drive out to see us just for that. Who are you having dinner with?" Kayla asked.

"Both brothers and their mates. I have to check in on how our sisters-in-law are doing."

"Oh, good. I need to do that too with Gabrielle. I just saw Nicole."

"Just have a good time tonight. You had time to do all the preparations for the Fourth of July activities you'd scheduled at the lodge, so no worrying about anything while you and Nate are having dinner," Roxie said and gave her a hug.

Kayla smiled. "Thanks. I know we'll have a lovely time." And really, after getting her other work done, she was feeling free for the moment.

She walked back to the house and got into her car. She'd already packed an overnight bag just in case she stayed with him and had put it in the trunk last night while Roxie was taking a shower. Then she drove into Silver Town where Nate lived.

As soon as she arrived and knocked at his door, he opened it and pulled her in for a kiss and hug. "You know, I only leave you alone because I know how stressed you are at work, but hot damn, when I get to see you, it's like a wolf's homecoming."

"I feel the same way about that with you." And

she truly did. Feeling warmed to her toes, she kissed him back, tonguing him for good measure. "Yeah, no regrets. This is just where I needed to be tonight."

He closed the door behind her, took her into the kitchen, and made them both strawberry daiquiris, her favorite. With drinks in hand, they headed out to the back patio and the grill. It was a hot summer night, though storms were coming through the area later and would cool things off a bit. He had already cooked the fries and put the hamburgers on the grill. "I should have made steaks."

"Oh, I love burgers. They smell delightful. Do you want to run as wolves later?" She sipped from her glass and purred. "So good." She hadn't run with Nate as a wolf in ages, and she really wanted to do it.

"Absolutely. I was hoping you'd say that."

They were soon sitting down to eat their burgers, corn on the cob, and fries, drinking their daiquiris. She smiled. "I love to cook, but I love it when you cook too. And I never have a daiquiri unless I'm dining out. This is so much fun."

"I'm sure you could use a break, and I wanted it to be fun for you. How are things going at work?"

"Oh, great. Landon and Blake ended up back at the lodge for the day, so I had time to work on marketing stuff. I don't know how you are about your work process, but I have kind of a schedule built in, and when I have to stop to do a ton of other things instead, it really throws me off. Before I forget, Roxie and I found some keys in a room safe that were left behind. The guest registered through a third party, and we wondered if you might be able to locate him."

"I'll sure do it."

"We'll pay you."

"Dinner will be enough."

She chuckled. "You can have dinners with me at any time. This is great, by the way."

"Thanks," he said.

———————

Nate had cleaned his place up completely in expectation of Kayla's coming over, hoping to reassure her he was the kind of wolf she'd want to be with in the future. And he'd had every intention of fixing her favorite cocktail for when she arrived. He liked them too, though he was also fine with a beer. But since her being here with him was special, he would enjoy having one with her.

When she'd arrived and he had welcomed her into his place with a hug and a kiss, he'd thought she looked tired. "I'm kind of like you and plan my day out as to what I need to take care of first. But with the work I do, it doesn't always fall into place like I hope it will. I can't find out anything on one lead, so I try some other things, get stumped, and begin working on another case when I'd rather just nail the first one, call it done, and go on to the next."

"Oh, me too."

He knew she'd feel better if she had her normal routine. With him, he could change plans with a snap of his fingers and deal with it without any real big issue. He had to be like that in the military.

He was glad she wanted to run with him as a wolf before the storms came, though if she changed her mind, maybe they could enjoy watching a movie after dinner. Just anything that meant she'd stay longer, and he was game.

"It's supposed to storm later tonight. Do you want to stay with me?" He wanted to extend their visit, to enjoy more time with her now that she was at his place. They tended to see each other more during family visits where he would try to carve out some time alone with Kayla. This was a refreshing change.

"The storms are not supposed to happen until much later this evening. Though..." She hesitated to say something.

"What?" He hoped she wasn't planning on running off right after dinner.

"I packed an overnight bag just in case I stayed."

He released the breath he was holding, so glad she was staying with him. He'd wondered if she was just shy about staying there. "You're not worried about what other wolves will think, are you?" He realized right away he shouldn't have mentioned it because if she had been, she might be convinced to go home instead of staying with him.

She gave him a heartwarming smile. "No. I'm not worried about what the other wolves will think."

He gave an exaggerated sigh of relief.

She chuckled and forked up a fried potato. "I might be needed early at work in the morning though."

"If you are, you can leave early. But I'd really love it if you stayed the night."

She nodded, he pumped his fist in the air, and she laughed. He loved hearing her laughter. It cheered him. Not only because of that, but it was the first time she'd agreed to stay overnight with him, and he felt he might be making real progress. He was always unsure what to say or do to make it right with her.

He wondered if he should bring up the next topic or just let sleeping wolves lie, but he wanted her to know he understood how she felt about her birthday and the ex, and he had to tell her what he wanted to do about it. "About your birthday party."

She finished another bite of her hamburger and cleared her throat. "I keep telling my sister and brothers it should be just one party for all of us. That way everyone can come to one celebration."

"I agree. If that's what you want, then that's the way it should be." Nate figured she needed someone in her court on the issue. He knew her siblings wanted to keep the status quo, but it really was Kayla's choice.

"Thank you. I didn't think anyone would ever agree with me. I just feel with the babies coming we need to... I don't know. Consolidate the birthdays because they're just one day after the other. And we're quadruplets, together, like it should be."

"Everyone enjoys going to both parties, I'm sure, but it really is up to you. You don't need to offer any reason for feeling that way either. Now, if it were me, I'd opt to have my own birthday party."

She smiled. "Because you and Nicole always have yours on the same day."

"Right. It's always been a two-for-one birthday party. I have a proposal to make. If you want, we can celebrate your birthday with your siblings and then the next day—or week, actually—I want to take you someplace special. Listen, I'm making kind of a muddle of this. I've just been worried about asking you and then you, um, saying no. I keep worrying you're not ready to stay with me yet. Maybe not ever."

She smiled. "Nate, you are the sweetest, most caring, and considerate man I know. It's not you. It's just me."

"Okay, well, if we keep an open dialogue, I believe we can talk through any issues we might have. We can talk about it more after we run as wolves if you'd like, okay?"

"Wait! Where were you planning on taking me for my birthday?"

He smiled. She sounded like a little kid ready for Christmas Day and unwrapping presents. That's one of the things he loved about her. "I thought we'd go to one of the pack cabins in the woods. I made reservations in case you wanted to do this—no pressure. It's the one with the view of the waterfalls, a river, and a lake. We can watch the sunset from the deck or climb up to the top of the cliffs and see the sunset up there. Hikes in the woods, run as wolves, barbecues, swim in the lake. We can just get away from it all."

"But can you afford to take off that much time what with work commitments?" she asked, frowning.

She hadn't jumped for joy at the prospect of being with him for a week at the cabin, he noticed. Maybe she didn't even like camping. He knew she was all for hiking. He'd been with her and several of the family members taking long hikes in the woods even when they weren't in their wolf coats.

"Yes. A couple of the PIs from the Green Valley wolf pack who have family here in Silver Town are willing to step in if Nicole needs some help while I'm gone. And the same with our pack leaders as far as ensuring everything at the ski lodge gets done while you're away if your siblings need extra help."

"Ohmigod, yes!"

Surprised Kayla had agreed to it and seemed

thrilled about the prospect, he was overjoyed. He was afraid she'd have to think about it for a couple of days and check with her family first just to make sure they were all right with it. Nicole was right—again. He had worried Kayla was going to reject his proposal, and that's why it had taken him so long to ask.

Kayla smiled. "That means we *have* to have my birthday party the day before with the others."

He laughed. "Is that the *only* reason you're going camping with me?"

"No, of course not. I need a break, and I am ecstatic about it. I've really gotten a bunch of work done, and we should be good. I know that the cabins don't have Wi-Fi, but that's okay. If I'm gone for a while, everyone will know how important I am."

He smiled. "They know. Okay, good. I told you it is totally up to you. If you want to have your birthday party the day before, that'll work. Or if you want to have it the day we leave, we can do that. It's your birthday celebration, after all."

She finished her drink, and he finished his. Then she rose from the table, and he did too, thinking they were going to clear the dishes, but she threw her arms around his shoulders and hugged him. "I believe you're my knight in shining wolf coat."

He pulled her close and kissed her mouth with eagerness and tenderness. "That's all I want to be for you." And he sure as hell wished he'd asked her sooner!

Chapter 8

ONCE THEY WERE FINISHED WITH DINNER, KAYLA kissed Nate and hugged him tight. She wanted to take this so much further, but she was worried about the incoming storm. Before the weather became too nasty, she wanted in the worst way to run as a wolf with Nate. "More of this later, okay?" She kicked off her sandals, ready to be a wolf with Nate. "Ready for a run?" She wasn't letting the fun end there.

"You bet." He smiled at her and yanked off his shirt.

She pulled hers off and then unzipped her jean shorts. That was the thing she really liked about Nate. He liked being casual, and so did she, so no sense in dressing up for dinner at his place or hers. Of course, if he took her out for dinner to the Silver Town Tavern, they both dressed up. They didn't have to. They could be as casual as they wanted to be at the wolf-run restaurant that catered only to wolves, but they still liked to dress up when they went there together—to show they were a couple, in case anyone was in doubt. Even though they always seemed to be meeting up with family when they ate there.

They eyed each other with intrigue. He was so hot—a well-toned body, tanned, and just sexy wolf material. They both smiled at each other, and then naked, they hugged before shifting, turned into their wolves, and raced out the wolf door, Nate letting her go first. It certainly wasn't like when she and Roxie were trying to get through the door at the same time. Of course with Nate, since he was a bigger male wolf, they probably would have gotten stuck.

Since the apartment building was wolf-run in a wolf-run town, they had woods behind the apartment complex they could run in, and all the apartments had wolf doors to make it easy to come and go.

They ran full out, enjoying the run, though they heard thunder off in the distance.

The wind began to whip up the leaves on the forest floor, the tree branches swaying with the force as Nate and Kayla ran toward a creek. They ran for about five miles, and she smelled rain in the air and felt the temperature dropping rapidly. It appeared the storm had decided to drop in sooner than the meteorologist had predicted. Clouds in the dark sky turned ominously green, and lightning flashed in sheets all across the dark sky, illuminating the trees and them. Rain, when it came, couldn't hurt them, but lightning and hail—if it was big enough—could.

They were too far from Nate's apartment when

the rains let loose, and then chunks of ice began to fall from the sky. Kayla hadn't expected that! She and he raced for the creek's bank with the same notion in mind. She hoped the creek wouldn't overflow, but an outcropping of rocks and an over-hang would give them some protection from the storm until it passed.

This wasn't how she had planned for their outing to go. They finally reached the overhang, lightning striking a tree nearby with a thunderous crack, making both her and Nate jump a little. Then she smelled smoke. The tree was on fire! She and Nate peered out to watch it, but the pouring rain soon put out the fire, and they both sighed with tenta-tive relief.

They snuggled together as wolves under the rock ledge providing them shelter. Their double coat of fur kept them warm, and cuddling together added to that. Only their guard hairs were wet, their undercoat of soft, downy fur keeping them warm and dry.

Nate licked her nose, and she licked his back. Despite the storm raging all around them—lightning forking into the ground, thunder boom-ing or cracking overhead and shaking the ground, ice falling and piling up all around the outside of their shelter, some as big as golf balls—she thought about her poor car. At least Nate's car was parked under a roof. Guests didn't have that luxury.

All that mattered for now was that they stayed safely under the shelter. She wanted to talk to him, but this was nice too, just being with him on a stormy night in their wolf coats snuggling to stay protected.

Then she realized the water in the creek was rising. Nate nudged at her, motioning to the creek, warning her if she hadn't already taken notice. But they had time before the water reached their shelter, and she was hoping the hail would stop by then.

The rain and chunks of ice continued to fall, the lightning never ending. Thunder blasted through the area. She had really wanted to run with Nate as a wolf, but they should have realized the thunderstorm might get there earlier and not have relied so much on the weather report, knowing it was often wrong.

The creek began to overflow the banks inches away from them. It wasn't going to stop. Then the water was at her paws, and Nate moved around her to protect her from the water.

She smiled at him for being so chivalrous. But when the water reached their bellies, he motioned with his head to leave the shelter and gave her a little woof.

She woofed back. They would run as fast as they could to the apartment. There wasn't any other shelter from here to there.

But to their surprise, the bank under their feet gave way suddenly. Nate slipped into the flooded creek, and Kayla followed right after him. The creek was moving so fast, she couldn't reach the bank, so she was just trying to keep her head above the water and saw Nate ahead of her struggling too. He kept trying to look back for her. She woofed at him, telling him she was all right. Just get out of the water!

He finally managed to scramble onto the bank, where he could finally get his footing, and she was relieved he was out of the water now. The hail was mixed, pebble-sized, which bounced off their fur coats, but larger pieces were still falling too. As she neared the location where he'd managed to get out of the water, he was staying for her. Though she appreciated the gesture, she wanted him out of this weather and not getting pummeled by the hail while he waited for her.

But when she reached his location, she didn't have the strength to get out on her own. She struggled to pull herself up on the shore with her front paws while Nate shifted and grabbed her by the body and pulled her onto shore.

"Let's run!" He shifted back and the two of them raced for the apartment complex.

Now she was glad he had stayed to help her out of the flooded creek.

A chunk of ice hit her shoulder, the fur helping to keep her from a worse injury, but she'd be bruised for sure. Luckily, their advanced healing abilities as *lupus garous* would mean the bruise would go away in half the time.

Another hit her butt. *Damn it. Now that hurt!*

Nate yelped, and she glanced over at him, keeping pace with her, watching out for her. He had blood on his muzzle.

The ice finally stopped falling, and it was all rain now, still pouring down, but she felt an overwhelming sense of relief.

They were getting close to his apartment complex. She didn't even want to see what had happened to her car. But she was glad they were nearly home.

She raced onto the covered patio and through the wolf door.

Nate ran through it right behind her. Then they both shifted.

"Man, I'm so sorry, Kayla," Nate said, pulling her into his arms. "Are you okay?"

"Yeah, but you've got blood on your face. Let me clean you up."

He kissed her right above her shoulder where ice had struck her. "You've got blood on your shoulder."

She glanced at it. "Uh, yeah, and bruising for sure, but it will go away fast enough. I'm just glad neither of us ended up with injuries more serious than that." She knew large hail had actually killed people out in it who were unable to take cover quickly enough, so it wasn't something to leave to chance. There hadn't been any reports of hail before they went for their run. She didn't want to look at her backside where she'd been hit.

"Me too."

"I hate to think of my car."

"Aww hell, I didn't even think of that." He ran his hand over her shoulder.

"Well, *we* are more important."

"That's for sure." He released her and turned her around to check her over all the way.

"All in one piece still, right?" she asked.

He smiled. "Yeah, in one beautiful piece." He leaned over and kissed her hip. "We need to shower, then bandage the wounds."

"Wait, I didn't get to check all of you out."

He chuckled. "It was rough out there all right."

"Thanks for helping me out of the creek. I couldn't manage, though I might have been able to some distance down the creek. But I really appreciate your help." She reached up and ran her hand over his back around where he had been struck a couple of times, bleeding, bruised. "We're a pair."

"Yeah, I agree." He took her hand and walked her into the master bedroom. "Why don't we take a shower. I had thought of watching a movie this evening before we called it a night."

"I'd like that." He got her a fresh bath towel, and she took a shower, planning on taking it quickly so he could shower afterward.

"I'm taking one in the other bathroom. Enjoy yours."

"Thanks! I will!" Though where she'd been cut was stinging like crazy. Still, she needed to wash away any germs from the creek that could infect the wounds. When she was done, she dried off and found him wearing a pair of boxer briefs, ready to bandage her injuries.

"Ouch," she said, when the bandage touched the sensitive wound on her shoulder.

"Sorry." He finished bandaging her, then tended to the spot on her backside.

Then she carefully took care of his injuries. "I think we deserve a drink." She started to bandage his back.

"I hear you. Ahh."

"Sorry."

"What do you want to watch?"

"A western?" she asked.

"You got it."

"Great. And to drink?"

"Glasses of wine, and we could have hot buttered popcorn?" he asked.

"Sure. That sounds good." She was so grateful they were in the apartment while the wind howled, the rain poured down, and lightning flashed, thunder sounding right afterward.

"I'll be right back." He grabbed a navy-blue terry-cloth robe for Kayla and helped her into it so she wouldn't have to put anything over her injuries that could cause friction.

"Thanks. Do you want to watch the movie in the bedroom?" she asked, surprised.

"Yeah, if that's all right with you. I figured after the night run we had, that might be the most relaxing."

"Oh, sure, that sounds grand. I'll come with you and help you carry the popcorn or wine or something."

After they microwaved the popcorn in the kitchen, they retired to the bedroom with a couple glasses of wine and a bowl of popcorn and their phones.

Once they settled under the navy-blue covers, he started the movie, and she leaned back against a pillow. "This is fun. I hadn't expected a movie in bed." The only place she ever watched a movie was in the living room of her home.

"Yeah. I hadn't really planned on it, but after what we went through, I thought it would be a nice change of venue."

"I'm all for it."

After they finished their wine and popcorn, they cuddled with each other, the rain still pouring down outside, thankfully no more hail though. "I need to get your bag out of your car once the movie ends."

"Good. I don't want to see what my car looks like. My bag is in the trunk."

He pulled her closer. "You can borrow my car if yours needs to be repaired. I can walk to the office."

"Thanks, but I'll just have Roxie come get me and take me to the lodge tomorrow. I have a much shorter walk to the lodge from our home than you do to work. And to do your job, you need a vehicle. I usually don't."

"All right. I'll take you to the lodge in the morning though."

"Oh shoot, after all the excitement tonight on our run, I forgot to call Roxie to let her know I'm not coming home tonight. She might worry I'm trying to make it home in this awful storm." Kayla grabbed her phone and called her sister while Nate paused the movie. "Hey, we're watching a movie, and I'm staying the night."

"Oh, good, I didn't want you coming home in this weather."

"We're good. But… Well, my car might be a little worse for wear. So depending on what it looks like, I might need to borrow your car or Blake's sometimes."

"Oh, sure. I'm so sorry. I didn't even think about that with you being at Nate's apartment."

"He's going to drive me to the lodge tomorrow."

"Are you sure? I can pick you up." Roxie sounded like she wanted to ensure Kayla wasn't too upset over her car.

Kayla glanced at Nate and smiled. "He wants to

take me in." She knew he'd be disappointed if he didn't have the opportunity. It would be out of his way, but it would be for Roxie too, if she came into town to pick Kayla up and take her back out to the ski resort. Not that it was all that far from town.

"Okay, well, that sounds good. See you tomorrow. No rush though. We have it covered," Roxie said.

"I'll be in." Kayla didn't want her family thinking that she was coming in late because she and Nate were getting it on. She had really loved the dinner, the wolf run, even the misadventure with taking refuge under a rock ledge and ending up in the swollen creek, and a movie—in bed, no less. So, yeah, it had been fun. And if she had time, she'd love to do it again, minus the part about running in a hailstorm and swimming for their lives in the creek.

———

After she ended the call, they watched the rest of the movie, and then Nate kissed her, knowing with Kayla, he could literally weather any storm. "I'll get your bag and be right back with it." He hated to see what shape her car was in. He left the bedroom and put on the clothes that he'd left in the living room before they had shifted to run as wolves. Grabbing her keys off the coffee table, he headed outside into the now-light rain with a flashlight, hoping her car was all right.

As soon as he saw it, he realized it was beyond repair. Golf-ball-sized hail had smashed the windshield, breaking it, and the rainwater was still pouring in. The whole car was dented with small and large pellets of ice that had ruined it. A few dents could have been cosmetically patched, but this was a disaster. The age of her car, the salvage value, the cost of repairs—it just wouldn't be worth trying to have it fixed.

He took pictures of the vehicle, hoping the car didn't have any sentimental value for her and figuring she would want to report it to her insurance agency right away to get a jump on having an agent out to document her claim. No doubt others who had vehicles out in this weather had the same issues as Kayla.

He noticed a couple of other cars parked at the apartment complex that were not in covered spaces with the same kind of damage. He wished he'd known how bad it was going to be. He would have given Kayla his covered parking space instead or even picked her up to bring her here instead of having her drive here. Though he knew she wouldn't have wanted to impose.

When they'd been out in the hail, his heart had nearly given out as soon as he fell into the creek and doubly so once he realized she had too. He kept wanting to ensure she was behind him, not going under until he finally could manage to climb onto the bank. But he could tell she couldn't make it on her own despite how hard she'd tried. He'd thought about grabbing her by the ruff of her neck as a wolf and pulling her out of the water, but he had been afraid he might lose her. Shifting into his human form hadn't made the job any easier, but at least he had succeeded in getting Kayla to safety. He noted she hadn't told her sister about all that they'd experienced. Maybe she was afraid of how Roxie and their brothers would react and that they'd want to see for themselves that Kayla was okay.

He got her bag out of the trunk, which was thankfully dry, and headed back inside. He set the bag on the floor in his bedroom and went to enjoy the rest of the night with Kayla.

"Don't tell me. How bad is it?" she asked, looking so beautiful in his bed, her head against his pillow, her dark hair spread across it.

He chuckled. "You don't want me to tell you or you do?"

"I don't. And I do."

"It's totaled."

"Good. I can get a new car then."

He chuckled and removed his clothes, then joined her in bed. "Here I was afraid you would be upset to hear the news."

"Only that I will have to pay for a new one, but no. No real sentimental value."

"Good. You didn't tell Roxie about our swim in the creek."

"No. She and my brothers would come here to

check me out. We can tell everyone about your heroics after I return home tomorrow."

He smiled. "Okay. I just wanted to know if it was okay to tell my sister about what happened."

"Yeah, absolutely."

He turned out his bedside lamp, and they cuddled together under the covers. They both said "*ow*" at the same time. Then they chuckled.

He had hoped to make love to her tonight, but he wasn't sure they could after the ordeal they'd been through.

"That was a great meal," she said. "And the movie was too."

He kissed her forehead. "I agree."

"And the run was an adventure."

He laughed. "Truly."

Then she turned on her side. "Our sides don't hurt."

He smiled, eager to make unconsummated love to her. Consummated love would mean they were mating, and he wanted to wait until they were at the lakeside retreat for that.

He faced her and cupped her cheeks. Then he began to kiss her mouth and deepened it. He always felt so attuned to her, so needy, so wanting. She ran her fingers through his damp hair and kissed him back, their gazes locked on each other. Bliss. That's what he felt when they were together like this.

He ran his hand over her hip, silky, warm, and

soft. He liked to think he was in charge of his own destiny, but when it came to Kayla, she influenced so much of what he did in a good way. He nuzzled her neck with his mouth, felt her pulse leap, heard her heart beating like thunder. So was his.

"Hmm," he said, and kissed her mouth, the burgundy wine and salty, buttered popcorn flavoring her tongue and lips. He deepened the kiss, hungrily spearing her mouth with his tongue. She teased back, slowly caressing his tongue, her eyes closing to his kiss.

He pressed his hand against her breast, felt her nipple peak, and moved his mouth down to lick and kiss it. She softly moaned.

Whenever he was with her like this, he felt alive, electricity zinging through his blood as he moved his hand down between her thighs. She immediately moved her leg over his hip, giving him easy access to her. He wanted to pleasure her as much as he wanted to claim her for his own for all eternity.

Her warmth reached out to him as he began to stroke her between the legs. She groaned softly, and he slipped a finger between her intimate folds. She was so wet, and he wanted to slide his rigid erection deep inside her. He was dying to mate with her, the yearning going deep.

Then he kissed her mouth again, hot and heady kisses, his erection itching to join her. Mating her during their cabin trip wouldn't happen soon enough.

She was tensing hard, his finger touching her harder, faster, until she cried out and he moved against her, wanting to be as one, but instead he just had to feel her body snug against his.

They were writhing together, kissing, tongues connecting in long, lingering strokes. Then she slipped her hand down to begin pumping his arousal. Oh, man, did that feel amazing.

———

Kayla couldn't believe they'd gotten themselves so banged up during the storm that they had to be careful of how they made love, but this was working out for them too. Nate made her feel well loved and she wanted to make him feel the same way. He had his hands in her hair, stroking, holding it, but then he was kissing her mouth again, driven like she was to bring him to climax. She could see his pelvic contractions, the intense pleasure in his expression, the growing need to explode. His gaze was dark and rapt, his mouth connecting with hers again, his kisses intoxicating, his body tightening.

She loved making love to him like this, but she was ready for more. Every time she hinted at a mating, he only smiled and shied away from saying yes. She thought he wasn't ready, or he was afraid she wasn't. Then again, maybe their trip to the cabin was all a plan to ask her and to finally mate her.

But this was grand, being with him, giving in, holding each other close, his eyes closing in bliss just as he groaned out loud and came in a burst.

"God, am I glad that you stayed with me tonight," he said, pulling her into his arms and holding her snug.

"So am I. This feels so good," she said, keeping him close. "So good."

"Hell, yeah. How do you want to sleep?"

"With you."

He chuckled. "That's a given. I was thinking more in line of our injuries."

"This works for me. Front to front. All your sexy bits pressed against all my sexy bits."

He chuckled. And ran his hand down her backside. "All of you is sexy."

She smiled. "Yeah, you too."

Then they took a shower, together this time, bandaged their injuries, and returned to bed, closed their eyes, cuddled together, and finally slept.

At first morning's light, she woke. They were still snuggled together, her chest pressed against his, while he was on his back, and she guessed his back wasn't feeling too bad, for which she was glad.

She sighed. "Hey, I guess it's time for me to go home and get to work."

He sighed too and ran his hands through her hair. "After a hearty breakfast."

"I can go for that." But then they settled down to

snuggle some more, and before they knew it, they were both late to work, hopping out of bed, groaning, and laughing.

She knew just how this would look to her siblings, and the same for Nate with his sister and his parents.

Chapter 9

THAT MORNING, AFTER NATE AND KAYLA MADE pancakes, he was amused to see her rushing through breakfast so they weren't *too* much later to work. Then he drove her to her house and parked, and she rolled her bag inside while he carried in all the things she'd had in her car since it would be towed away as soon as Desmond Reynolds, the insurance adjuster, took a look at it and released it.

Roxie was at work, so she wouldn't know exactly what time Kayla had arrived home, only that she showed up late for work this morning. Nate knew Kayla was embarrassed about it, but he figured they'd be late, and there wasn't anything further they could do about it. Not that there was anything wrong with it either.

"I'll look into the situation with the owner of the keys that were found in the room safe. Roxie sent me the third-party booking information already," Nate said.

"Okay, good. I should have thought of that when I asked if you could do it. Oh, I forgot to ask. Does anyone know you were planning to invite me to go with you to the cabin?"

"Jake Silver might have figured out what was going on. I had to reserve the cabin through him. Though I didn't tell him I was taking you. And he didn't ask. He might have thought I was taking the family."

Jake was the pack leader's brother and second in charge, so that was one of the jobs he took care of for the pack. Nate said it with a teasing light in his dark eyes and a smile on his lips, dimples appearing on both cheeks.

She loved his dimples. They made the rugged Army Ranger approachable. She wrapped her arms around his neck. She wasn't sure if she should tell him that Nicole had already let the cat out of the bag with Roxie or not.

"And Nicole knows because I had to tell her so I could take off and make arrangements with the Green Valley wolf PIs to help out. But I didn't tell those PIs who I was going with on the vacation. Nicole would have known I was taking you, or I would have said I was going with some of the guys in the pack," Nate explained.

"Okay, so since Nicole knew, Blake would know. And if he knew, Roxie and Landon would know." There. She hadn't given away Nicole, not wanting to get her in trouble. Roxie had slipped up by telling Kayla the news. Kayla kissed Nate. "If there's any chance of a storm, we're not going for a run in the woods."

He chuckled. "No, you're right. Only fun stuff this next time. Let me know if we're on for two birthdays or—"

"One. Four on one day. That's it."

"Sounds good to me, but don't be shocked if I have a birthday surprise for you after that."

"I would be surprised if you didn't, and it will be welcome." Then she kissed him until he parted his lips and she tongued him.

He groaned.

"Oh, are you hurting?"

"No. I just wish"—he smiled—"we didn't have to get up so early to go to work."

She laughed. "We are late to work." She knew what he meant though. At the cabin, they could make love to each other the whole week long, go to bed when they wanted, get up when they wanted. No sisters or brothers or jobs to worry about and they'd be all healed up.

"If you'd like, I can take you to Green Valley to look for a car," Nate said. "This afternoon or tomorrow afternoon?"

"I need to speak to the insurance adjuster this morning. Then he'll release it and it can be towed off." She had figured she'd just get one of her brothers or Roxie to go with her, but it would be nice to go with Nate. "But sure, that would be great. Look at your schedule and see which would be best for you."

"Okay, I'll see what Nicole says too."

"Sure." She liked how he was eager to help her with her car and didn't put things off. She could always borrow Blake's or Roxie's car, but she'd rather have her own in case they needed theirs.

As soon as they said goodbye, she locked up the house, then walked to the lodge and saw Landon's car parked there, so he was in. Blake would have walked from his place already if he wasn't home with Nicole.

Kayla walked into the lodge through the staff entrance. If she was bringing Rosco and Buttercup, they always went through the front doors to show off the arrival of their lodge mascots. When she entered the lobby, Rosco hurried to greet her with licks and body rubs. Kayla gave him a big hug. "I missed you too."

"Hey," Roxie said, joining Kayla and giving her a hug. "If you can't tell, Rosco missed you last night. So did Buttercup. I'm so glad you stayed with Nate after that storm hit though."

"Yeah, it was a wild night all right. Uh, sorry for getting in so late."

"Hey, I told you I didn't expect you to come in early this morning. I mean, what with your car being totaled—so sorry about that, by the way—but you had to get Nate to drive you here, and I'm sure he was dragging his feet."

Kayla laughed.

"Do you need me to help you with the car?"

"Yes, taking me to see the insurance adjuster in an hour at Nate's place would be great. Then I'll have a tow truck haul the car off and I'll ride home with you. And thanks, Roxie."

"What are sisters for? What about shopping for a new car? Or did you want to wait a bit on it?"

"Nate's going to take me to Green Valley to look for one."

"Oh, great. Even better. A lot of the guests' vehicles in the parking lot at the lodge were hit too. Luckily, Landon had already driven home, and his car was parked in his garage. The same with the rest of us. But here, we had a whole lot of unhappy guests. Not with us, just with the hailstorm causing so much damage to their cars. We've been helping them contact insurance investigators, and we set up a lemonade stand out there to cool off tempers."

"What a great idea. Oh, by the way, before you hear it from Nicole once Nate tells her, we're having *all* the birthday parties on your birth date." Roxie opened her mouth to speak, but Kayla quickly added, "Nate finally told me he's taking me to the cabin near the Silver Falls. You didn't tell me it was *that* cabin."

Roxie's lips parted, and then she smiled broadly. "Oh, wow. Yes! That's great. I didn't know it was that cabin either. Maybe Nicole didn't know it. Or she might have been at least keeping that secret."

Then she frowned. "You didn't let on you knew already, did you? I don't want to get Nicole in trouble or for her to be mad at me for accidentally not keeping the secret."

"No. I let on that I didn't."

"Oh, great." Roxie sighed and put her hands on her heart. "For a whole week. You're going to have a great time, and it will be so well deserved."

Blake came back from the indoor swimming pool area and must have overheard Roxie's enthusiastic comment. "What's the good news?"

"Well, our very own Kayla is going on a camping trip for a whole week with Nate. And they're staying at the Silver Falls cabin."

"Whoa." Blake winked at her.

"It's just for a fun trip." Kayla hated that she became so easily flustered over things.

Landon joined them from the restaurant with a cup of coffee in hand. "Family meeting?"

"Oh, for heaven's sake. It's just a camping trip. Is everything else covered? I'm going to get a jump on our winter promo," Kayla said. "And I'm celebrating my birthday on the same day as all of you are." Then she headed for the office.

"Wait," Roxie said, looking at something on her phone, "Nicole just texted me that you and Nate ended up in the creek during the storm. In the middle of the hailstorm?"

"Yeah. And he saved me." Kayla smiled and

headed into the office, and Buttercup wound her way around her legs. She'd missed Kayla too. She lifted Buttercup into her arms and sat down on her office chair, stroking a purring cat.

"I hear wedding bells ringing in the not-too-distant future," Roxie said, loud enough for Kayla to hear.

"What did I miss out on?" Landon asked.

Kayla smiled. She'd gotten her way. She was having her birthday celebration with her siblings. Of course that had a lot to do with going to the cabin with Nate. She hadn't expected her family to be so excited about it. But she knew she'd have a great time.

She began drawing up plans for when winter arrived at the ski resort. Oh! She needed to make her camping list first. She started a new page and began listing everything she needed to take with her so she wouldn't forget anything.

Chapter 10

LATER THAT MORNING, KAYLA AND ROXIE headed over to Nate's apartment to get this business over with concerning her totaled car. Desmond Reynolds, their insurance adjuster, was a wolf, so there was no problem with him saying the car was totaled, though after she'd seen it, she didn't think there was any doubt of that. Wolves helped each other out whenever they could.

"Ohmigod, I'm so glad you weren't driving it when the hail demolished your windshield," Roxie said, taking pictures to show their brothers, Kayla figured. "I can't imagine the two of you being out in the storm during a wolf run."

The adjuster shook his head. "Damaged property can always be replaced. Wolves? That's a whole different story." He had Kayla sign the documents that she needed to. "We'll be sending you a check in a couple of weeks, hopefully, though it can be as long as forty-five days, but I'll try to expedite it."

"Thanks, Desmond."

Then the adjuster left, and Kayla called Ollie's Auto Body Shop and Towing Service. "Hey, Ollie, this is Kayla Wolff. Can you come pick up my totaled car at Silver Town Apartments?"

"Oh, you too, eh? So sorry to hear it. Though I've had a jump in business a hundredfold. I'll be right there. I just picked some up from the ski lodge and impounded them," Ollie West said.

"Great. Thanks."

Shortly thereafter, Ollie drove up with his tow truck, wearing his trademark red-and-white tow truck shirt and blue jeans and work boots. When he was working on cars, he wore his green-and-white auto-body shirt. Red-haired and red-bearded and with bright green eyes, he was a character. He'd sweet-talk a car into doing anything for him, and everyone trusted him to take care of their vehicles as if the cars and trucks were his own family members'.

Ollie had Kayla sign a release of the car, and then he towed it off for her. She brushed her hands together, as if washing her hands of one more task that had to be done, and then got back in Roxie's car and they returned to the lodge.

"That was easy," Roxie said. "I can't wait to see what you'll get this time."

"Something bright red."

Roxie smiled. "I guess you're not too upset about it."

Kayla sighed. "I'd be lying if I said I was. It guzzled gas and gave me fits half the time. I'll be glad to get a replacement, though seeing it so damaged was upsetting. Like you, I was just glad I wasn't in it at the time."

When they arrived at the lodge, Roxie went to see where she was needed.

The phone began ringing, and Kayla answered it in the office. "This is Kayla Wolff at the Timberline Ski Lodge. How may I help you?"

"I need to speak to a manager," a man with a gruff voice said.

"You're speaking to her."

"I left my keys in a room at your lodge. I need to pick them up." He was very authoritative as if *they* had made the mistake of keeping his keys.

"Uh, sure. If you have some ID, you can come in and do that anytime. Which room was it?"

"I don't remember the room number."

"Okay. Your name?"

"Durham Manning."

"Can you describe what was on the key chain?"

"A car key, house key, safe deposit box key."

"Anything else?"

"Might be. I can't think right now. I just need to get my keys."

Kayla thought that was strange. She knew exactly what she had hanging off her key ring. And why wouldn't he have mentioned he had two safe deposit keys on the key ring, not just one? "Can you describe the key ring?"

"Silver."

Why wouldn't he mention a skull dangled from it too? "Okay, it'll be here. Just ask for me, Kayla, or one of the other managers when you get in."

"All right." He hung up on her.

Kayla left the office to speak with Blake. "Hey, a guy by the name of Durham Manning says that he's coming in for those keys we found in the guest room safe, but I don't have a good feeling about this guy. He didn't tell me that there was a smaller key that looked like a mailbox one or *two* safe deposit keys on the ring, and he couldn't say what else was on it. He said it was silver, but you know how often key rings are silver. And he didn't mention the skull hanging from the key ring, which is pretty noticeable as far as helping identify them as his own. He didn't say the keys were in the safe either. You'd think he'd mention that first in case we hadn't looked in there and found them but also to help further identify them. And he didn't know what his room number was."

"Okay, well, if he drives here, we can see if the key belongs to the car he's driving. If it's a duplicate key. If not, we need to make sure they're his keys. Have we had any success at locating the person who stayed in the room?" Blake asked.

"Not yet. I'll check with Nate. I figured I'd give him a chance to look into it first. But if we have the possible owner of the keys coming in, we don't have a lot of time."

"I'd go with your wolf instincts, and we'll have to do everything we can to verify they're his before we hand them over," Blake said.

"Right." Kayla called Nate next and told him what was up. "I suspect you haven't learned anything about the man who registered for the room and left his keys in the safe."

"I just got some information right before you called me. The man who made the reservation was named Durham Manning."

"Okay, so that's the name the man gave me who said he's coming to pick up the keys." She explained what was bothering her about this man's claim. "Maybe I'm just reading too much into this."

"I don't blame you. I do the same thing. On another topic, is there anything special you'd like to eat at the cabin?"

"No, nothing special. You know what I like, and that will be fine. Just whatever we usually eat."

"All right. Now that I know a Durham Manning reserved the room, I'll look into who he is as much as I can in the meantime. And give you any information on him that I can find."

"Thanks, Nate. I sure appreciate it."

"No problem."

They ended the call, and she went out to speak with Blake. "Nate said the guy's name is Durham Manning, which is what the guy coming in for the keys said his name was over the phone. But because of my concerns, Nate's going to look into the man further."

"Good show. If he can get a picture of him, we'll know if it's the same guy who shows up."

"Okay, sounds good." She went back to working on winter promo ideas. It wasn't long before Nate sent her a picture of Durham Manning that he'd found on Facebook. Ohmigod, that was the muscular, black-haired, and bearded man she and Roxie had seen when they'd run as wolves the one day, speaking to another man, trespassing on their land. She printed the picture out and shared it with Blake. "Roxie and I saw this man and a blond-haired guy talking on our land when we came upon them as wolves."

Blake stared at her in disbelief. "And you didn't tell Landon or me?"

She sighed. "They would have been gone by the time we returned home, dressed, and called anyone. Besides, we scared them off, and they were having a discussion, like they wanted to get away to somewhere private."

"You should have told us."

And then he and Landon would have left their mates to run with Roxie and Kayla from then on when they could have been needed at home. "We never saw them again. Just the one time."

Blake still looked disgruntled. "You still should have told us. You went running the next day, correct? What if they'd been there again?"

"They weren't. But we were cautious."

Blake scoffed. "Next time—"

"We'll tell you." Kayla conceded only because she knew he'd tell Landon and the two of them would give her and Roxie grief.

"All right. We'll tape the picture right here with a note to verify the identity of Manning when he shows up." Blake was already writing a note to their clerks and the siblings, though only the siblings—as management and owners of the lodge—would actually hand the keys over to the owner due to liability issues. "What exactly were they talking about?"

"A job, I think." Kayla shrugged a shoulder. "Nothing really specific." She gave Blake the description of the other man, and he wrote it down. "I'll come to back you up as soon as the man arrives to get the keys," Kayla said. She returned to the office, but before she could thank Nate for the photo, she got a slew of attachments from him. She began opening them up, then printed them out.

Then she got a call from Nate, and he sounded worried. "This Durham Manning has committed a number of armed robberies of jewelry stores."

"Are you sure this is the same Durham Manning who rented the room? What if it's some other?" But now she was thinking that the "job" the men had been talking about in the woods had to do with a robbery.

"Yeah. It's the same man."

"But they released him from prison? Or he's never been caught?"

"He was in prison for eight years. And now he's out and wanted for questioning about the new armed robberies."

Kayla's jaw dropped. "You mean he might be involved in the armed robbery in Green Valley?"

"He could be."

"And he stayed here at the lodge?" That was the thing about having a lodge like this. They had no idea who was staying here—good guys or bad. Though most of the time they were just everyday normal people on a vacation. Silver Town and the ski resort weren't on any of the major highways— which was just the way the wolf pack wanted it—so they didn't often get folks who were driving through to somewhere else unless they were taking a more scenic route.

"It appears that way."

"Okay, well, I need to call Peter." Sheriff Peter Jorgenson had sworn in Landon and Blake as reserve deputies when he needed more deputies while pursuing criminals, so technically, they could arrest the man. But with prior warning like this, they needed to tell Peter what was going on and let him handle it with his full-time deputies.

"And Darien or Lelandi."

Darien and Lelandi Silver, their pack leaders,

always needed to be made aware of any trouble the pack members might be in for.

"Right. Thanks so much, Nate. I'll let my brothers know right away too." She got off the phone and was hurrying out to see Blake and warn everyone about Durham Manning when someone approached the counter, a man with a shaved head from what she could see under the cap, his face free of whiskers. He didn't look like the man in the photo—who was bearded and whose hair was black and curly. The man at the counter's eyes were hidden behind dark glasses, and he had a cap worn low, the bill shading his features. He asked for the set of keys he had left in the room, his voice gruff and commanding as if he could intimidate Blake into giving them up just like that.

Kayla immediately slipped the rap sheet Nate had sent to her below the counter for Blake to see, then hurried back into the office to call Peter. She shut the door, not wanting to leave her brother out there by himself to deal with a potential armed robber but needing to get a hold of the sheriff right away before the guy left.

"Peter, we might have a situation here." She briefly explained what was going on.

"On our way."

She loved that about the sheriff's department. They would come at a moment's notice. Not that they didn't have other situations to take care of in town, but Peter would make sure everything was covered pronto. She opened the office door to see the man holding his hands out, palms up and shaking his head. She texted Landon and Roxie about a potential emergency.

"I don't know what the big deal is," the man said at the front desk. "I told you who I am."

"It's just a formality. We don't want to hand over the keys to the wrong person. It could constitute a liability issue. Do you remember where you had left them?" Blake asked.

The man tilted his head to the side a little. "In. The. Room."

If he'd left them there, he would have known they were in the safe. Not just in the room lying on the dresser or some such place.

Kayla saw Landon stalking across the floor—ready to take care of any troublemaker in their midst. Both her brothers were six feet tall, muscled but not outrageously, and they wouldn't take any guff off of anyone.

"Do you have the vehicle with you that these car keys belong to?" Blake asked.

"No. I rented the car after a plane trip to Colorado. That's why I didn't realize that I had left my keys behind until I reached the airport. What else do I have to do to prove to you these are my keys?"

Kayla was listening to everything that was being said as she checked in another guest. The main doors opened, and she glanced in that direction to see Peter and the pack leader's brother Tom and Tom's cousin Deputy Sheriff CJ Silver enter the lodge to speak with the man talking to Blake. She was relieved to see them and hoped there wouldn't be a fight between them and the shaved-headed guy.

"You're going to need to come with us so we can have a little talk," Peter said, showing his badge and identifying himself as the sheriff of Silver Town.

"What the hell," the man said, practically growling. "I come to get my car keys that I'd accidentally left in my room, and I'm interrogated as if I'm a common thief?"

"Come with us. We'll talk down at the sheriff's office." Peter was firm.

The shaved-headed guy's face grew crimson. "What? Are you going to arrest me? You have no cause. I know my rights."

"You're claiming you're Durham Manning, and he happens to be wanted by the FBI for questioning. They're on their way to Silver Town now to speak with you. Put your hands behind your back," Peter said.

"All right. I'm not him."

Kayla had known he was lying when she had spoken to him on the phone.

"So who are you then?" Peter asked. "Have you got any ID on you?"

"No."

Convenient.

"I mean, how could I say I was him when we don't look anything alike? So I left my ID with him. So what happened was I'd met him on a hike a few days earlier and we walked together and he said his name was Durham Manning. He told me that he was staying at the lodge. Anyway, he'd left his keys in his room, and he said he'd pay me a couple hundred bucks to get them. Then I came to get them for him. I didn't figure it would be a crime or any damn thing."

"Just like that? Did he give you a reason why he didn't want to return to get the keys himself?" Peter asked.

"Nope. I just figured he had his reasons. I didn't realize he was wanted by the FBI, or I wouldn't have done it."

"Okay. Well, since the FBI is on the way to Silver Town, they'll want to question you about everything you know concerning Durham Manning," Peter said again.

"I told you. I didn't really know him. I just met him on a hike, and we were mostly just…hiking."

"Yeah, that's what you told me," Peter said, but he didn't budge from doing his duty.

The man shook his head, muttering obscenities. But he finally complied. Peter and the others took him out to one of the deputies' vehicles and drove him to the sheriff's office.

Blake sighed. "Well, they'll let us know what they discover about this man. I don't believe his story about just meeting Manning and then coming for his keys so he could earn a couple hundred dollars."

"Me either." Kayla heard the door open again, though people were always coming and going, but when she looked, she saw Nate hurrying into the lodge, headed straight for them, warming her all over. He was like a bit of sunshine in her life, no matter what was going on. She smiled at him. "Don't tell me you came to rescue me."

Nate gave her a hug. "Yeah. Well, and I'm deputized too, so I thought if you all needed me, I would be here for you. Where is he?"

She knew he'd wanted to come and check on her personally, which she thought was truly heroic. "Well, I appreciate it. You just missed him. Peter hauled him off."

"Oh, good. I'm glad they've taken him into custody to learn what this is about."

Roxie quickly joined them. "I was dealing with a plumbing issue in the lobby restroom with our plumber. I can't believe the guy who left the keys in the safe was an armed robber. Blake texted me and sent a photo of Durham Manning. He was the black-haired, muscle-bound guy in the woods we saw talking to the blond while we were on our run, wasn't he?"

"Yeah," Kayla said, not wanting to bring that bit of news up again.

"Which you should have told Landon and me about already," Blake scolded.

"What's this?" Landon asked.

Blake told him what Kayla had revealed earlier about running as wolves and encountering the two men.

"Hell, Kayla, you and Roxie should have told us about it," Landon said.

They would *never* hear the end of it.

Roxie turned her attention to Nate and smiled at him to avoid responding to Blake's and Landon's comment. "Did you come to rescue Kayla?"

Nate was frowning, looking as serious as could be. "Yeah. Of course. If Blake can't go running with you, just call on me."

Kayla and Roxie sighed.

"But who is this other guy then if he's not Durham Manning?" Roxie asked.

"That's what Peter will have to discover. He said he'd called the FBI to take care of him though. The man's not a wolf, and if this guy truly knows the armed robber, the FBI will need to question him thoroughly, learn his identity, and go from there," Blake said. "He didn't have any ID on him. I guess he just thought he could waltz in here, and if he was aggressive enough, we'd fold and take him at his word."

Not long after that, Tom Silver came back into the lodge. "Hey, if you've got that set of keys belonging to Manning, we need to turn them over to the FBI agents. I figured they wouldn't want them because the real owner might still come for them. Though, if the real owner *is* Manning, they'll want to take him into custody for questioning anyway, so they need the keys."

"I'll get them," Kayla said and retrieved them from the safe in the office. She handed them over to Tom. "I hope we get to learn what this is all about."

Tom nodded. "The two agents are wolves, and they'll definitely let us know what happened. If they hadn't been wolves, they wouldn't have shared what was going on."

"Good show," Nate said.

"I'll let you know as soon as we learn something." Tom saluted them, then headed out of the lodge.

"What happened to you?" Roxie finally asked Nate, looking at the wound on his face.

He'd removed the bandage, but the area where the chunk of hail had hit him was still cut and beginning to heal. "Uh, that was due to the fight with the hailstorm. Don't worry though. I won."

Roxie's mouth gaped, and then her gaze shot to Kayla. And, no, Kayla hadn't told her sister or her brothers about the injuries they'd had in the hailstorm.

"Were you hurt too?" Roxie asked.

"Not bad. We're both healing up just fine. Luckily, we found protection under that massive stone ledge next to the creek," Kayla said.

Blake and Landon were frowning. "The creek was a raging river by the time the storm let up," Landon said. "That's how come you went swimming in it?"

"Yeah, the earth gave way, and we ended up in the creek, but"—Kayla patted Nate on the shoulder—"he rescued me. If you ever get caught in a hailstorm and are swept away in a raging river, be sure Nate is with you."

"Kayla Marie Wolff, you never even mentioned the two of you were hurt by the hail," Roxie said, scolding.

Kayla smiled and hugged her sister. "We made it out just fine and watched a great movie afterward."

"Okay, so I need to get back to that retirement party I'm in charge of catering, if you don't need me," Landon said.

"Yeah, go ahead," Blake said.

Landon stalked off to one of the banquet halls.

"Hey, it's lunchtime," Nate said, as if he wanted to get Kayla out of hot water with her siblings. "Can I buy you lunch at the lodge, Kayla, if you're free?"

"She's free," Roxie said, shaking her head. "Next time…"

"There won't be a next time like that," Kayla said. "Dinner, drinks, wine and popcorn and a movie, a run as wolves, sure, but no hailstorm issues." She took Nate's hand. "You know how this works. We own the restaurant, so the lunch is on me."

"Even better." He winked at her, and they headed off to the restaurant. "Sorry about mentioning the hailstorm, but I didn't know what else to say when your sister asked how I was injured. Besides, my sister asked me first thing about my injury this morning at the office, and when I told her we took refuge next to the creek, she said the same thing as your brother. The truth would have come out."

"You're right. I'd mentioned it, but not that we were hurt." She kissed his shoulder with affection. "You know you really didn't have to come here and rescue me."

"Yeah, I did. I would have hated myself if hadn't shown up and you were harmed. How are your injuries from the hailstorm? I didn't even think to ask you about them this morning."

"Much better, thanks. Your face is healing nicely."

"Yeah. And the rest of me too."

"That's good to hear."

Nate opened the door to the restaurant for her. "All right, so what's today's special?"

"Lobster tails, baked potatoes, and corn on the cob."

"That sounds good."

Today was already perfectly special, she thought, because she had a hero of a wolf trying to rescue her again.

"Then we'll go to Green Valley and look for a car for you. I already discussed it with Nicole, and she said she could manage since I was coming here to help out anyway."

Kayla smiled. "Oh, yeah, perfect."

Chapter 11

AFTER HAVING LUNCH AT THE LODGE, NATE drove Kayla to see cars at some of the dealerships in Green Valley. He hadn't bought a new car in several years. He loved haggling with car dealers and had done the same for his mom when she'd needed a new car and for Nicole too when she left the army. "What about this one?" Nate asked Kayla, while they looked at the cars at the first dealership she wanted to check out, thinking a minivan or hatchback would be useful.

He was peering in through one of the car windows when a salesman came out to sell them a vehicle. "We just want to look around on our own for a while. She's not sure what she'd like to get this time around."

"Yeah, sure, my name is Zan Jenkins. Just call on me if you need some help."

"Sure thing."

Once the salesman walked off, Kayla let out her breath, sounding relieved. "I hate high-pressure salesmen, so I'm glad you suggested that we just look on our own for now."

"Yeah, me too. Okay, so what about this one?"

Nate showed Kayla another hatchback and was reading all the items included with the package deal.

"I'd like to have a red car. Then I can see it in the snow."

He smiled. He was thinking more in terms of style and use, not color. He started looking at a Honda Odyssey. Man, it had room to spare. Just perfect.

She folded her arms while he slid back the side door and climbed into the rear back seat. With three rows of seats, it was perfect for family outings. A pair of twins, grandparents, parents, and room for another person in the last row. And storage room in the trunk for whatever they needed.

He was sold on it. For the price, and it was red, he thought it was perfect. But when he saw her raised brows and folded arms, he figured Kayla wasn't buying it.

He sighed, and they began to look at two-door coupes.

"These are cute," she said, "but it would probably be more practical to have a four-door, or I wouldn't be able to take all the ladies—Nicole, Roxie, your mother—to the tea shop."

"I'm sure one of the other ladies would volunteer and you could have the sporty car for running around in."

She smiled at him. "Let's look at some of the four-door sedans."

Then she and he began to check them out. While she was sitting in the driver's seat of one of the red sedans, he glanced back at the Odyssey. He was thinking if he took his parents and his sister and brother-in-law and the babies and Kayla anywhere, *he* could use the vehicle.

"Is that the one you like?" he asked Kayla as she checked out the trunk of the sedan.

"I want to look at the others too."

"Even if they're not red."

She chuckled. "I will give up a red one if one of them has everything else I want." Then she saw a Honda Civic on the showroom floor in red. "Let's see that one."

He smiled.

And it turned out to be just the one she wanted.

"Okay," Nate said to the salesman. "How much will you take off of the price if we get both the Honda Civic and the Honda Odyssey?"

Kayla frowned at him, looking puzzled.

The salesman offered a reduced price but said he could go no lower than that.

"Ask the manager," Nate said.

The salesman went off to speak with him while Kayla and Nate drank some complimentary bottled water in the office. "Why do you want the Odyssey?" Kayla asked Nate.

"With my sister having the twins, I could take the family places. I can't now."

She sighed. "You know if you get that van what will happen."

"What?"

She took another swig of her water bottle. "Our families will think something else is going on."

He had to admit when he'd asked Kayla to mate him and they were expecting their own babies, they'd need a van. But truly, he figured it would help out with his own family for now.

The salesman returned and made a counteroffer.

"Do you want to check out the Ford dealership?" Kayla asked Nate, rising from her chair. "We just started looking. There are three other dealerships in Green Valley." She shrugged. "We can go to Denver after that. We're in no rush."

Nate stood, following Kayla's lead. She was really good at this bargaining business.

"I'll talk to the manager again," the salesman said, and hurried out of the office.

"Damn, Kayla, I should have let you do all the bargaining."

She laughed. "You got us down that far on the price. If we're going to get two vehicles, they should give us a better discount than that. And I really am ready to check out the other places."

Then the manager came back and met their offer.

"What about your car?" Kayla asked Nate.

"I'll sell it." They filled out all the paperwork on the new cars, and Nate made arrangements for a friend to take his old car to a used car sales place that would give him a better price than if he'd used it as a trade-in.

His friend was one of the PIs with the Green Valley wolf pack, Bryan "Phoenix" Wildhaven— who happened to be a cousin of their pack leader, Lelandi—and met him there. Nate handed him the title, registration, and car keys. "Thanks, Phoenix. I owe you one." Nate was glad he had brought the paperwork with him, just in case he had decided to get a bigger vehicle for himself. It always paid to be ready for anything.

"You bet. And like we said, while you're on your vacation at the cabin, we've got you covered," Phoenix said.

"I sure appreciate it."

When Phoenix drove Nate's car off the new car parking lot, Kayla took Nate's hand and squeezed it. "You seemed to know him."

"Yeah, he's Army Special Forces. I know him from the army. We were on a few hairy missions together."

"That's really great then. He's really named Phoenix?"

"That's what we call him. He came out of a burning building when everyone thought he hadn't made it, and after that we all called him the Phoenix, rising from the flames."

"Wow, that's amazing."

"It was."

Their new cars were finally ready to go, and she gave Nate a hug. "Thanks so much for helping me with picking out a new car. I'm usually a lot more indecisive than this, but when you started to get him to come down on the price, it was all a go for me."

"Well, we made a team. I never thought they'd come down any lower until you said we'd shop around. They didn't want to lose two car sales in one day."

"You know, I'm going to have to tell everyone you bought the car to take your sister's babies on trips," Kayla said, pulling her new car door open.

"See, if you had just gotten the van, you wouldn't have to do that."

She laughed. "Then they'd ask why *I* had bought a van with all that seating."

"To take your brothers' double sets of twins places."

She kissed him. "I can't wait to go to the cabin in your new van."

He chuckled and kissed her back.

"I'm headed back to the lodge. I'll see you later," she said.

"I'll follow you back to Silver Town, and then I'll be going to the PI agency."

They headed out, but they ended up talking all the way back to Silver Town on Bluetooth.

"So what's the first trip you're going to make with your sister and the babies and Blake?" Kayla asked.

"The zoo. They have one in Green Valley. It's not real big, but...well, maybe when the kids are older, we can go there. I'll figure out somewhere to take the whole lot of them. Any special plans to take your new car out for a spin?"

"Oh, I'll probably take the ladies all for a teatime social. Everyone's going to want to see it, but when I'm not driving it, it's staying safe and secure in the garage."

He laughed. "After what happened to your last car, I don't blame you."

When they finally arrived in Silver Town, he said goodbye to her and parked at the agency and Nicole immediately came out to see his vehicle. "Ohmigod, Nate. Have you been telling me *everything* that's been up with you and Kayla?"

"Yeah. This way I can take you and the whole family places if you need the extra seating."

"Uh, right. I thought you were just helping Kayla get a new car."

"I was. Then I got this really great bargain for us by getting the two vehicles."

Nicole laughed. "When I need a van, let me know when you're available, though Blake might be able to get the salesman to come down on the price."

"Kayla can too. She did a great job. I'm going to work on getting some witnesses lined up to see if we can learn who was the last to see Phil and learn more what his frame of mind was before he went missing. Then I'll be driving into Green Valley to do the interviews."

"Okay. I'll go with you. I finished the last three cases we were working on. And you can drive us in your new vehicle. I love the new smell of a car."

That's why he hadn't talked to more witnesses before picking up Nicole. He knew she'd want to help him with this. "You'll love this one."

"I already do. Now I'm going to have to talk Blake into getting one too. But maybe we'll just let you be our chauffeur."

Nate smiled. "I'd be glad to." They took off to speak to the other witnesses but didn't get anything further from them concerning the missing Phil.

———

When Kayla arrived at the lodge—she was parking there before she parked in the garage at the house so her siblings could see her new car—she figured she wouldn't be explaining about Nate's Odyssey to anyone anytime soon. Unless Nicole mentioned it to Blake and Blake asked her about it or told Roxie about it and she questioned Kayla. They were sure to think more was going on behind the scenes between Kayla and Nate than she was letting on.

Her brothers and sister were amazed at the deal she'd gotten on the car and loved it. Then she drove it home to leave it in the garage to protect it from the world. She walked back to the lodge after that.

This had turned out to be the best day ever. But then Blake walked into the office and showed Roxie something on his phone. Both of them looked at Kayla.

"What?" Kayla asked.

Landon joined them and grabbed a bottle of water from their office fridge. "What am I missing out on this time?"

"Look at Nate's new van," Blake said and showed him the picture of the Odyssey. Nicole must have sent it to him.

Landon looked at Kayla.

"He bought it to take Blake, Nicole, the kids, and the grandparents places," Kayla said.

They all smiled at her.

———

"So where is our birthday party being held?" Kayla asked Roxie as they got ready for bed that night. "I haven't heard a squeak from anyone about it." Which meant Nate and his sister and parents were probably planning it as a surprise. Once Nicole had married their brother Blake, Nicole and Nate's parents had adopted the Wolff brothers and sisters as part of their family. Nelda and Gary were the sweetest couple.

"Well, Nicole said we need to dust off our Hula-Hoops."

"Ohmigod, a fifties party? I'm so ready. But we don't have any costumes for the party."

"I can't be certain that's what it is, but I think so. Nicole said they've got it all covered. So we're just supposed to show up and that's it."

"Where is it being held? At Nate's place or his parents'?" They were keeping everything so secret, Kayla figured they had to be having it at one of their places. "The night after tomorrow, right?"

"Yeah. The invitations will be delivered, and we'll know all. I have no idea where they're even holding it."

Kayla was so excited about it and couldn't wait. Enjoying the party together with her siblings would make it extra special.

Roxie smiled at her. "I've never seen you so excited about anything."

"Of course you have."

"I'm glad we're celebrating all our birthdays on the same night, especially since you're taking off with Nate the next day for the week."

They straightened up the kitchen and headed up the stairs. "I can't wait to spend the week with him." Kayla sighed, then thought about their mystery man. "I wish we could learn about the man who came to get the keys at the lodge. There has been no word on him. I even called CJ to see if he knew anything." She walked into the bathroom to brush her teeth.

Roxie joined her and used the other sink to brush hers. "I heard the FBI agents took him into custody and left with him."

"Right. That's what CJ said." He was good at his job, and she knew he or the sheriff would inform them right away, once they knew anything.

"Are you all set for camping? Do you need to borrow any of my things?" Roxie asked.

"I'm good. As long as we don't have any sudden storms. Well, we'll have a couple of days of bad weather in the middle of the week, but the rest of the time it's supposed to be good."

"Just don't do any running in a hailstorm."

"No plans to. Or falling into a creek either. Night, Sister. See you bright and early in the morning." Then Kayla retired to her bedroom. She couldn't wait to get her invitation to the party and see the details.

"Night, Sis."

———

The next morning as Nate was driving to the PI office, he was so glad Nicole had been in charge of the birthday party celebration for the Wolff siblings. He would never have thought of having a fifties party, and he was glad to help. Thankfully, she'd mentioned it early to him and he was able to reserve one of the three banquet rooms at the Timberline Ski Lodge through Lelandi, since he and his family had wanted to make this a surprise for the Wolff siblings. The rooms opened up into one large one for weddings and other events that required more than one room, but they'd only needed one room for this event. The Sleepy Hollow banquet room had a view of the outdoor swimming pool. The Wolff Park and Mountain View banquet rooms looked over the ski slopes, but one was booked, so he had picked Mountain View.

"Hey," Nicole said in greeting when Nate arrived at the office.

"You're early." He was surprised to see his sister at the agency this early since she'd been having bouts of morning sickness for weeks.

"Yeah, I was feeling great this morning, and I'm excited about tomorrow night. Are you all packed up for your camping trip?" Nicole asked.

"I sure am."

"Okay, I figure we'll begin setting up the party tomorrow afternoon and be ready at five. Mom and Dad said they'd come over early to help us out, and they've got someone in the pack handling the stationery store for us until closing."

"Sounds like a good deal. And costumes?"

"Being delivered to the lodge's office at three.

Also, Jake Silver is coming to take pictures of the event," Nicole said, sounding excited to do this.

Nate was glad Jake would do that since he and the rest of the Silver adults were invited. As one of the pack leader's brothers, Jake was second in charge and a professional photographer. His artwork was even featured in several Colorado galleries. He would do a great job.

"Are you getting together with Kayla today?" Nicole asked.

"No. After taking time off yesterday to help her with purchasing a car and the other issue with the man at the lodge and then the birthday party tomorrow, I'm trying to get some work done on these cases and plan to do it until late tonight." He hoped not to leave too much undone before he left for the week with Kayla.

"I'll be fine with the workload. The Green Valley wolf PIs will help out if I need it." Nicole sighed. "I hope you plan to ask Kayla to be your mate soon."

He looked up from the file.

"You're perfect for each other, and waiting isn't going to change things. I know you don't want to go all alpha male on her because you think she's so introverted, but you have been seeing her since you got here last year. She doesn't date anyone else. And it's not just because she's shy."

He had to admit he had felt that way to an extent, but he knew Kayla wasn't a real pushover;

when she wanted something, she got it. He smiled at his sister. "Kayla doesn't jump into things, like *some* women I know." He had been surprised when Nicole hit it off so well with Blake and, in a whirl-wind of romance, mated him. He was glad she had. They were a fun couple. "When it comes to romancing Kayla, she's…cautious. I've asked her out a number of times, and she's—"

"Turned you down?"

"Been too busy with work."

"So what do you do? Take her a box of her favorite chocolate-covered almonds as a quick pick-me-up? Order a lunch and have it with her at her office? No. You dive into your own work like the devil is after you."

"Nicole, if she's busy, then I don't want her to feel I'm pushing myself on her. She needs some space sometimes."

"Okay, next time that happens, you do something special for her. You don't have to have lunch with her, but take her a boxed lunch from the Victorian Tea Shop. She loves their soups and sandwiches, and the teas and special pies are to die for."

Nate smiled. "All right. Next time she turns me down, I'll do something special for her, and if it blows up in my face—"

"You try something else next time."

He chuckled. He was going to say he would give her the space she needed, but maybe Nicole was right. When it came to women's feelings, she was much more attuned to them.

Though if things worked out for him when he asked Kayla to mate him, he would be doing all those things for her, and more, to perk up her day—just because he loved her.

Chapter 12

BECAUSE KAYLA WAS GOING TO BE OFF FOR A week, she wanted to do her part and worked late that night. Then she ran with Roxie, Blake, and Nicole as wolves. Afterward, they went to their respective houses, barking their good nights to each other.

When Kayla and Roxie had shifted at their home, Kayla said, "I can't wait to see what Nicole and the others have planned for us tomorrow for our birthdays, can you?"

Roxie laughed. "No. I think she's gone all out this year. See you in the morning."

"Night, Roxie."

The next morning when Kayla and Roxie arrived with Rosco and Buttercup at the lodge, a smiling Blake raised a handful of pink-and-black envelopes and waved them at them. He was beaming.

Kayla quickly removed Rosco's leash so he could settle in his dog bed next to the fireplace. Kayla ran to get her invitation from her brother. Blake laughed and handed another to Roxie. She ripped hers open like Kayla did.

"Did you read yours already?" Kayla asked Blake.

"No. Landon and I were waiting for you both to get here." Blake opened his invitation.

Landon came out of a ballroom to get his invitation and opened the envelope addressed to him. He laughed. "A fifties rock 'n' roll party. That should be fun."

CJ dropped by the lodge and joined them with news about the man who claimed he was Durham Manning. "I don't have the best of news. The mystery guy overcame the FBI agents and escaped."

"No way," Kayla said, shocked that he'd escaped.

"Yeah, the agents were pretty incensed that they lost him. They hadn't been able to get fingerprints or DNA on him, and they weren't able to learn who he truly was," CJ said. "He had been careful not to have any ID on him."

"Wow," Kayla said. "That's not good, but at least he won't be coming back here. The agents still have the ring of keys, right?"

"They couldn't find them."

"Okay, but if he took them, he still won't be returning here," Kayla said. The man still needed to be apprehended, but at least it would no longer involve them here.

"Correct," CJ said. "They have search parties looking for him because he attacked the agents. They hope to still bring him in to learn who he is."

"But what about Durham Manning?" Kayla asked. "He's still at large too?"

"As far as we could confirm, he is," CJ said. "But we looked into the booking of the room, and he might not have actually booked it. Maybe the guy claiming to be him had actually registered the room in Manning's name. Maybe the keys really belonged to the shaved-headed guy who came for them. We're still checking into it."

"Roxie said she'd smelled the black-haired man had been here at the lodge, but not the blond-haired guy. Have there been any more robberies that you know of?" Kayla asked.

"No, they're probably lying low or got caught at something else or somewhere else, but we still haven't been able to connect the crimes to them," CJ said.

———

The next day, Kayla and Nate concentrated on doing their respective jobs, but Kayla was too excited about the party that evening. She didn't know when she'd been this happy. Nicole had even sent over the outfits for the fifties party that afternoon, and Roxie and Kayla changed into pink poodle skirts, black-and-white oxford saddle shoes, and white shirts. They pulled their hair back into ponytails.

And then Nicole arrived at the office dressed as if she were their triplet—though she had an expanded waistline because of the twins—and they hugged her.

"This is so much fun, Nicole. Thanks so much," Kayla said.

"We've had a blast getting ready for this. Mom, Dad, and Nate are in the Mountain View banquet room setting up. I need to go help them."

"We will too," Kayla said, eager to assist them. "I can't believe you were able to keep the party location a secret when it's at our lodge."

Nicole laughed. "We had to work at it. But it's your birthday surprise. We'll set it all up."

"All right." Kayla and Roxie went out to help at the front desk until the party began.

Their guests were snapping pictures of the three ladies in their poodle skirts.

Kayla smiled. "This is so neat." She felt like the party had already begun once she had put on the fifties-era clothes.

Wearing a black leather jacket, jeans with the cuffs rolled up, sneakers, and a white T-shirt, his hair all greased up in a ducktail, Nate came to escort them to the banquet room. "It's time to party."

"Ohmigod, you look just great," Kayla said, adoring him for going all out for this.

"He does!" Roxie hurried off ahead of them.

"You look beautiful." He reached around and slid his hand down Kayla's ponytail.

Kayla gave Nate a hug, and then they kissed.

"Thanks to you and your family for going all out for our birthdays."

"We've had a wonderful time setting this all up." He took her hand and walked her to the room.

Inside, red-and-white-checkered tablecloths covered the tables. Hamburgers, french fries, deviled eggs, and watermelon were displayed on one table. A dance band was playing "Yakety Yak," and immediately Nate took Kayla to the dance floor and began dancing with her.

"This is so much fun," Roxie said, Blake agreeing.

"Did you have any clue they were going to do this?" Kayla asked Blake.

"I sure didn't, or I might have let it slip. Nicole was being really sneaky about it all."

Kayla laughed.

Gabrielle arrived, and she was already dressed in her costume, her blond hair twisted, swept up, and pinned into a poof on top of the head to give her the curly bob look. Kayla guessed Nicole had arranged for her poodle skirt and shirt to be sent to the veterinary clinic. Like Nicole, her waistband accommodated the twins she was carrying. Her green eyes alight with excitement, Gabrielle smiled at Kayla, Roxie, and Nicole as she joined them.

They hugged her like they were all sisters and best of friends, which they were. They loved to go together to Silva's tea shop when they could all get away from their jobs. A Silver Town theater was opening around Christmastime, and they were eager to see some flicks together that the guys weren't all that interested in going to.

Landon hurried over to give Gabrielle a hug and kiss. He leaned over and kissed her belly. "I'm glad you could get away from the clinic."

"Dr. Mitchell is taking care of the clinic and the animals if there's any kind of emergency. I wouldn't miss your birthday celebration for the world," Gabrielle said.

Everyone was thrilled Gabrielle was their new veterinarian in town and even gladder that Dr. Mitchell, though retired, helped out whenever Gabrielle needed him to.

Nate and Nicole's parents, Nelda and Gary, hugged each of the Wolff siblings, and everyone wished them a happy birthday. Nelda wore a swing dress with a petticoat—all in pink with high heels to match—and her hair pulled back into a French twist. Gary was having fun as a greaser, sliding his hand over his slick hair periodically to be in character. Kayla loved them for joining in on the fun, and she thought Nate looked so much like his father, dressed the same except a younger version.

Soon Darien and Lelandi arrived to participate in the celebration. So did Tom and his wife, Elizabeth, and Jake and his wife, Alicia. A couple of the Silver cousins who were living in town came too: CJ and his mate, Laurel, and Brett and his mate, Ellie.

Kayla hadn't expected so many members of the Silver family to come to their birthday party, but it was great having them. They had all this food, the music, dancing, and everyone was dressed in just the right clothes for the period. Some of the guys were wearing camp shirts, wide-legged pants, two-toned oxfords, and fedoras.

Even Rosco joined the party in a fifties greaser leather jacket. Buttercup was wearing a pink skirt, only instead of an applique of a poodle on it, it had one of a little black kitten.

Kayla snapped a couple of pictures of Rosco and Buttercup, thinking this would be a fantastic idea for a Valentine's party next year.

"Jailhouse Rock" started playing, and Nate took Kayla back to the dance floor, where most of the couples joined them in the dance. Even Jake did with his mate while Roxie was taking some video of the dancers. "Splish Splash" played after that.

While "Oh Carol" was playing, most of the dancers started to eat dinner. "Dream Lover" followed, adding to the fifties ambience.

Jake took a moment to shoot some photos of everyone, including Rosco and Buttercup.

"This is just too cool," Kayla said. "So much fun."

Everyone agreed. Then as soon as "All Shook Up" started to play, the partygoers headed back to the dance floor, doing the jitterbug and then swing dancing to more of the music.

Kayla realized the twin brothers Kemp and Radcliffe Grey, who were ski instructors during the winter but in charge of the zip line for the summer, had slipped into the party with their hair greased back, wearing sneakers, jeans and T-shirts, and black leather jackets. Both twins were vying to dance with Roxie, the only one who didn't have a partner.

Kayla loved that they had shown up to dance with her sister, and it looked like Roxie did too. Nate's family must have invited them so Roxie wouldn't feel left out. Though Blake, Nate, and Landon all took turns dancing with Roxie too.

After dancing to a few more oldies, Kayla and Nate sat back down to eat some more. "I love dancing with you. The food is great too. And everyone looks wonderful in their costumes," Kayla said.

"Yeah, this has been terrific. I helped with some of it, but Mom and Nicole were the driving force behind it."

She noticed a few lodge guests peeking in to see the party that was going on. A few were snapping some shots of them in their costumes on their phones.

She laughed. "This is definitely something I'm going to set up for a promo for next year."

Nate smiled at her and grabbed another fry. "Do you always think in terms of promos?"

"Often."

"About tonight… Do you want to come home

with me, and we'll leave together in the morning to head out to the cabin?"

"Yeah. I kept thinking I might need to do some work at the lodge tonight, but I don't think anyone's going to let me. So I'll go home with you. My gear's all packed and sitting by the front door of the house. I'll just need to grab an overnight bag with some things for this evening."

"Okay, great."

They danced some more before the band played "Happy Birthday."

Then gifts were opened. The brothers and sisters got everything from ski clothes for the upcoming season to housewares and supplies for grilling.

After the night's revelry, the Wolff siblings thanked everyone for the beautiful party, and then Kayla, Roxie, Nate, Rosco, and Buttercup went to their house while everyone else went home to theirs.

Nate parked his car at Kayla's place so he could pack up her things. He was glad she was staying the night with him. It would be nice to wake up with her and have breakfast with her too.

"That was so much fun," Kayla said, detaching Rosco's leash from his collar. "I'll be right down after I change into regular clothes."

"It *was* great," Nate said. "I'll take your bags out to the car."

Kayla called out, "Thanks."

Roxie released Buttercup on the floor, and Rosco curled up in his bed. Buttercup hurried to join him and snuggled up with him. She had her own bed, but she preferred sleeping with him.

Nate thought the two of them were cute, the huge Saint Bernard and the orange tabby cat sleeping together.

"That was the best birthday party ever! Having Kayla's celebrated along with ours worked out just great," Roxie said.

"See? I told you so," Kayla called down from upstairs.

"It was," Nate said.

"You were right," Roxie yelled up to her.

He finished loading up his car with Kayla's camping gear, and she came down to join him with her overnight bag. "That's the way we'll celebrate my birthday from now on. One big family birthday party." Kayla gave Roxie a hug before she left with Nate.

"That works for me. Have a great time," Roxie said to the two of them.

"Thanks, we will," Kayla said.

Rosco lifted his head to see what was going on, but he was too worn out after the party to get up and say goodbye. Buttercup was already sound asleep.

Then Kayla and Nate left and climbed into his van.

"Have you got anything in mind to do tonight?" she asked.

Nate smiled at her. "You betcha."

Once they arrived at his apartment, they took out her overnight bag, leaving the rest of her gear in the van for the night, and headed inside and locked up.

Then she was kissing him, and he was so ready for the next phase of Kayla's birthday celebration. Before they got carried away, though, he took her into the bedroom and motioned to the blanket-covered hope chest at the foot of his bed. She'd never even noticed it when she'd been there the other night. He was glad about that.

Wanting her to see the chest for her birthday first, he pulled the blanket off it with a flourish. "Happy birthday."

"Ohmigod, it's beautiful. You... You made the chest?" Kayla looked thrilled, and he was glad she appreciated it.

"Yeah, and Nicole and Mom made the wolf quilt-covered pillow seat."

"How? All of it's just gorgeous." She pulled him in for a hug, her warm body tight against his, and immediately his hardened against her delecta-ble softness.

She was just so perfect for him, and he loved

her inside and out. "The picture of the wolves was digitally created and then transferred to the fabric. Then they quilted the rest of the pillow seat cover."

"It's just exquisite. The hand-carving of the wolf howling and the mountains in the background on the front of the chest is gorgeous too. It looks just like me."

He smiled. "It is. It's you, telling the whole world you are there. Big as life."

"It's amazing." She had tears in her eyes as she released him and opened the chest and smelled the fresh cedar. "I just love it."

He pulled her into his arms for another hug and kissed her. "It's not supposed to make you sad."

"No one has ever done anything this special for me for my birthday. It's just gorgeous." She hugged him and began pulling off his shirt, and he knew she was ready to celebrate her birthday in another way. "Hmm." She ran her hands over his bare abs, and he began removing her shirt, kissing her neck, ready for the intimacy to evolve between them.

He pressed his lips against her soft mouth. He wasn't falling in love with Kayla. He was already there. She was his one true love.

He lifted her off the floor and she wrapped her legs around his hips. Then he sat on the bed, Kayla on top of him. She and he were kissing, her svelte body grinding against his arousal, and he was so ready to just say screw it and tell her he wanted to mate her.

Whenever he was with her like this, that inferno just started to build between them. He kissed her lips, and her mouth pressed his for more. He was eager to fulfill her need. He slipped his tongue between her parted lips, stroking her tongue with long, luxurious strokes, loving her reaction to him. He was the luckiest wolf in the whole wide world.

He reached behind her to unfasten her bra, slipped it off her shoulders, and tossed it aside. Then they were back to kissing again, her beautiful breasts pressed against him. God, she felt so good.

She moved off him and ran her hands over his crotch and his erection straining against his pants. His arousal jumped against her exploration, and she smiled infectiously.

He unfastened her shorts, pushed her onto her back, and pulled off her flip-flops and shorts and then her panties. She quickly unfastened his belt, unzipped his pants, and tugged them off. He yanked off his shoes and socks. Once she removed his boxer briefs, Nate and Kayla were sandwiched naked together again, kissing and hugging, their hearts beating furiously. She was irresistible.

He loved how physically connected they were, how passionate she was with him, just like he loved being with her.

Then he separated enough from her that he could move her legs apart and found her wet and receptive. Again, he wanted to jump the gun and just ask her to mate him despite also wanting to hold off until they were at the cabin tomorrow.

When it came to going all the way with Kayla, it was difficult to contain his craving. But he wanted to make the mating location even more special. He began stroking her clit; she writhed under his touch, and he loved it. She gripped his shoulders, her mouth connecting with his in a hot, searing kiss.

This was the best—leaving their cares behind, connecting with each other on a hot note. He continued to stroke her until she began to tense up and arch her back. He stroked her faster, harder, her fingers digging into his shoulders.

She cried out loudly with her orgasm and pulled him hard against her body, snug, then mischievously wriggled against him. He groaned. She smiled and pushed him off her, then slid her hand down his chest. "You are so hot."

"So are you, honey."

Then she closed her hand around his sex and began stroking him, kissing his throat, his chin, his cheek, and he was lost in her love. Cupping her face, he kissed her deeply, but she was slowing her strokes and he wanted her to speed them up. He was dying here.

He moved his hand over hers and tightened her

strokes on him and quickened them. She smiled and kissed his mouth, then without further guidance from him, she began stroking him harder and faster.

Then he was coming, and he couldn't hold back. With release, he groaned out loud. "Kayla." That's all he could get out. He still desired telling her he wanted to mate her. He wanted to take her to the cabin right this minute, but someone else was staying there through tonight. He smiled and kissed her. "I'm going to hit the shower, and I'll rejoin you in bed in a couple of minutes."

"No. Way." She was out of bed in a flash. "You'll get lonely or might lose your way back to me."

He chuckled. "Never, but this is even better." He knew he should have just mated her. He swept her off her feet and hauled her into the bathroom, kissing her the whole way.

She was the only one for him.

Chapter 13

AFTER EATING BREAKFAST TACOS THE NEXT morning, Nate and Kayla packed up the van with his hiking gear and the groceries Nate had bought the day previously. She and he were sweating from the exertion. It was hot out—92 degrees the last time he'd looked on the weather app. And then they finally got on their way. At least they had a cool, air-conditioned van to ride in.

"Have you been out to the cabin before?" Kayla asked, wiping her brow with a tissue.

"Once since I've lived here. Someone broke into the cabin while it wasn't being used in the winter time, and the pack leaders gave me the job of searching for clues to learn who had done it. I tracked three men and two women's scents to the bed-and-breakfast. They'd gone for a long hike, broken into the cabin, eaten a bunch of the food, vandalized the place, and stolen some things from it. We found them in their guest rooms, laughing about the whole thing. Our local judge insists on speedy trials for out-of-towners, and our wolf lawyers do a great job of seeing justice is served. The party of thieves had to clean up the cabin and pay hefty fines for vandalizing it and for stealing property. Plus they all have criminal records now. If they get caught committing any further crimes, they're in the system."

"Good. That's what I like to hear."

"The pack usually doesn't have any trouble at the cabins, but they have safes to lock up any valuables for when guests are hiking or swimming and away for a while."

"Okay, that's good to know. I didn't bring my purse, but you could put your wallet in there while we're running as wolves or out hiking." She looked out at the pine trees and sighed. "The first thing I want to do after we arrive at the cabin is swim in the lake. It's so hot out."

He felt the same way. "I'm all for that."

Up ahead, they saw two men walking on the private road, carrying hiking packs, tents, and sleeping bags, scruffy, bearded, both dark-haired. Nate pulled over onto the shoulder of the road. "Hey, this is private property out here."

The one man shrugged. "Didn't see anything posted."

"No trespassing signs are posted all over." Nate hated when people who trespassed on the pack's private land always claimed that. Hunters, hikers, you name it. But the land was privately owned, and they didn't want humans trespassing on it, should some of the pack members want to run in their wolf coats during the day—or night.

"Well, we're on our way out of here. Nice to meet you. Have a great day." The men continued to hike back toward town as if they could do whatever they wished and get away with it. Not in *their* pack territory.

"They lied about not seeing the no trespassing signs, don't you think?" Kayla asked.

"Yeah, I'm sure of it." Nate called Sheriff Peter Jorgenson on Bluetooth. "Hey, Kayla and I are about a half mile from the Silver Falls cabin, and we ran into two human hikers who are trespassing on the private road. They both have dark-brown hair and beards and are wearing jeans and hiking boots. One is wearing a black T-shirt; the other has a gray T-shirt."

"They are loaded down with camping gear," Kayla added. "So it appears they've been in the woods for a while. With the van window open, we smelled their pungent, sweaty body odor. We could smell they'd been drinking—beer, whiskey—and smoking pot too."

That was the thing about their sense of smell. It was heightened as wolves, and they could smell odors more intensely. Nate might have brushed it off because he just wanted to enjoy this time with Kayla, but they had to let trespassers know there were consequences for trespassing. Otherwise, they were bound to do it again and share with others that they had done it, and then the trespassing could spiral out of control. They had to think of their wolf pack's safety above all else.

Peter said, "We'll intercept them on the road."

"Great." It was always a good idea to be vigilant to keep their wolves safe.

As soon as Nate and Kayla reached the cabin, she sighed with relief. "We're here. I haven't gone camping since I moved to Silver Town."

"Neither have I. Each of us just needed the perfect camping partner."

She smiled. "We sure did. Now, let's hope it's a success. What if we find out we *don't* make compatible camping partners?"

"Not happening. We're going to have a blast."

"We will."

With a couple of boxes of groceries in hand, Nate climbed up the steps, set the boxes on the porch, and unlocked the front door. He opened the door and set the boxes inside on the island counter in the kitchen while Kayla hauled in more groceries. Then he grabbed the straps of Kayla's hiking pack and eased it off her shoulders and set it down on the floor. They finished unloading the groceries and his backpack from the van. He shut and locked the door while she got them some water to drink.

"Boy, this is going to be so nice," she said, looking around at the cabin.

"It sure will be." He pulled her into his arms and kissed her.

"Really great. No interruptions."

They drank their fill and then put away all the perishable groceries. Afterward, they carried their packs into one of the bedrooms with a beautiful view of the blue lake surrounded by woods on three sides.

The cabin had three bedrooms so that families could stay there in comfort. A large fireplace took up most of one wall, perfect for winter and chilly nights. The living area had three brown couches, one that folded out into a bed for additional guests, and a bookcase filled with books and board games for all ages. A stack of blankets could be used for cuddling on the couches on cold nights.

The cabins were about half a mile apart, and each had electricity and running water, but none of them had Wi-Fi. The cabins were meant to be a getaway for wolf families and friends and not a place to conduct business. It was a way to reconnect with their wolf halves and with nature—though they had all the comforts of home life too while staying at the cabins, more so than if they went tenting. Which, for mating, worked out better for them.

"I almost feel guilty that it's just the two of us staying here when I know this is the most sought-after cabin and it's the prime season for rentals," Kayla said.

Though the cabins were used year-round.

"I reserved it months earlier," Nate said.

She smiled and shook her head. "And you kept it secret from me all this time?"

"Yeah, I even kept it from Nicole until a few weeks ago. I was afraid she'd mention it to Roxie or Blake, and they'd make the mistake of mentioning it to you. I really wanted it to be a surprise for your birthday."

"Well, this is fantastic. I'm just glad we could both get away and enjoy it."

"Me too."

They opened their packs and began digging through them for their bathing suits.

Nate figured they'd go for a lake swim to cool off, then shower, have lunch, and take it from there. He was so glad she'd wanted to do this with him.

As soon as they had their swimsuits unpacked, they began stripping out of their street clothes. They'd worked up a sweat just from packing and unpacking the car in the heat, so he knew she wouldn't want to strip and make love in bed just yet.

They hurried to take off all their clothes, and then she pulled on her boy-short bottoms and her bikini top. "Last one in is a rotten egg." She raced for the back door.

Trying to hurry, Nate lost his balance while pulling on his board shorts so quickly to pursue her. But he thought about Kayla's comment about putting his wallet in the safe and hurried to lock it up. Then he took off after her, grabbing a couple of beach towels from the linen closet. He knew he'd catch up to her, but she was out of the door in a flash.

He laughed and bounded out after her and raced to catch her, dropping the beach towels on the sandy beach, then swept her up in his arms before she could step into the water, startling her. She screamed out and laughed.

"We tied," he said, carrying her into the lake.

She just laughed again. He loved her laughter.

He waded out until they were deep enough in the lake that he was treading water, but he wasn't letting her go. She was all his for the whole week long, and he was going to enjoy every minute of it. He had every notion of asking her to mate him, and she had to know that's what this was all about too.

She seemed to love that he was keeping her close and not releasing her to swim on her own. "It's going to be a lovely night this evening. A sky-filled with stars. But...I–I might have trouble with shifting nearer the end of our vacation."

"I know." It was something he often thought about. He kissed her on the forehead, just enjoying this time with her. He didn't want her to worry about having little control over her shifting during the full moon. "I had thought of reserving the cabin for when we had a new moon and no chance of you turning. But I wanted to do this for your birthday.

And I wanted to run with you during the week too, which we couldn't have done during the new moon." Well, he could have; she just couldn't have.

They had never really discussed the business of her not being a royal like him. She and her siblings' grandfather had been human before he was turned, so they had more humans in their background than Nate had.

"Speaking of which, it doesn't bother you that we're not royals? I know it's fine with Nicole or she wouldn't have mated Blake. But...you and I have never really spoken about it."

He assumed Kayla had figured he felt the same as his sister. It didn't matter to him in the least that Kayla wasn't a royal. "Yeah, I'm fine with it, Kayla. Just like my sister is. I always have been." In the beginning, Nate and Nicole's parents had some reservations, knowing that their grandchildren wouldn't be royals, not for generations for their offspring. But they loved the Wolff siblings just the same—like their own children.

Kayla ran her fingers down his chest in a tender caress, her gaze lowered. "At least when Gabrielle and Nicole have their babies, they can control their shifting at all times. The babies will only be able to shift when their moms do when they're young. And since both of them—Nicole and Gabrielle— are royals with fewer human genes, it's not that big of an issue. But with me, if I have babies and suddenly shift—something I don't have total control over during the full moon—they would too. It puts the babies and me at a bigger risk."

He kissed her cheek. "That's what's great about living in a wolf-run town. Everyone looks out for everyone else. I don't have any issues with it at all and will be there for you and the babies at any time. And my parents will help out whenever we need them to. You don't have to worry about it."

She kissed his chest and looked up at him. "I'm not really comfortable with change."

He realized then that they had needed to talk to each other about a few things that they'd never made time for before. He was doubly glad he had brought her here where she felt she could discuss everything openly with him.

He nodded. He'd suspected Kayla hadn't liked change. "In the army, I had to move a lot. But I was ready to really settle down once I retired. Have a home, set down roots," he said.

"Roxie left the army before she retired, but she doesn't mind change. It took me awhile to agree with the rest of my siblings to even move from Vermont to Silver Town. There was nothing left for us back there—our parents were gone, and I knew all the benefits to being in a wolf-run town—but I still wasn't sure of the reception we would get when we moved into another wolf territory. Or how it would be for us dealing with a wolf pack's leadership. We didn't have that in Vermont, not in Killington, so we were used to being our own little family pack. I wasn't sure how it would be for us to run a new ski lodge either. We had managed the one in Vermont as a family forever. And even moving from Vermont to being in Colorado where weather conditions, plants, just everything is different was a big change. At least for me. The rest of the family doesn't get stressed out like I do about change."

"But you are all settled in and happy here now, right?" Nate was worried she felt homesick for Vermont, but everyone she cared about was here. What if she wanted to leave and return home?

"Oh, absolutely. Sorry. I was just…" She let out her breath. "I was just thinking about… Well, if you and I mated, I would have to move again. I mean, it's just that I get stressed when I think of things like that. I know it's silly and I can do it and be happy, but I just wanted you to know that's the way I am."

He smiled. "It's about moving into my apartment, isn't it?"

"I know it's crazy, but—"

"No, I totally understand. My dad doesn't like change at all either, so I'm used to that. Even though my parents wanted to move to Silver Town from Denver because both Nicole and I were settling down here, my dad wasn't ready to move, to get a new home, to open a new stationery store, to become part of a pack and have pack leaders' rules to follow, though Lelandi and Darien are great leaders. So in that respect, you and he are a lot alike. I totally understand how you feel. Anyway, what can we do to make this work?" Because no matter what, he knew they were right for each other, and he would do anything to make it worth it for them.

"Thanks for understanding."

He thought for a moment, and then he smiled. "Okay, I got it. We need to find Roxie a mate first. Then she'll move out and you'll get the house, and you won't have to move."

Kayla laughed, and her laughter echoed across the lake. She kissed him. "She'll find a mate herself when she's good and ready. We might have to wait for years though."

"That wouldn't do. What if we build a home beyond Blake and Nicole's home? That was always the plan for the next sibling who found a mate and was staying here, right? Then whoever was still single would have the house nearest the lodge."

"Are you asking me to mate you?" Kayla sounded surprised.

He thought Kayla had figured that was why he had brought her out here for a week. "Hell, yeah, and I will do anything to make the transition the easiest for you."

"You are asking me to mate you?" she asked again as if she couldn't believe it.

He sighed. "Hell, I'm not good at this. Yeah, I

love you, Kayla, so much, with all my heart. You are the yin to my yang. I've just been waiting to ask you when I thought you would be ready. From the very beginning, I was fascinated with you when I first met you at the lodge. Here you were, so eager to help me with a case of theft at the lodge, and I knew it was because I intrigued you too. I felt a spark of interest in you as soon as I met you. I knew you would change my life forever. I was eager to help you and your family out, sure, but especially because I got to work with you."

"Yeah, I felt the same way about you. Like we had this magical connection. Believe me, it takes me awhile to really want to meet someone new— especially a bachelor male wolf—but as soon as I saw you, there was just something about you that drew me to you. I was eager to work with you too when normally I would have been a whole lot more reserved about it. And, knowing the way I am with meeting strangers, my brothers and sister were delighted that you and I seemed to hit it off right from the start."

He smiled. "I'm so glad. I adore you."

"I love you too. And adore you just as much. You're so…virile but tender too. I just wish I wasn't such an introvert."

"*I'm* not an extrovert either."

She looked surprised he'd say that. "But you get out all the time, and you're around people and—"

"I'm still not an extrovert. We're great together. We both need the time to chill after seeing tons of people. But when we're together, we're so attuned to each other that I just feel comfortable. I don't know about you, but I just feel good, better, relaxed, and happy around you. I don't feel like I have to put on any pretenses with you, and you seem relaxed too whenever we're together. What we have is something really special. Together we're—"

She smiled. "Hot."

He chuckled. "That's for sure. Do you want to swim some more laps, return to the cabin, and then see just how hot we can be together?"

"I sure do."

Then he kissed her, and he released her. They swam in the lake some more. The top layers of the water were warmed by the hot sun, but deeper, the water was cool. Still, it felt really nice to cool off, as high as the temperature was. After swimming for about an hour—playing, sitting out, getting in again, clinging to each other, and just floating on the water—they heard people approaching the lake. He wondered if they were wolves or just human hikers who shouldn't be here. He would be annoyed if they were trespassers when he just wanted to enjoy this time with Kayla.

Chapter 14

NATE CAUGHT KAYLA'S ARM AND PULLED HER close, hugging on her, kissing her wet cheek, adoring her, hating the intrusion of the hikers. "We are probably turning into a couple of prunes. Are you ready to return to the cabin?" He was ready to mate her.

"Are we mating?"

"Yes! Are you ready?"

"I sure am."

"No problem about the housing situation? If you want, we could use the guest room in your house for the two of us while we build a new home like Blake and Nicole did. Then you won't have to leave your home until ours is ready for us to move in."

"We'll figure it out." Kayla took his hand and headed in to shore, and they finally saw the hikers—two men and two women—reach the lake. "Wolves or otherwise?"

"Not sure. The way the hot breeze is blowing in the direction of the couples, I can't tell. If they were local wolves, we'd know them for sure. But not if they're wolves we haven't met who are just passing through."

"Well, if they're human, then they're trespassing," Kayla said.

"Yeah."

"So before we call Peter on them, we need to check to see if they're wolves. We don't want to give the sheriff a false alarm."

"Agreed. It's the perfect time to leave the lake, go inside, and shift into our wolves. We'll go out the front door of the cabin. We can go around and get downwind of them so we can smell them. They won't even see us." He grabbed up Kayla's beach towel on shore and shook it out, then wrapped it around her and kissed her. She kissed him back, but they wanted to learn if the people were wolves or not before they got down to the more pleasurable business at hand. He grabbed up his towel and wrapped himself up in it; then they headed for the cabin and walked inside.

"We could scare them off as wolves—if they're not wolves. Otherwise, they'll just wave at us and be friendly. If they run out of the water screaming, we'll know they're human, and we can sic Peter on them," Kayla said.

Nate laughed. He really hadn't expected Kayla's wolfishness to come to the forefront like that. He'd never seen that wilder side of her. He loved it.

"Well?"

"Yeah, let's do it." He locked the cabin door, and then they tossed their towels on the back of a couple of kitchen chairs and both of them pulled off their bathing suits and shifted.

Then as wolves they raced out the front door and headed around to the lake through the woods, first to get downwind of the people to see if they could smell their scents. They were definitely human.

Kayla licked Nate's face, and he licked her cheek back. Then he howled, and she stared at him, appearing a little surprised that he did that. She howled then too, and he loved her for it.

The people who were making out in the lake turned immediately to see the two wolves howling.

"Holy shit! They're wolves," the one guy said.

"Are you sure?" one of the women asked.

"Yeah, they are howling like wolves," the other man said. "Hell, look at them. Those are two bona fide wolves."

"Will they swim out to eat us?" the other woman asked, sounding terrified.

Nate nudged Kayla's face, she licked his muzzle, and then they both ran off into the woods, hidden from the humans' sight so they could go in through the front door of the cabin.

As soon as they were inside, they raced into the bedroom and headed for the windows, shifted, and peered out to see if the people were vacating the premises. The foursome was still in the water, looking in the direction that the wolves had run off.

"I thought about stealing some of their clothes,"

Kayla said. "It would have served them right for trespassing. But then they might not leave the lake."

He chuckled. "Yeah. I don't think they would have chased us down to get their clothes back."

"Okay, so do we call Peter and have them charged with trespassing?" Kayla asked. "Or let them believe it's too dangerous running around here further and they won't be back?"

"I'm calling Peter," Nate said. "The problem is they may be too scared and never leave the water anyway."

She laughed. "True."

"Hey, it's me, Nate," he said to Peter on the phone.

"Have you got more trespassers?"

"Yeah, swimming in the lake. We sort of gave the two couples a wolf scare, and they aren't leaving the water."

Peter laughed. He always had a great sense of humor. "Naked?"

"Yeah. I'm glad I'm not the sheriff."

Peter laughed again. "We'll be there shortly. We don't want anyone suffering from hypothermia because they're afraid the wolves are nearby and they stay in the lake for too long." Then Peter said goodbye.

"We're really doing this," Kayla said to Nate. "I mean, the mating?"

Nate smiled. "We sure are. Unless you want to change your mind."

"No. Way. You're not getting off the hook that easily."

"Hey, you had me hooked from the beginning," he said.

"You know, for being a hard-charging Army Ranger, you're a real softy."

"I am, am I?"

"Yeah." She rubbed her naked body against his. "Well, this part of you is really hard. But in here"— she placed her hand on his heart—"you're a real softy where it counts." She took his hand. "Let's get a quick shower."

About showering first, he wholeheartedly agreed. The lake was filled with melted snow and ice in the spring, but it was warmed up now, and it was better to wash off a bit. He scooped her up and carried her into the bathroom and set her down. She pulled her shampoo and soaps out of her bag.

He started the shower, and then they both stepped under the heated water, soaping each other up. He loved smelling her fragrant vanilla soap, which was why he didn't bring his own into the shower this time. He wanted to wrap her scent around him the whole week long.

Once they'd rinsed off, they dried off, and he heard his phone ringing.

She groaned.

"It won't be about work," he promised her.

"Nicole said if she ran into any trouble, she'd let Darien and Ryan know. She won't be calling us."

"Who then? Peter? Calling about the people in the lake? Okay, we need to know what's up then." She peeked through the window blinds, and Nate joined her at the window. They saw Peter holding his phone to his ear, and his deputy CJ Silver standing nearby. Their backs to the people quickly getting dressed lakeside, Peter and CJ were standing some distance away from them to give them some privacy.

Nate answered the phone.

Peter said, "Hey, we didn't want to disturb the two of you, but they're going to be leaving soon with citations for trespassing."

"What did you tell them?"

"That they will also be charged with indecent exposure. Anyone with kids could come along and witness a bunch of naked adults in the lake."

Of course, wolf kids were used to the wolves stripping and shifting, so that was a way of life for them. But humans wouldn't know that.

"All right, thanks, Peter. We appreciate it."

"Yeah, hopefully, it'll be quiet from now on. But you did the right thing by calling me. Talk later."

They said their goodbyes and then ended the call.

Nate realized Kayla was no longer at the window with him and had already slipped under the blue sheet, having folded the quilt at the foot of the bed.

Yeah, it was time to warm up the sheets. He set

his phone on the bedside table, climbed into bed with her, and moved on top of her, eager to become her mate. He began kissing her, their mouths melding in synchrony.

"This." She pulled his lower lip gently with her teeth and licked his lip. "Is." She nuzzled his cheek. "Nice."

He rubbed his body against her hot one. "Yeah, it sure is."

Then they were kissing, working up the heat, his fingers spearing through her silky hair. He loved the softness of her curls, the delightful smell of her—of sweet vanilla, of the wild, the woods. She excited every sense of his being and intoxicated him. Their kisses grew more persistent, deepening, desperate. She appeared to be eager to enjoy the tumult of emotions swamping them in an exhilarating way.

Their blood was pumping hard, their breaths coming fast as he moved his mouth to her breast and kissed her, licking her aroused nipple, and sucked. She moaned softly, and he savored every bit of her as he licked a trail across her chest to the other breast and kissed her in the same manner.

She ran her hands over his shoulders, through his hair, barely breathing before he moved back to her mouth. She eagerly kissed his mouth with raw desire, and he felt a deep connection with her. He loved her as much as she loved him.

Then he slipped his hand over her hip, caressing

her belly just above her short, curly hairs. "Oh," she said breathlessly, "don't tease."

He smiled at her and ran his fingers through her curls and found her wet bud, swollen, eager for his touch. She lifted her pelvis a little, wanting more contact, he figured, and so he gave it to her, stroking her, intensifying his stroking her. He moved his mouth to hers, and she licked his lips, then opened hers, inviting him in. He kissed her deep, all the while stroking her, working faster, harder, attempting to coax a climax out of her. She responded with eagerness, caressing his tongue with hers, stroking his. He was so pumped up, his arousal full to bursting, ready to take a deep dive between her legs once she'd come.

She was moving under his touch, and he was certain she was going to come, as much as she was tensing, her eyes glittering with lust. Then he slid his finger into her, swirling it deep inside, and that was enough to shatter her, and he felt her contractions. She cried out with jubilation.

Then she let out a long sigh and smiled at him, caressed his shoulders with her soft touch, and kissed his cheek. "I love you."

"I *so* love you. Are you ready?" He held his body over hers, hovering, waiting for her to say the word, eager to fulfill their destiny.

"Past ready. We should have done this a long time ago."

Smiling, he so agreed. He leaned down and

pressed his mouth against hers, their lips fusing in a sensuous kiss. He pushed his stiff erection into her gently, until he was seated to the max, and began to thrust. Their bodies rubbed against each other, her soft body molding to his, and she felt so good against him like this. He couldn't believe how incredible it was to finally be deep inside her, making a new bond with her, joining with her, taking her with him to the point of no return and mated bliss.

She was his and he was hers through and through. She squeezed her inner muscles, caressing his thrusting arousal, making the journey that much more riveting.

Nothing else intruded on this special time with Kayla—just the two of them making love, loving each other in the same space and time, beginning their mated life in a glorious way.

Then he was coming, and he groaned out her name, his love for all time. "We should have done this a long time ago," he managed to get out and continued to thrust until he was completely spent.

"Yeah, like I already said. Why did we wait so long?" She was smiling up at him, pulling him into her arms in a welcome embrace, and this felt so right.

"An overabundance of caution on my part."

She sighed. "And on mine."

They would be together now day and night when they weren't working. And hell, he had every intention of filling that new van up with little wolf pups, as long as she was feeling the same way.

"Yes," she said, as if she were thinking the same thing.

"Yes?" He raised a brow.

"I want kids too."

He chuckled. "I knew we were meant to be together from the first time I laid eyes on you."

"Ditto for me. And that's why you really bought the van."

He chuckled. "Yeah."

Then he pulled out of her, but he wasn't letting go of the closeness he craved to have with her, the unbreakable bond they had. She rested against him, cuddling, just perfect for him in every way.

Chapter 15

"LET'S GET SOMETHING TO EAT FOR LUNCH, AND then we can go for a hike or go swimming again?" Nate asked Kayla after making love to her and taking a refreshing nap.

"Oh, swimming. It's so hot out that appeals. In the morning, we can take a hike after our wolf run, before the day heats up too much. But I do want to run as a wolf tonight."

"Okay, that works for me."

They made tuna fish salads, finished lunch, cleaned up, and changed into dry swimsuits.

"We need to leave our damp ones outside. They'll dry faster," she said.

"Yeah, these too after we swim. We got side-tracked what with trespassers at the lake and—"

"Making love."

Looming over her, he hauled her against his chest and held her close. "Yeah, making love. The most important thing." He kissed her thoroughly.

Then they separated, and she ran her hands up his chest. "Yeah."

She pulled out some fresh beach towels while

he grabbed their damp ones and bathing suits and hung them on the railing on the back deck to dry.

Then they raced off the deck to reach the lake and dove in.

The air was still hot, and this was refreshing. They swam out until they couldn't touch the bottom of the lake. Then they treaded water, clinging to each other, feeling so intimate, sexy, intriguing. She just loved being with him like this.

She pressed her lips against his mouth, wrapping her legs around his hips, savoring his kisses. "I'm glad you like the water as much as I do."

"When can I play with you in it? Even better."

They kissed each other again, their tongues sliding over each other's, and then they finally separated and played tag with each other for about a half hour. He was so good at it, and whenever he came after her, she panicked. When she went after him, she swore he would slow down so she could catch him and then cuddle and kiss again. She loved it. Afterward, they rinsed off with a hose outside the cabin, went inside, made love, and then cooked grilled hamburgers, corn on the cob, and fries for dinner.

After eating and cleaning up, they settled on a settee on the back porch, watching the sun set over the lake while they sipped margaritas, the orange and pink colors caressing the rippling waters. "This is sure nice sitting out here like this," she said, snuggling against him.

"Yeah, I'm glad we're doing it before the storms come," he said. "The same thing with taking a swim while it was so hot. Just perfect."

"I agree."

They listened to the cicadas and crickets singing in the woods, an owl hooting nearby, and the sound of the branches stirring in the breeze.

He held her hand, and she was ready to return to bed with him, but she did want to run as a wolf too. It would be safer at night, especially after they had seen so many trespassers on the property of late. This would be their first mated wolf run, and she was eager to run and play with him as a wolf.

He leaned over and kissed her mouth, and she enjoyed the sweet, tangy flavor of tequila, orange liqueur, lime juice, and sugar from the rim of the glass on his lips. "Hmm, you taste so sweet. Are you ready to run as wolves?"

"You bet." Then she and he grabbed their empty drink glasses, dry bathing suits, and beach towels and went inside. They left their bathing suits and towels in the bedroom and took their glasses into the kitchen. She kissed him, and he wrapped his arms around her and kissed her back.

She kissed him again, and then they quickly stripped out of their clothes, shifted, and raced out the wolf door and into the night.

The sound of the river drew them, and they ran that way, reaching the bank finally, and sprinted into the water. Wearing their fur coats, they stayed warm despite the chillier temperature. Their outer guard hairs were wet, but the rest of them stayed dry.

This was so much fun with Nate. Kayla couldn't believe they were mated now. He nipped at her, and she nipped back at him. They were having a great time.

She howled, and he howled too. They were alone out here, or other wolves would have howled in greeting.

They licked each other's faces, and she rubbed against him, loving being wolves. She still couldn't believe they were actually mated, and she couldn't be any happier. This was one change she'd been completely ready for.

———————

"Hmm, I could lie in bed with you all the rest of the day, but I'm hungry," Kayla said, waking up in Nate's arms early the next morning. She rolled over to rest her chin on his naked chest and smiled at him.

He stroked her hair and smiled back at her. "I was feeling the same way. It's our vacation, and we can stay in bed or play in the water or run as wolves— whatever you want to do."

She sighed. "I want to eat."

He laughed. "Okay, food it is. We need our strength too."

But they didn't move from their relaxed state, her arm draped over his abdomen and her cheek against his chest. This was just too nice.

"Man, this is going to be a lazy second day here." Nate kissed the top of her head.

"I know. Isn't it great? I didn't realize how stressed I was until I came here with you and just relaxed, putting aside all the work issues."

"I know what you mean. Besides, we're going to be up late doing a wolf run, so it didn't hurt to stay in bed a little longer this morning." He moved the cover aside, and she and he climbed out of bed.

She pulled on a pair of black, lacy panties and fastened the matching bra while he slipped on some boxer briefs and then they headed for the kitchen.

"This is something I normally don't do. Cook in my underwear," she said.

He smiled. "I do. I like the look on you."

"Huh. You're pretty provocative." The way his boxer briefs hugged his package and his toned butt was impressive. "That's something I didn't know about you."

He pulled out a frying pan, and she got the sausages out of the fridge. He put the sausages into the pan. "When you stayed overnight at my place, we were in a rush to get dressed and go to work the next morning. Now you can see me on my days off just like this."

"I like the look." She kissed his bare shoulder. "Just be careful about splattering grease."

He pulled out a grease cover to place on top of the frying pan. "Have it covered."

She smiled and began making the pancakes. "I can't believe the fridge and pantry are so well stocked."

"Yeah. Everyone contributes. Whatever we don't use that isn't perishable, we'll just leave here for whoever stays here next. Though I brought a lot of the more perishable items to use during the week. Some staples are always stocked at the cabins."

They finished making their pancakes, sausages, coffee, and tea and sat down to eat.

"I thought since it's cooler this morning, we'd go on our hike first thing along Wolf Run Trail and see the two Silver Waterfalls that way. It's a five-hour hike round trip. We'll have a snack along the way and then enjoy both falls. Afterward, we'll hike back in time to have lunch at the cabin, then go swimming during the heat of the day." Nate started cutting into his pancakes.

"That sounds great. And then we can nap." She smiled at him and forked up one of her sausages.

"Or do other stuff."

She laughed. "I'm all for doing the other stuff most of all."

Wolves could travel around thirty miles a day, so she was enjoying the hikes as a human and taking runs as wolves and swimming too. Working at the lodge meant she didn't get as much exercise as she'd like to sometimes.

After they ate, they cleaned up and put away all the food—conscious that black bears could be in the area and they didn't want to attract them since they'd been known to break into cabins looking for food. Kayla and Nate dressed for hiking—shorts, hiking boots, light backpacks filled with bottled water, protein bars, lightweight jackets, first aid emergency blankets, flashlights, wildlife deterrent spray, cell phones and the satellite phone, and first aid kits. They were always prepared in case they came across someone who had been injured or was in distress on a hike, wolf or otherwise. Or if they ran into trouble themselves.

During the summer months, they had to watch out for rattlesnakes, which are common in Colorado both in the woodlands and on rocky terrain. Not so in Vermont, so they had to be more vigilant here.

Once, as a wolf running in the mountains, Kayla and her siblings had come across a yellow rattlesnake, nearly giving her a heart attack, and she'd leapt out of its path. Since then, she and her siblings had learned about the different species of venomous snakes in Colorado in case they ran into any more.

Nate pulled a couple of hand-carved, cool wizardry walking sticks out of an umbrella stand to use in case they ran into a predator but also to aid them if they needed to cross a stream or just in general.

They headed out then, and Kayla was glad they were hiking this morning nice and early because it was so cool. She loved immersing herself in the sounds of birds twittering and singing, the fragrance of pines and firs, and an occasional rabbit scent and even a black bear, which meant they were keeping an eye out in case they ran into one.

"This is so nice," she said. "I'm just thoroughly enjoying myself."

"It really is. And I am too."

"I guess we should tell everyone we're mated." She glanced over at him to see what he thought of the prospect.

He chuckled. "You don't think we should keep them guessing?"

"Do you think they'll believe we'll wait, since we've been dating for so long already?"

He leaned over and kissed her. "Nah. They'll probably figure the moment we got in, we were stripping off our clothes and doing it."

She felt her face heat with embarrassment. The way she always blushed, she swore she had redhead genes in her makeup even if she didn't have the red hair. "I was thinking we could go across that swinging bridge at the stream west of here and see the flowers in the meadow tomorrow morning. After that, we have the issue of rain and the full moon; I might be shifting later. But tomorrow should be good."

"Yeah, that sounds great."

They followed the trail up the east side of the river toward the waterfalls and would hike the same way on the return trip. The clear mountain streams fed into the two unique, eighty-foot and sixty-foot waterfalls and then flowed into the river snaking by the hiking trail.

She smelled the fresh falls' spray way off in the distance and was beginning to get hot and sweaty. She welcomed a dip underneath the falls to cool off.

They paused beside the river where a bench sat on the bank. Some of the townsfolk had carved it from a fallen tree trunk, smoothed the top, and varnished it to give wolf hikers a place to take a moment to sit and enjoy the river. As they went farther north, they eventually would be out of pack territory and into the San Isabel National Forest.

She and Nate sipped from their water bottles and reached into the river to splash some of the water on their arms and faces. Large rainbow trout swam just below the surface, and Kayla smiled. "I hope we're scheduling some fishing so we can have grilled fish for a couple of meals."

"Yeah, I was thinking about it for sure. They have fishing poles at the cabin. We can do it in our wolf coats too."

"Okay, well, if one doesn't work, we can switch to the other."

"That's the great thing about being able to do either."

They returned to the hiking trail and continued through the woods. Nearly two hours into their trek, Kayla smelled something really awful. Whiffs of something dead. She knew it was bad news.

She frowned at Nate. "Do you smell something foul? Dead? Human?"

"Hell, yeah," he said darkly. "Whoever the unfortunate victim is, he or she's been out here for some time, if we can accurately go by the smell of the stage of decay he's in."

They continued to follow the scent, which was growing more pungent the closer they got to it. That was the problem with their sensitive sense of smell. Bad odors were enhanced way too much. They didn't want to give up the search. They had to find the body.

"Let's call this in." Nate stopped and dug his satellite phone out of his backpack and handed it to her. "I'm going to keep searching until I can find where the scent is coming from. Call Peter and let him know where we are and what we're looking for."

"Okay." Following Nate, she really hoped this wasn't a case of homicide. She didn't know what else it would be if it wasn't that though. Not at this time of year. In the middle of winter, someone might have gotten lost, maybe, become hypothermic, run out of water and food. Then again in summer, if the person had suffered heat stroke, a heart attack, dehydration from lack of water, or even a bear, cougar, or coyote attack or had been bitten by a rattler, he could have died purely by accident.

She called Peter on the satellite phone. "Hey, it's Kayla."

"Don't tell me you and Nate are having trouble with more trespassers. We're going to have to start patrolling the area from now on," Peter said.

"No, I'm afraid it's something much worse. We smelled human remains about two hours north of our cabin. The location is the Wolf Run Trail heading up to the Silver Falls. We're about a quarter of a mile from taking the trail up to the cliff overlooking the Greater and Lesser Silver Falls."

She was still following Nate when he suddenly turned around and returned to her. "The smell is strongest where we came from, and it's coming from across the river. That's why we were smelling the odor so strongly back there," Nate said, rubbing her arms in a soothing caress and kissing her forehead.

"Okay. Peter, I'll give you our coordinates as soon as we reach the spot where we smelled the odor the worst." She and Nate backtracked and then headed to the river. She gave Peter the GPS coordinates. "We're going to swim across the river and make sure there's no one injured over there."

"Okay, I'm getting an investigative team together as we speak."

"All right, thanks."

"Be careful crossing the river."

"We will be."

Kayla wanted to wait for the sheriff and his men to come to investigate this, but because Nate was a private investigator and a reserve deputy sheriff in case of emergencies, she knew he had to check it out and learn what he could. If someone was in need of help, she also wanted to assist. He was an excellent swimmer, and so was she, so she didn't worry about the two of them navigating the river, though that could always be a hazard too.

They left their walking sticks on the ground and pulled off their backpacks. She tucked the satellite phone in his backpack while he removed his shirt. They kept their hiking boots on in case there were any submerged logs or branches, jagged rocks, broken glass, even fishing tackle stuck in the rocks and hidden in the river. Then he gave her a hug and kiss, and she gave him a heartfelt hug and kiss back before they entered the water.

They began to wade into the river until it was deep enough and then started to swim against the strong currents.

She felt awful that anyone would have died out

here. As she swam across the river, she watched Nate fight the strong current like she was doing. He kept looking back over his shoulder to make sure she was okay. "Don't worry about me. I'll be fine. Just go. I'll get there," she called out to him. But he wasn't taking any chances and continued to glance back to ensure she was still making it. She loved him for it.

Then he stopped and treaded water, fighting the current. "I'm waiting for you." He looked ready to return to rescue her if she needed it.

He didn't need to. She was getting there. As soon as she caught up to him, he swam toward shore again, more slowly though, trying to stay with her.

Before she reached the shore, she belatedly worried that they might run into a predator eating the remains.

After fighting the current for about twenty minutes, he finally reached the targeted shore and climbed out. "Do you see anything?" she called out to him. Bare-chested, wet, his shorts clinging to him... Despite the situation, she thought how sexy he looked.

He motioned to the woods. "The odor gets stronger in that direction. The person must be in the woods."

"Okay." As soon as she was close to the shore, he stepped into the water to help her out and pulled her into his arms and hugged her tight. She took a deep breath. "Let's do this."

"Yeah. Let's get it done."

They headed into the woods and could smell the odor of decay grow stronger.

"Do you see the body yet?" she asked as she and he started looking in different directions, but they were staying within sight of each other. She was also smelling for any sign of anyone else.

"Not yet, but it's somewhere near here." Then a few minutes later, he said, "I found him over here, covered with twigs, leaves, and pine needles. He's...uh, in a bad state of decomposition. You don't need to see this."

"Are you sure you can't use my help?" She wished Nate hadn't seen the victim either.

"No. Not on something like this. There's nothing you could do anyway. I'm just looking for evidence to see if I can learn who the victim is and trying to determine what happened. I don't think anybody else is over here."

"You're right. I don't smell any sign of anyone else either."

"Just the one man and he's wearing a black ski mask."

"In this heat?" She couldn't believe it.

"Yeah, it's chilly at night, and if he was trying to stay hidden from whoever shot him before he expired, wearing the ski mask could have hidden his face better."

"Shot him? Someone murdered him?"

"Yeah. I can see three gunshot wounds."

"Oh, that's awful." She frowned. "It still seems odd that he had been carrying a ski mask during the day in this heat unless he had been up to no good. Can you tell how and when he died?"

"It looks like he died about a week ago, though the doc will have to confirm the actual time frame of his death. It appears he was shot twice in the chest and once in the leg."

"Okay, well, that isn't good. That means we have a murder on our hands."

About twenty minutes later, she heard men coming on ATVs on the trail across the river and hoped they were the sheriff and others of their pack and not trespassers whom they wouldn't want to get involved. Thankfully, with their superior wolf hearing, only second in strength to their sense of smell, they could hear sounds six to ten miles away.

"I'll go see if that's Peter," she said.

"All right. Let him know where we found the body," Nate said. "I'm still looking for some ID."

"Sure thing." She backtracked the way they had come and headed to the river. She saw Peter in the lead and waved at him and the other men from the shore. "Peter's here with a team of investigators," she called out to Nate.

Peter pulled up and parked on the trail. CJ, Tom,

and Jake Silver were all behind him with a raft and other gear.

"Did you find the body?" Peter asked Kayla.

She motioned to the direction the body was located. "That way, a hundred yards into the woods."

"Some of our men are taking the bridge south on the river to reach the area. Though it's even more rugged to travel on that side of the river. Our medical examiner, Doc Featherston, is on his way to examine the body," Peter said as they began to get the boat ready to launch.

"Oh, good," Kayla said. "We didn't find anyone else here."

"Hey," Jake said to Kayla, "do you want one of us to take you back to the cabin so you can wait for Nate to return there?"

"No, thanks. I'll wait until Nate comes back." She wasn't leaving without Nate, and she wanted to finish her hike with him to the waterfalls if he still wanted to. She'd feel better if they did what they had come here to do.

Peter and the other men got into the boat and began rowing over to meet up with them.

Then Nate came out of the woods and headed for the shore. "Hey, I'm done here, honey."

"We'll ferry the two of you across," Jake said.

"What did you find?" Peter asked.

"The man was shot three times. There are no bullet casings anywhere around the area that I could find. It appears he was shot somewhere else and then most likely swam across the river, managed to crawl or stumble into the woods, cover himself up with a few twigs and other forest debris, and died. It doesn't appear like anyone covered him up to hide his body, and we smelled no signs of anyone else who had been in the area. He's wearing a black ski mask, maybe to hide himself from whoever shot him. But it makes you wonder why he had a ski mask in the heat of summer. I didn't find any ID on him, no car or house keys, but I did find a key card. It's for the Timberline Ski Lodge."

"Oh, great," Kayla said, not in a good way.

"I'll take it into evidence," Peter said.

"I figured that. I left it in his pocket. I didn't disturb anything, except for finding the key card, and I was careful not to leave fingerprints on it. Kayla's family can probably determine which room it went to and maybe identify the man."

"Okay, we'll take it from here. Good job," Peter said, and slapped Nate on the back.

CJ and Tom ferried Nate and Kayla back across the river, while Jake and Peter headed into the woods.

After dropping Nate off on the shore, CJ and Tom headed back across the river to join the others in investigating the death of the man.

Nate hugged Kayla. "Knowing what we do now,

I figure we could have waited for Peter and his men to arrive."

"Oh, no, I'm so glad we found him. Making sure no one else was there was important too. He could have been there for who knows how long. His family and friends need closure."

"Yeah, once Peter can identify him." Nate pulled on his shirt and then lifted his backpack onto his shoulders.

He helped her on with hers, took her hand, and then turned on the path in the direction of the cabin.

"I still want to go to the waterfalls unless you really don't want to. Are you going to be okay?" She realized after he saw the remains, Nate might feel somewhat traumatized.

"Yeah."

"So what do you think?"

"Well, he was wearing hiking boots, a black T-shirt, and blue jeans, and he had nothing on him that I could easily locate—like ID, water bottle, hiking pack. Just the key card. I'm wondering if it happened at night, he was shot and crossed the water, or even if the gunman fired at him when he was trying to cross the water or had reached the other side and the gunman couldn't locate him afterward."

"Oh, how awful. If he'd been shot on the other bank, we would have found shell casings on the other side."

"Good point."

"The ski mask sure doesn't fit. Why would some-one wear it during the heat of the summer?"

"I agree. Peter will take the key card back with him to see if your sister or brothers can determine who stayed in the room." Nate looked down at Kayla and rubbed her arms with a gentle caress. "Do you want to keep going?"

"Oh, yes. We're so close now to the falls. I want to remember something good about this hike and not that we just found a dead body." She couldn't believe the man could have been one of their former guests. That made it seem worse somehow—like they should have protected their guest better.

"Yeah, I agree."

"I sure can't wait to hear who the key card belonged to."

Nate nodded. "You're just like me, loving to solve mysteries. Of course, when it involves your lodge, I'm sure you have even more of an interest."

"I do. It's driving me crazy. I want to know just who it is and if we might have seen him on the security videos with someone who could have been the last one to see him alive, once we learn who he was. Though he's probably not recogniz-able right now."

"Yeah, I was thinking the same thing. He was wearing the ski mask, so I couldn't see his features. Once we get back to the cabin, which will give your siblings time to research it, why don't you call them and see if they've learned anything?" Nate asked.

She laughed. "We are a pair. Here we are on a vacation from work, and we are both itching to help solve the case."

"Yeah, but that's because it sort of fell into our laps."

"That's true. At least we got cooled off in the river after our swim."

"We did. By the time we reach the falls, we'll be thoroughly dry in this heat."

"And ready to stand in the spray of the waterfall and dip our hands in the spring before we climb to the top, and that'll cool us off again."

"That's just what I'll do."

Chapter 16

NATE AND KAYLA HEADED UP THE TRAIL AND had to navigate over rocks, being careful to watch for rattlesnakes. With their enhanced hearing, they could hear the slightest rattle shaking, though the delightful sound of the rippling flow of the waterfalls was filling their ears too.

Signs were posted up here for hikers to stay off the edge of the waterfalls. Loose, slippery rocks could mean a hiker's death if he fell from the top of either of the waterfalls. Of course that didn't stop some people—humans or wolves—from wanting to take pictures close to the edge. At least three humans had paid the price in the past for being daredevils, but that had happened before Kayla and Nate moved here.

When they reached the bottom of the waterfalls where they poured into the river, she and Nate navigated over mossy stepping stones and stood in the light spray. Their clothes were already dry, and they didn't want to get drenched again, just to cool off.

Then they climbed up the rocky cliff to the top of the waterfalls.

They had just reached the crest where they

could see the water spilling over the edge of the cliff, and she had to admit it was tempting to wade into the stream of clear water and peer over. Not that she would do it, but she did have the natural urge to do so.

"It's tempting, isn't it?" Nate asked as he pulled out his cell phone and took some pictures of her smiling at him.

"Yeah."

He wrapped his arm around her and took pictures of the two of them kissing each other.

She leaned down at the stream and dipped her hands in and splashed the cool water on her arms and her neck. "Hmm, that feels cool and refreshing."

He did the same. "Yeah, it does."

They heard hikers arriving, and Kayla sighed. The hazard of taking a vacation like this in summer. Even though the resort had lots of skiers all winter long, there were tons of visitors to the area hiking in the summer, even more guests than in the winter. All the lodging in town and their own ski lodge were full at this time of year.

At night, that was different. They could run as wolves with most humans settled down at campsites in the San Isabel National Forest or having fun in town, not hiking out in the wilderness. Too treacherous. Too easy to twist an ankle or break a leg. Kayla and Nate would run as wolves on private pack territory at night, and they shouldn't have any trouble with humans. They might end up bumping into other wolves though—out for a run in their wolf coats, having a good time. But wolves were okay.

"Do you want to go to the cabin now and get some lunch?" Nate asked.

It was later than they had planned to hike because of them swimming across the river and checking on the deceased man, so by the time they hiked back, it would make for a late lunch.

"In a moment. The men coming up the path will be in our way when we make the trek down." Plus, she didn't want to be "chased" off when they had come all this way to enjoy the waterfalls from the top of the ridgeline.

"Bet you won't get close to the edge and take a selfie, LJ," a black-haired man taunted his buddy.

"I'm not that foolhardy, Chris," a blond-haired man said.

"Hey, LJ's getting married, Chris. He doesn't want to do anything to mess that up. Besides, his bride-to-be would give him hell," another dark-haired man said.

The others laughed.

"You go first, Chris," the dark-haired man said. "You're always the risk-taker."

"I will, Alex. Watch me."

"Whoa, we're not alone," Chris said as he saw Kayla and Nate up on the rocks beside the stream.

He gave her an appreciative smile, like he was some kind of lady's man and could change her mind about being with Nate. As *if*.

They all greeted each other.

Chris dropped his backpack on the bank before he started to walk across the stream as if to prove to his friends and Kayla and Nate that he had what it took to impress everyone.

"Hey, Chris, we agreed before we made the climb that none of us were going to wade out there," LJ said.

"Seriously, LJ?" Alex said, removing his backpack, setting it on the rocks, then walking across the stream, slipping immediately on slick rocks and falling on his butt, water splashing everywhere.

Everyone laughed. Kayla couldn't help it. She hadn't meant to, but it *was* funny.

"Do you want to leave?" Nate asked her.

She wanted to say something to the guy who was getting closer to the edge of the waterfall, the other sitting in the stream finally standing up and taking another spill. She and Nate didn't laugh this time, but their friend who was standing on the rocks next to them did. It was dangerous, the rocks slippery. As wolves, they could navigate it, but as humans, it could be treacherous.

She figured it didn't matter what she said to the black-haired man who was still inching his way to the edge. The signs were posted. They didn't pertain to him. Maybe he had a death wish. What did she know?

Nate finally spoke up. "I wouldn't get too close to the edge. The rocks are loose there, they're slippery, and if you fall the eighty feet, it's to your death. Over the years, three people have died that way." Then before anyone could say anything, Nate raised his brows at Kayla, silently asking her if she wanted to go now.

She was glad he'd warned them. Hopefully, the guy would have enough sense to return to the safety of the rocks where they were standing. Then she and Nate headed down the rocks to the narrow path and made their way to more level ground.

"I figured if I said anything, they'd ignore me because I was a woman," Kayla said to Nate.

"I almost didn't say anything. The signs are posted, warning of the danger. People like that don't care. They just have to prove something to themselves or others. Or they believe it will never happen to them. Probably if he wasn't trying to show off to his friends how brave he is, he would not have done it."

"Well, hopefully, we won't be finding any more dead bodies—this one downriver from the waterfall." She took Nate's hand as the path widened. "I'm so ready to have lunch. I'm starving. And I can't wait to take a swim and cool down!"

"Oh, hell, look what I found. Wait, I lost it. Grab

it!" Alex shouted from up above the falls. "It's got to be worth a fortune."

"It's too close to the edge of the falls," Chris said. "Wait...I–I got it."

"Damn, good job. Toss it here," Alex said. "Got it!"

Then they heard a man yell out. Nate and Kayla paused. Looked up at the waterfall. Waited.

"Shit, no! Chris, hold on!" Alex shouted.

"Help! Help! We need help!" The man's voice was strained, frantic. It sounded like LJ's voice.

"Do you think they're just playing around with their friends?" Kayla asked Nate, concerned but not wanting to be pulled into these men's idea of a prank either.

"Help! We need help!" That was LJ again, and he sounded even more desperate.

She and Nate were eyeing the waterfall from down below, looking for anyone in trouble, and that's when they saw the black-haired guy, Chris, hanging from the rocks at the top edge of the waterfall as the water rushed past him and over the edge.

"Damn it anyway. I'm going to see if I can help." Nate began running up the narrow path until he reached the rocks and was climbing up them to get to the top as fast as he could.

"Me too." Kayla was trying to catch up to him, her backpack thumping on her back, and she thought of ditching it. But they might need her medical supplies.

Nate had already ditched his backpack next to the other men's.

As soon as she reached the top of the cliff, she dropped her pack next to Nate's and pulled the satellite phone out of his bag. Then she called the park ranger's office. This was out of the pack's jurisdiction, and the park ranger could take care of this, though she and Nate would do what they could to save the man's life.

Chris's eyes were wide, and he looked terrified as he clung to a couple of rocks that had held in place—lucky for him—his body dangling over the falls. He couldn't hold on like that for long. The water was cold, and he'd get hypothermia before long. The friend who'd kept falling in the water earlier was lying down on his belly in the stream, holding on to Chris's one arm, but he didn't have the strength to pull him up all on his own.

LJ was inching his way through the stream, trying not to fall, appearing terrified of being in the same predicament as his friend. She could smell their frightened scents. Nate began to make his way carefully and as quickly as he could across the stream. It was deep enough that someone could be swept away if they lost their footing and didn't stop themselves from being pulled over the falls in time.

"Just hold on," Nate said.

Kayla got hold of the park ranger's office, and

Eric Silver, their pack leader's cousin, said, "I'll be there as soon as I can."

"Nate is trying to reach him, and so is another friend of his. One of his friends has hold of his arm, and the man is holding on to a couple of rocks, but he can't get any purchase to climb back up."

"Okay, Kayla. We're on our way."

Then she got the emergency blankets out of their packs and told Nate, "Eric Silver is coming with a rescue team." But she didn't think they'd arrive in time to save these men. It was up to her and Nate to rescue them for now.

Chapter 17

As Nate made his way to Chris, hanging precariously from the edge of the waterfall, he couldn't believe the guy had gotten himself into such danger. Well, Nate guessed he could, the way he'd been going and acting all macho in front of his friends. What would he tell the folks back home if he and his buddy Alex could save his life? How cool, exciting, and adventurous it had been? Unless they couldn't manage to get him to safety before he slipped to his death.

Then again, Nate wondered what the business was with finding something that was worth a small fortune. A nugget of gold? Silver? Miners had mined both in this area until they shut the mines down. Every once in a while, someone found some gold in the river, streams, or creeks. It might be worth something, but not losing a life over it!

"Why don't you head back to the shore?" Nate said to LJ, who seemed terrified of the stream—and for good reason after the trouble both his friends had gotten into. Nate didn't ask it as a question, but more of a command to do what he said. If they had listened to him in the first place, LJ's friends wouldn't be in this bind.

"But I gotta help Alex pull Chris up." LJ sounded more like he felt he had to aid his friend to save face, but he was too scared to really get close to where they were.

"If the stream carries you over the edge, you could knock your friend off the rocks, and both of you would fall to your deaths." Nate knew it was going to be hard enough to save his friend without worrying about this guy too. And Nate had already passed him and was several feet closer to his friend who was in jeopardy than LJ was now.

"Yeah, yeah, okay." He sounded like he knew his friends would give him a rough time about copping out, but if he caused more trouble, it just wasn't worth the risk.

Nate slipped once but regained his footing, and when he reached Chris dangling dangerously over the edge, Nate lay down on his belly in the cold water next to the other man and grabbed Chris's other arm. He looked over at Alex, who appeared stricken. He was shivering from the cold water, already hypothermic himself, Nate figured.

"Alex, we're going to pull your friend up at the same time. You can do it. If we don't, your friend's going to die. So we have to do this. Okay, now, slide back, digging your toes into the rocks on the stream-bed. Keep pulling back." Since Nate wasn't hypothermic, he was making much more progress, but Chris wasn't out of danger yet. And Alex appeared to be in peril himself. "We'll get you both warmed up as soon as we pull your friend up and into the stream. Come on. You've got this. Keep going."

They were pulling Chris up inch by inch. Nate was able to get him up to about his waist on the cliff, but he was so cold and his lips so blue that Chris looked like he didn't have an ounce of strength left in him to make it the rest of the way on his own.

"Come on, man, you can do it. We're almost there. We have Search and Rescue coming for you too."

"I–I...was"—Chris's teeth were chattering something awful—"such...an...idiot."

"Yeah, well, we all make mistakes. We just don't want this to be your last." Nate glanced at Alex. He really didn't look good either. "Come on, Alex, help me with your friend. The sooner we can get him out of here, the sooner you can both get warmed up."

They kept pulling until they were able to get Chris onto the streambed, but they had to hurry and move across the stream and onto shore. The men weren't able to stand up, they were so cold, and Nate was afraid he wouldn't get them both across the stream in time to rescue them. To Nate's further distress, Kayla started crossing the stream to help him with the men. He wanted to tell her to go back to shore, but she was keeping her footing, and he was struggling just to get Chris to his feet.

Then she reached them and helped Nate get Chris onto his feet. Nate started to navigate the stream with him, struggling to keep Chris upright while Kayla helped Alex cross the stream.

As soon as Nate got Chris to the shore, he handed him off to his friend. "Get him out of his wet clothes and into dry ones and then wrap him in one of the emergency blankets." Then Nate went back into the water to help Kayla with Alex.

Once they pulled Alex out of the stream and onto the sun-warmed rocks, Nate and LJ began helping him out of his wet clothes. A diamond necklace on a gold chain fell out of Alex's jeans pocket. Everyone stared at the necklace for a moment, and then he reached for it, but his movement was sluggish, and they still needed to get him out of the rest of his wet clothes.

"Leave it," Nate said. Then he and LJ helped Alex strip the rest of the way and dress in some dry clothes.

Kayla picked up the necklace and was examining it.

Nate covered Alex with the other blanket. Kayla handed the necklace to Nate to inspect. She brought out some of their protein bars, and LJ pulled bottles of water out from their own backpacks.

"Are the bottles warm?" Kayla asked, and she was right, Nate was thinking. Warm drinks and energy-rich foods were fine for someone who had hypothermia, as long as they weren't going into shock. But with mild to moderate hypothermia, it could help them passively rewarm their own bodies.

"Yeah," LJ said. "They've been sitting in the sun."

"Okay, they'll be fine," she said.

"You found the necklace in the river," Nate said, looking up from his examination of the necklace, not asking a question.

"No, I got it for my girlfriend," Alex said, stuttering from being so chilled.

Nate could smell his deception. "Why would you carry the expensive necklace in your jeans pocket on a hike?" They could have been faux diamonds, but even those could be expensive. "Okay, here's what really happened and why Chris nearly lost his life. You found the necklace in the water, thought it was worth a fortune—we heard you yelling about it from where we were—and you lost it. You shouted at Chris to grab it. He did, tossed it to you, and you shoved the necklace into your jeans pocket. Then he lost his balance, being too close to the edge of the cliff, and went over it."

LJ and Chris looked at Alex, waiting for him to tell the truth.

"Okay, yeah, but it's for my girlfriend. I found it, so finders, keepers..."

Nate shook his head. "The way it works is this. You turn it over to the police, and they determine if it's been reported stolen."

"There have been several jewelry store heists in neighboring towns, so it could be from one of those," Kayla said.

"Uh, okay." Alex and his friends looked at the necklace as if it were cursed now.

"A park ranger we know is coming to get you guys, so he can take the necklace into custody and turn it over to the police. The heists were armed robberies, so you probably don't want to have anything to do with the necklace if it was taken during one of the thefts," Nate said.

"Uh, no," Chris said.

"Thanks to you both for saving my friends," LJ said, quickly changing the subject. "They're both my best men at my wedding."

"I think we'll stick to a girl in the cake next time we have a bachelor party," Chris said, still shivering badly. "But hell yeah, thanks so much for saving my ass back there. I would never have made it up that cliff if you hadn't come back to aid Alex in helping me. All I could do was just cling to those slippery rocks. I kept thinking of what you'd said to me about those people dying and how it would never happen to me. Ever. But then, you know, I'm thinking LJ was going to be going to my funeral, delaying his wedding, and then dealing with me not being in attendance. And the whole thing would really have sucked. Especially since it was all because I was trying to save the damn necklace that probably was from a jewelry store robbery." He cast Alex an annoyed look. "For your girlfriend?" He scoffed.

"Sorry, Chris. Yeah, thanks for helping me save

Chris," Alex said to Nate. "I would never have gotten Chris up that cliff on my own. And I might not have made it back on my own either. Thanks to both of you. And for calling for help. Chris lost his cell phone in the river; mine and Alex's were out of juice."

Kayla asked them about the wedding, getting their minds off Chris's near-death experience. But Nate was thinking if they didn't even have phones that worked, that was truly foolhardy.

Within the hour, Eric Silver and his rescue team arrived and took all three men off Nate and Kayla's hands. Nate was glad to see Eric there. He couldn't believe he'd be seeing so many of the Silver brothers and cousins today.

"We have a bit of a situation," Nate said. "The men found this diamond necklace in the stream and were trying to grab it before Chris went over the falls. It could be from one of the recent jewelry store heists in the area."

"I'll turn it over to the local authorities, and we'll do a search in the area for any other signs of more jewelry," Eric said privately to Nate and Kayla.

"Good because Nate risked his neck to save that man and his friend," Kayla said.

"So did Kayla," Nate said.

"That's why they'll be charged and fined for not obeying the rules. People like that need to respect the rules for their own safety and others. On another subject, I heard you found a dead body."

Eric would have since his brother CJ and cousin Tom had been at the crime scene.

"We did," Nate said.

"And he was wearing a ski mask," Kayla quickly said.

"A ski mask in this heat?" Eric shook his head. "Sounds like he might have been one of the robbers."

"That's what I'm thinking," Nate said.

"I'll alert Peter about the necklace. I heard you two were on a honeymoon of sorts. Congrats are in order."

"Thanks," they both said.

Then Eric wished them well and headed out after the rescue team, calling Peter on his way.

Kayla and Nate headed back down the trail. They had really gotten their exercise today. He figured they'd just play in the water, not go swimming laps to exercise. Running as wolves? That wasn't exercise. It was just pure joy.

They paused for a break after an hour of hiking and then finished off the last hour and half back to their cabin.

"Quick shower and then time to have a very late lunch?" Nate asked, opening the door to the cabin.

"Yeah, I'll make us some grilled ham and cheese sandwiches after we get cleaned up."

They dumped their backpacks on the floor, put their walking sticks into the umbrella stand, and raced each other for the bathroom.

Then they were stripping off their clothes and jumping into the shower, quickly soaping up, rinsing off, and drying off, then putting on some clean clothes.

After they made lunch, they collapsed on the dining room chairs with big glasses of water and their sandwiches and pickles.

"I feel like we did enough activities today to make up for the whole week," Kayla said.

He smiled at her. "We could skip swimming, just sit on the porch enjoying the beauty of the lake, drinks in hand. Then go running as wolves after dinner."

"Nah. We have to at least get in the water. No swimming laps though. If we can't drag ourselves out of bed in the morning, so be it."

He chuckled. "Hey, do you want another sandwich?"

"Yeah, sure. They really hit the spot."

He started making them another grilled ham and cheese sandwich while she served up more pickles and refilled their water glasses.

Then Peter called Nate's cell phone. Nate put the call on speakerphone. "Hey, sorry to bother the two of you, but be sure if you see anyone that seems suspicious at all to give us a call. The murder happened so far away from your cabin that we don't suspect the murderer would be running around where your cabin is. If anything, and he's trying to find the body, he would be nearer to the location of the body. Even so, he had a week to locate him and hide him or move him, so we suspect he won't be out there."

"Okay, thanks, Peter. We'll certainly be contacting you if we see anyone who seems out of place," Nate said. "Did you find any bullet casings?"

"No. Which either means the shooter took them with him when he left, we just haven't found them, or he shot the man when he was in the river and the shell casings are underwater."

"Okay, well, while we're out hiking, if we come upon anything that looks like evidence, we'll let you know."

"Good. Thanks for all your help. You need to be working with us," Peter said.

Nate smiled. Peter had said that often enough to him, but he loved being a PI and working with his sister in their own agency.

"Have you heard from my brothers or sister about the key card yet?" Kayla asked.

"Not yet. Roxie said she's looking into it, and your brothers are scouring security videos to see if they can find anything unusual," Peter said.

"Okay, that's great." Nate suspected Nicole was helping with the investigation. He sure wished he was too if he hadn't been enjoying this special time with Kayla.

"Oh, and Eric called me to tell me about the

necklace. One of my deputies is picking it up from him and taking it to the Green Valley Police Department to see if it matches any of the stolen items from there or from the other heists in nearby towns. I had Eric interview the hikers about their whereabouts on the days of the robberies. Not that we really believed they had anything to do with the jobs, but since they had the necklace, most likely from a robbery, we have to be sure. Their alibis checked out."

"Okay, that sounds good," Nate said.

Then they finally ended the call, and Nate and Kayla went into the bedroom to change into their swimsuits.

"I was wondering—do you want to stay here at the cabin the rest of the week?" Nate asked. "There's bound to be a flurry of activity while the sheriff's department investigates the murder."

"Yeah." She reached out and took his hand in hers and squeezed his hand. "We're here to enjoy being with each other. I'm having a wonderful time here with you at the cabin. This is like being on a honeymoon. I'm thrilled to be here despite what we found today. Just think, if we hadn't been on the trail, that body may not have been found."

"Okay. I feel the same way about being with you here. We could go to my place, but it just wouldn't be the same."

"You're right. Oh, and I've been thinking

about our living situation. I'll move in with you," Kayla said.

"Are you sure? I thought I could stay with you in your guest room on the first floor on the other side of the house. It's practically soundproofed from the second-floor bedrooms, Nicole said. When she and Blake stayed there, it was perfect for them while they were building their home. Then you won't have to travel from town out to the ski lodge every day."

"What if we split our time at each of the places? I could come to your place, and we can go out to dinner or grill at your place. Other times we can go to Roxie's and my place, and we can have dinner at the lodge, or I can fix something for us to eat. In the meantime, we'll have our dream house built."

"That sounds good to me. If you decide you want to stay at one of the places and don't want to go back and forth all the time, I'll be happy to do whatever you want."

She leaned over, smiled, and kissed him. "I knew you were the one for me. Do you want to swim in the lake now?"

"Yeah, I sure do. And we can run as wolves in the other direction from where we went for our hike today."

"Absolutely. Unless—"

He raised his brows.

"You want to learn more about what happened. And we can go together to see if we can find any scent trail the killer might have left behind. Even bullet casings."

Nate laughed. "No. I mean, yeah, if Peter needs my help investigating this, but not while we're here on vacation."

"Okay, just making sure because I'd be fine with it. I just want to call Roxie in case she learned anything."

Smiling, Nate shook his head. "You're as bad as me."

"I know. That's why we're right for each other." Kayla called Roxie and put the call on speakerphone.

Before she could say anything, her sister said, "You are on vacation with Nate. You're *not* supposed to be investigating murders."

Nate smiled since Kayla hadn't spoken a word yet, though Roxie knew her too well.

"Yeah, so we stumbled on a dead body. It wasn't part of our planned fun excursion, believe me."

Roxie laughed. "The news has spread through the pack like wildfire. Of course, mostly everyone was warned we might have a murderer on the loose in Silver Town, though Peter believes whoever killed the man probably didn't stick around. Even so, Peter's deputized a bunch of men and a few women to look for trespassers on pack lands because of all the ones you've encountered during your stay at the cabin."

"That's good news," Kayla said. "The key card, Roxie? Who did it belong to?"

"I'm not finished."

Kayla looked at Nate and rolled her eyes. He smiled and rubbed Kayla's back.

"Did you or did you not mate Nate?" Roxie continued.

Kayla laughed. "What do you think?"

"Yes! You did it. Ohmigod, Kayla's mated," Roxie said to someone.

"Are you surprised?" Landon asked in the background. "We all knew they would. And congratulations to both of you."

"I'm surprised. And yes, we're thrilled for you."

Blake said, "Congratulations! Now, Roxie, you're the only holdout."

Roxie just laughed. "Okay, about the key card. Remember the guy who left his keys in the room safe?"

"Are you kidding?" Kayla asked, sounding like she couldn't believe it.

"The armed robber? That would explain maybe why he was wearing a black ski mask when he died." Still, Nate was surprised that it was him too.

"Yeah, Peter said they're running his... Hold on." Roxie said to someone else, "What's Peter got to say?"

Landon said, "It will be a while before they can learn the identity through the DNA. But the key card had fingerprints on it, and they're running it through the system to identify whose prints were on it."

Frowning, Kayla glanced at Nate.

"I used a leaf to pull it partially out of his pocket and then saw it was one of your lodge's key cards. It won't have my fingerprints on it."

"Once the coroner removed the ski mask, they were able to see his long, black curly hair and beard, matching the hair and beard in the photo of Durham Manning. They're also searching for dental records to match, but they're pretty sure it's him," Landon said.

Kayla patted Nate's shoulder and kissed his cheek to comfort him, since she knew he wanted to be the one who was involved in searching for all that information.

"What about security videos?" Nate asked.

"Blake is still going over them for all the time we figure the guy was here at the lodge," Roxie said.

"Wait," Blake said. "I've got this man checking in at eight in the morning at the registration desk. After comparing the video with the picture Nate sent us, I'd say this is the same man who reserved that room. Or at least stayed there. Peter's sending a team to go over the room, searching for any fingerprints or anything else that might help identify who all was in the room. I'm still looking to see if I can identify anyone who might have spoken to him in the lobby. No luck so far. I've seen him on video a few times, coming and going, but no one with him. The other guests who were staying in Manning's former room were moved to an upgraded room—no additional cost to them—so Peter and his men can do a thorough examination of the room."

"Okay, good," Kayla said. They sure didn't want to spook other guests while Peter was conducting a criminal investigation nor oust someone from their room when they'd paid good money for it and were here trying to enjoy their vacation.

Roxie said, "Hey and, um, we've been talking about the living situation and—"

"I think we've got it figured out if it works for you," Kayla said. "Sometimes we'll be staying in the guest room at our house, and sometimes I'll stay in town with Nate. And then we'll build a home on the other side of Blake and Nicole's house."

"Are you sure?" Roxie asked. "I was thinking I could give you the house since we all know how you are about being uprooted."

"Thanks, Roxie." Kayla glanced at Nate, probably realizing he might want to have some input too.

"Whatever you want to do is fine with me." Building a new home could stress anyone out, and Kayla did love the home, but he also knew she didn't want to make her sister move when they'd had the plan to leave it to whichever sibling was mated last. "We can build the house just the way you want it. And it will be brand-new."

Roxie laughed. "This one is only two years old. Just think on it. Everyone will pitch in to help me build a home on the other side of Blake and Nicole's place, so don't worry about that. Or they'll do the same thing for you, just like they did with Blake and Nicole's home. You have time to decide since everyone has accommodations for now. You two have fun and don't worry about this murder business. We—well, Peter—has it all covered. And congratulations again! We couldn't be any happier."

Then Landon and Blake added their congratulations again, and they ended the call.

Kayla sighed. "Now that my siblings know about us, we need to tell Nicole and your parents."

"Then we'll swim." Nate pulled out his phone and called his parents first. "Hey, Kayla and I are mated." He put it on speakerphone.

"Good, we knew you would finally come to your senses." His mother said it in a lighthearted, fun way. "When are you getting married?"

He knew that was coming next. "We haven't gotten that far with any wedding plans."

"I'll say. Not with finding a dead body on your vacation," his dad said.

Nate should have known that word would have reached his parents, too, via the pack grapevine. "Yeah, that was all a little unexpected."

"Well, you and your siblings are already part of our family, but we're so glad you mated our son, Kayla," his dad said. "We didn't think Nate would ever settle down and give us grandkids."

Kayla blushed.

Nate wrapped his arm around her and hugged her.

"First comes the wedding," his mother said. "I know, you don't need a wedding, but you do want one, don't you, Kayla?"

Kayla smiled. "I sure do. We'll have it at the lodge. We'll just have to schedule a time when I can't shift."

"Right. We'll help you with everything, dear. Just don't you worry," his mother said.

"Okay, well, we know you two are on your vacation, so we'll let you go, or your mother will be making all the arrangements for the wedding with you before you know it and you'll never get back to your vacation activities," his dad said.

Then Nate's parents congratulated them again, but before they could call Nicole, she was ringing Kayla. "I know you had to be on the phone to Mom and Dad so I called you instead of my brother. Blake told me the great news."

"Thanks, Nicole. Now we're even more like sisters," Kayla said.

"Yes, we are, and I can't be more thrilled. I'm going to let you go because I'm helping Peter with the investigation into Durham Manning, the murdered guy. Boy, the two of you have all the fun."

Laughing, Nate shook his head. "I knew you didn't have enough on your plate."

They finished up the call, and before anyone else called—like their pack leaders—Nate and Kayla grabbed their beach towels and raced out to the lake to swim.

Chapter 18

After dropping their beach towels on the shore, Kayla and Nate ran into the lake, splashing and having a ball. They swam out a way until they could tread water. He loved spending time with her like this when they both could be carefree and enjoy life, though he suspected she was thinking about this business with the murdered man like he was. He was trying not to think about it though.

"Do you want to go fishing after this? We could try our luck at fishing with poles while it's still light out, and if we're unsuccessful, we could fish as wolves when it gets dark out," she said.

He pulled her into his arms as they treaded water. "I think that sounds like a winning plan."

"You know, Durham Manning was an armed robber. I was thinking about the jewelry store robbery in Green Valley again." She licked the dripping water off Nate's chin.

He smiled. He'd known she was thinking about the case. She'd make a great PI, though he knew she loved the work she did now. She was so creative. "I figured you might be thinking about that." Nate tilted his head down and nibbled on her ear.

She giggled. "That tickles." She nibbled his chin. "Yes, and remember the robberies Ryan mentioned that had occurred in other towns nearby?"

"Yes. So would Manning have put some of the stolen jewelry in a couple of the safe deposit boxes? And the guy who was after his keys wanted to get into those safe deposit boxes?" Nate asked.

She wrapped her legs around Nate's hips, and that felt damn good. "Possibly. Or he might have sold them and put the cash in there. Then again, safe deposit boxes aren't insured, so if anyone got into them—"

"Like—"

"Like the shaved-headed man who most likely stole the key from the FBI agents when he escaped. Now, if he had access to the safe deposit boxes, he could have stolen the cash and/or jewelry inside them, and no one could do a thing about it. No one would even know what had been inside them."

"If either the jewelry or the cash hadn't been in the safe deposit boxes, then he could have stashed... Wait, what if that's the reason he was murdered? He kept all the jewelry or the money from the sale of them and didn't share them with his partners in crime," Nate said, his legs treading water while his hands cupped her buttocks. He was thinking he'd sure like to make love to her.

"Then the murderer would have wanted to keep him alive, not kill him. Unless he got the truth out of him about where the money or jewelry or both were stashed before he shot him. Manning must have gotten away, and then the shooter couldn't find him in the dark and left him for dead. But why would the shaved-headed man come looking for Manning's keys at the lodge then unless the keys gave him something he needed? A home could easily be broken into. A car, the same thing. He wouldn't have to have the keys to either the house or car. It wouldn't be as easy to break into a safe deposit box without the keys though."

"Exactly. Since the FBI agents lost him, there's been no sign of him either. But with a name and a picture of the deceased man being widely circulated, maybe the personnel at some bank will recognize he had banked with them. Or someone else will come forth saying they even know who might have wanted him dead. The man who came for his keys could be the murderer, and since the FBI lost not only him but also the keys, he might have managed to get into the safe deposit boxes and emptied them." It gave him chills to think Kayla and her family had spoken to the man when he could have been armed and dangerous.

"But he'd have to have signed Manning's signature on a sign-in sheet to get in."

"That's true," Nate said. "Maybe he knew him well enough to copy his handwriting."

"Yeah, that could be." She shivered. "I don't know about you, but I'm getting a little chilly."

The temperature was starting to drop. "Are you ready for a hot shower and a nap?" he asked.

"Just what I had in mind. Let's go in," she said.

Then he released her, and they swam toward the shore. Once they got out, they dried off, then raced each other to the cabin, but a van pulled into the drive, and they realized right away that reporters from Green Valley had arrived because of the logo on their vehicle.

"Oh, great. The story of the murder must be on the news," Kayla said, and they entered the cabin and shut and locked the door before anyone could question them about anything. "Okay, here's another scenario. What if Manning buried the jewelry out here?"

"That could be bad news, and if that's the case, a bunch of people could begin trespassing on pack land to try to find it." He grabbed his phone and called Peter. "Hey, we've got reporters from Green Valley out here at the cabin."

"We'll get right on it. Sorry, the story got out, and we couldn't stop it at that point."

"I figured it wouldn't be long before that happened. Thanks, Peter."

"But I have an idea. Brett could come out and get an exclusive interview with you, since he's one of our wolves, and that will stop the human reporters from bothering you. We'll make sure we don't reveal any crime details we shouldn't during the interview."

Since Brett Silver was one of the pack leader's

cousins and a reporter for their local newspaper, Nate figured that would work. "Yeah, we can do that. I need to talk to Kayla about it, but I think she'll be fine with it. We'll make sure we say only what we need to."

Saying they had found the dead body was fine. Even humans could smell one that was that pungent.

"Okay, I'll have Brett call you in a little bit," Peter said.

"Make it a couple of hours." Nate had every intention of making love to Kayla first and then napping with her.

"Yeah, sure, sorry about all this."

"It's not your fault that we found a dead body. Talk to you later, Peter." Then Nate realized Kayla was already in the bathroom showering. He hurried for the bathroom and quickly slid his board shorts off and put them on the tub next to her wet bathing suit. He walked into the shower, pulling the glass door closed, and enveloped her soapy body in his arms.

"Is Peter sending someone to get rid of these reporters?" she asked, rubbing her soapy skin against his, his erection already growing with desire.

"Yeah, but Brett's going to come and inter-view us."

Kayla didn't appear pleased with the notion.

"We'll rehearse what we're going to say, and it'll be based on the truth. At least we weren't running in our wolf coats, and anyone could have smelled the dead body as a human, so we should be fine."

"Okay, and then it can be exclusive to him and no one else will bother us."

"Hopefully."

They dried off and ended up in bed and began making love, so glad they hadn't waited to mate any further, and then slept.

When they both woke, they dressed and checked to see if the reporters were gone, and they were. Before they gathered their gear to fish, Brett called. "Hey, is this a good time to for me to get that interview?"

"Yeah, sure. Come on out. We're going fishing afterward."

"That sounds like fun. I'll be there soon. Peter said he sent CJ to get rid of the news reporters who were trespassing."

"Good. We noticed they were gone, but I figured they would have needed some persuading."

"CJ can be persuasive, that's for sure," Brett said.

After a quarter of an hour, Brett arrived in his truck with Jake, who was taking the pictures.

Nate explained how they had smelled the dead body and then had swum across the river to locate the victim after Kayla called the sheriff's department.

"Okay, we know we can't give any details on the crime scene. But what were you both thinking when you swam across the river?" Brett asked.

"That if the person who had died wasn't alone and that someone else who might have been with him had been injured, we might save him or her. We didn't have any idea what could have happened. But it wasn't to be the case," Nate said.

"What about the situation with you rescuing the men at the Silver Falls?" Brett asked.

"I didn't think this news story would be about that," Nate said.

"Brett hadn't planned on it being any more than the case of the murdered man. Before we got here," Jake said, "we heard the news about the waterfall incident on TV though."

"No," Kayla said.

"Yep," Brett said. "The men you rescued told the news about it as soon as they could, once they learned you had found the dead man. I think they wanted to be part of all the news, and they took this opportunity to go to the press."

Nate shook his head.

"Hey, it makes for great press," Brett said. "Our own hero and heroine, and you were both human the whole time. Thankfully, they didn't mention the diamond necklace. Peter said Eric read them the riot act and said if they mentioned anything about the jewelry, whoever stole it might want to eliminate them. So that must have convinced them not to speak of it."

"That's good," Kayla said, "or we could find a

bunch of treasure seekers out here, along with the jewelry store robbers."

"Exactly," CJ said.

Then they talked about the rescue, and Brett read over the interview questions and answers to make sure they all were in agreement, and then Jake took a few pictures of Kayla and Nate.

"We will be out of your hair then," Brett said. "Have a good time."

"And congratulations are in order," Jake said.

"We will, thanks," Kayla said, squeezing Nate's hand, and glanced at Nate as if they were in trouble for not mentioning this to the pack leaders.

"Uh, yeah, we meant to tell Darien and Lelandi," Nate said.

Jake and Brett laughed.

Jake said, "They know you're busy. The word is spreading throughout the pack that you're both mated. Your parents are thrilled and have told everyone. You know how it is. Lelandi and Darien both are delighted and wish you well."

Brett smiled. "Yeah, though there were still some others who were sure hoping the two of you wouldn't mate."

Nate and Kayla smiled.

"But we knew it was to be," Jake said.

Then he and Brett said their goodbyes and left.

"Well, the news of the other men telling the press you saved them was unexpected. Not to mention that your parents have told the whole pack about our mating. They're so cute," Kayla said.

"I agree about the other news. We will be hearing more about this, I'm afraid. As to my parents, they loved you from the moment they met you, so I'm not surprised they wanted to share the good news with the whole pack right away." Nate smiled and hugged and kissed her.

"Well, I love them too. They already treat me like a daughter. So...are you ready to fish?" Kayla asked.

"I sure am."

They put their damp bathing suits and beach towels out on the back patio to dry out, then retrieved fishing poles from the storage shed and filled a cooler with ice. After grabbing their backpacks and water, they headed out to the river with their gear in hand. Then they baited their hooks, stepped into the shallower water, and cast out their lines.

It wasn't long before Nate was reeling in a 15-inch rainbow trout and glad he'd caught at least one of the fish they'd need for dinner.

"Wow, that looks great," Kayla said. "I didn't know you were such a lucky fisherman."

He chuckled. "It has nothing to do with luck. It's all in the wrist, and it's all skill." He put the trout in the ice chest, rebaited his hook, and cast the line out and got a nibble, his bobber bobbing.

"No," Kayla whispered as the river rushed on by

and the sun glinted off the water. "Not another one. Luck, I tell you."

He laughed. He felt another tug, and then he began reeling in another rainbow trout. This one was a couple of inches smaller. He pulled it off the hook and put the fish into the ice chest.

"Do *not* toss your line back in the water. The next one is all mine," Kayla said.

He smiled. "It sure is."

Then he sat back on the bank and watched her. He loved her.

She waited and waited and waited. Then she turned to him. "Did you use different bait than I'm using?"

He laughed. "No."

"Okay, I figured you might have sneaked something else on your hook when I wasn't looking that's really getting the trouts' attention."

He chuckled and got up and joined her in the water and wrapped his arms around her waist and nuzzled her cheek.

"Hmm, this is an awfully nice way to fish. I like it. I'm not sure I'll catch anything, but—"

"You already caught me."

She turned her head and kissed him. "Yeah, I did. And you're the best catch of all."

After a half hour, he didn't think she'd catch anything, but then her bobber moved, and she startled. "Oh, oh, I've got one."

Then she began reeling in the trout. "Oh, my, it's bigger than yours."

He chuckled. Size-wise it was in between the two he'd caught, and it was a good size. "You did it. The perfect number of fish for dinner. You got lucky."

"Ha! It was strictly skill. You were fishing upriver from me, and you kept catching the fish before they could see my bait," she said.

"You are precious."

"So are you. Let's take these back to the cabin and cook them. My favorite recipe is lemon-butter herb-baked trout. In less than twenty minutes it's done. Succulent, melts in your mouth. We can add asparagus, chopped cauliflower, or broccoli to the same pan and just cook it all together."

"Broccoli sounds good." He carried the ice chest while she carried their fishing poles back. He knew she was thrilled she'd managed to catch a fish for dinner. He was glad too.

They made a good team.

Once they returned, they both cleaned the fish. He had planned to clean them all himself, but she wanted to clean her own, which had amused him. He suspected she wanted to eat her own too.

The meal was delicious, and they cleaned up, then sat on the back patio watching the sun set over the lake, having glasses of wine.

"This is so wonderful," Kayla said, clinking her glass with his.

"I so agree." He took a sip of his wine and leaned over and kissed her.

Once the sun went down, they went inside the house, set their glasses on the kitchen counter and stripped out of their clothes, then shifted into wolves and ran for the wolf door. She went out first, and then he followed her.

They raced each other through the woods, not on any path used by humans or wolves in human form. But as wild animals would make their own trails. The deer had made several trails through the woods, and the wolves would use them too.

Nate and Kayla were chasing each other—it just was part of being wolves—and for now, he was glad she had control over when she could shift or not. That meant they could run as far as they wanted, and she wouldn't suddenly have the urge to shift and have to walk back through the woods naked as a human.

She nipped at him as he came up toward her, and he nipped her back. He adored her. He bumped her, and she bit at his neck in playful fun. He was glad they could just play after all that had gone on today. Tomorrow, they were sleeping in, as long as she wanted to. She'd always made herself scarce when it was the week of the full moon, and he knew she had felt insecure about him seeing her when she had less control over her shifting. Now, she was his and he was hers, and he would prove to her that he loved her just the way she was.

Then she tackled him, and he wasn't expecting it. He loved it. He tackled her back, both of them growling at each other in playful fun, though to humans, they probably sounded rather vicious.

Then they ran off again. He hadn't expected her to run this long or this far after all the other exercise they'd had, but she kept running and running. He stayed with her, letting her decide how far she wanted to go until she finally made her way to the river and took a drink from the water.

He drank from the river next to her, and for a moment, they just stayed there, panting in the cool, sixty-degree temperature, their fur keeping them warm.

And then she licked his muzzle, and he licked hers. She nuzzled his face and appeared not to want to leave this spot. Was she all worn out? He didn't think so. He thought she was just enjoying the wilderness as a wolf, like he was. With him. And he was happy to do anything that she wanted.

Then she stood, turned to leave, and he was right next to her the whole way back. He figured she was ready to finally get back to the cabin and call it a night. He was glad, though he didn't want to admit *he* was worn out. But he wanted to climb into bed with his mate and love on her the rest of the night.

Chapter 19

IN THE MIDDLE OF THE NIGHT, NATE WAS DREAM-ing he was chasing Kayla as a wolf. She was keeping out of his reach for a while, but then he caught up to her, pounced on her, and she rounded on him. He was having so much fun with her, growling and nipping at her, and she was doing the same with him. He licked her face, and she licked his, play sneezing as a sign of happiness. But then something pulled him out from his dream, and he listened. What had disturbed his sleep? The wind blowing a shutter and banging or scraping it against the log cabin?

Still asleep, Kayla had her head and hand resting against his chest, but then she moved, opened her eyes, and looked up at him and saw that he was awake. Frowning, she whispered, "Did you hear something too?"

"Yeah, something woke me from a dream, but since I began listening, I haven't heard anything more."

They both were quiet, listening for anything further, their hearts beating hard, their soft breaths exhaled, and that's when he heard the same metallic sound again—a clicking sound as if someone was using a lockpick.

"Someone's trying to break into the cabin. Our phones are charging in the living room," Nate whispered to her, hurrying to get out of bed and wishing they were charging their phones in the bedroom now.

"I guess you don't want to chase them off as wolves." She carefully climbed off the bed, though if the housebreaker was human, he wouldn't be able to hear them. Not while he was still outside the cabin.

"Not if he is armed with a gun. We'll run off through the woods as wolves though." He rushed across the floor and shut and locked the bedroom door just as he heard the front door open.

Kayla was struggling to open the window. "It's stuck."

"They have to be in one of the bedrooms sound asleep." The male housebreaker's voice was hushed.

Frustration etched in her brow, Kayla was still struggling to open the window. It probably hadn't been opened in years. Nate hurried to join her and helped yank it free and pull the window up. Of course it had to creak and groan.

He helped Kayla onto the windowsill. They were already naked, so there was no sense in trying to get dressed and run through the woods as humans. They could run much more easily, faster, and farther as wolves, and if the people who broke in came after them, they'd be looking for humans, not wolves. Kayla jumped to the ground below the window.

"You hide in the woods. I'm going to puncture all of the vehicles' tires, and then I'll join you." He quickly followed her through the window.

"I'll help you."

Someone twisted their bedroom doorknob and found it locked.

"All right." Nate didn't really want her to be exposed to any more danger than she had to be, but he knew when her mind was made up, she wouldn't change it. Not if she felt she could help him and keep *him* safe.

Both of them shifted into their wolves. Then they carefully moved around the cabin to make sure no one was by the strangers' vehicle—a blue Ford pickup. It was Randy's truck, the man Nate had interviewed about his friend Phil going missing. Then Nate smelled Randy, Everest, Ann, and Sarah's scents out here too.

Nate bit into the driver's side tire on the pickup, and Kayla attacked the rear tire behind it. They peered around the back of the truck to see if anyone was watching it, but everyone involved in the break-in must have gone inside the cabin.

Nate and Kayla raced around the truck to bite the other tires, and then Nate went after his own van tires. He hated to do that to his brand-new van's tires, but his keys were sitting with his phone in the living room, and the housebreakers could very well steal his van, especially once they learned they couldn't leave here in Randy's truck. Not without changing out all the tires. Nate began biting his van's tires, and then Kayla got the rest of them. He was glad she'd helped, and they'd finished the task more quickly.

Afterward, they tore off into the woods, but both of them glanced back at the cabin and saw a man peer out the window. "Hell, they climbed out the window," Everest said.

"Are you sure they're not just hiding?" Randy sounded irritated with his friend.

"I checked already. They're not anywhere in the bedroom, and the window's open wide enough for them to climb out of it. Come on, let's get them. We have to stop them before they alert anyone," Everest said.

Nate had considered closing the window, but opening it made so much noise and the housebreakers had already gained access to the house, so he hadn't wanted to alert them to what he and Kayla had been doing at the time.

"You said we'd have them right where we wanted them," Randy said.

What in the hell were Phil's friends doing here? The news. It was on the news that Nate and Kayla were staying at the cabin. But why would Everest and his cohorts be after them? Unless Phil's friends had something to do with Durham Manning's murder or Phil's disappearance and they believed Nate and Kayla knew something about it.

For now, Nate just needed to get Kayla safely to the closest home he could reach, which was Darien and Lelandi's place. Then they'd have Peter and a ton of wolves arrest the housebreakers.

Kayla seemed to have the same notion in mind and kept running with him in the direction of the pack leaders' house, which was located out of town in the country.

After a while, she slowed down her run, and Nate did too. The men looking for them would never find them, and Nate and Kayla needed to conserve their energy. But he sure wanted to take the men down himself for coming after him and Kayla and forcing him to ruin his tires.

He brushed against Kayla, letting her know he wanted to detour to the river. She nuzzled him and turned in that direction. They needed to drink. He was feeling parched, and Kayla had to be too. They finally reached the river and drank their fill.

For a moment, they just stood there together, sharing the space, and he loved her so much. But he felt awful that he'd dragged her into all this, just because he'd been working on this case and then they found the body and it was reported in the news.

She nipped his face and turned and headed back into the woods and loped toward the pack leaders' house again, but then she paused. She lifted her chin and howled.

She was right to call on their pack. He howled too. Their howls warned of trouble, and it wasn't long before they heard howls in return. Some of their pack members had heard them and would be there to help them. Good.

They kept running until they ran into Darien, Tom, and Jake racing toward them in their wolf coats, and Nate quickly shifted to tell them what was going on. "Men broke into our cabin and were coming after us, maybe because we were on the news for finding the dead body. I recognized a man by the name of Everest, who I had spoken to about another case—a missing man from Green Valley. Another man who was speaking was Randy, and the truck belongs to him. I smelled the scents of their girlfriends Sarah and Ann too."

Darien shifted. "Hell. All right. We'll go to my place, and we'll call up the forces to take them into custody. Let's go."

They shifted and headed off to the pack leaders' house, and once they were there, Lelandi got Kayla and Nate something to wear.

Once everyone was dressed, Tom and Jake began calling Peter and others to rally a group of deputies to arrest the people who had broken into the cabin.

"Just don't alert them beforehand that we're coming to arrest them," Darien said. "We don't want them getting away."

"We bit their tires and my van's tires so they will have to be on foot. We can probably track them down without any trouble if they run off through the woods, unless they call for someone to come pick them up," Nate said.

"Are you going with us then?" Darien asked.

"He and Kayla are supposed to be sharing mated bliss," Lelandi said.

Kayla smiled. "We will as soon as we can take back our cabin."

"You're going to still stay there?" Lelandi sounded surprised.

"Yeah. Once the bad guys are rounded up, we won't have any more trouble, and we're going to enjoy our stay at the cabin no matter what," Kayla said.

"I need to go to identify those who broke into the cabin if they're not wearing any ID or have a false ID. I know them by scent, while none of you would." Nate kissed Kayla, glad she was ready to persevere. He felt the same as her, but he would have made other arrangements if she hadn't wanted to return to the cabin so they could still have fun together for the rest of the week. "But you'll stay here for now, won't you?"

"Yeah. I'm not all army-trained like you. You can

come back for me when the place is clear, and we can return to the cabin."

"All right, honey." Nate hugged and kissed her again as they heard other vehicles gathering outside Darien and Lelandi's house.

"Be careful," Kayla said.

"Yeah, and you stay safe." Then Nate went with the others to drive to the cabin. He hoped they wouldn't be chasing down the bad guys all night. He wanted to be snuggling with his mate and spending the rest of the week just enjoying it with her. Though he couldn't believe he might be able to help the police solve the murder mystery—if that was what this was about—once they captured these men.

He rode with Darien, Jake, and Tom, as Sheriff Peter and several others led the pack. When they finally arrived at the cabin, Nate really expected to see Randy and the rest of his friends had returned there, but a search of the cabin revealed everyone was gone. He smelled Everest's scent but also Randy, Ann, and Sarah's scents. The whole gang, except for Gerald and the missing Phil. Nate was glad he had gone with Darien and the others so he could help catch them.

"They said they were going after us," Nate said to Darien and his brothers and Peter. Some of the other men had managed to unlock Randy's truck and were searching it. "I'm certain they wouldn't believe we could run through the dark woods and reach help, so they're still looking for us in the forest. They probably think we're hiding in the woods."

Darien nodded. "Most likely they're still close by the cabin. They probably don't know the woods like we do, and as humans in the dark, it will be hard for them to go very far without getting themselves lost. We should be able to find them easily enough."

"Unless they had someone pick them up and they've left." Nate didn't think they'd leave their truck behind though.

"I also called the auto body shop to get replacement tires for your van," Jake said.

"Ah, hell, thanks. It killed me to have to tear up my tires like that when they were brand new."

"Yeah, but it was good thinking on your part, or they might have just taken off with your new van," Darien said.

"That's exactly what I was thinking. I wanted them stranded here so we could easily pick them up."

Tom said, "The tow truck is coming to confiscate Randy's pickup. We'll have to impound it."

"If I hadn't been worried about getting Kayla to safety, I would have hung around to try to learn what they had to say," Nate said. "Though I needed reinforcements to apprehend all of them."

"I believe some of us need to turn into our wolves anyway. Easier for us to run and locate them now that we've gotten their scents," Darien said.

"We'll howl if we see any of them to pinpoint their locations for those who are in uniform or others searching in human form."

"I'll run as a wolf." Maybe Nate could sneak up on them as a wolf and hear some of them talking, revealing just what they had been up to.

"I will too," Tom and Jake said.

Peter raised his brows at Darien. The pack leader smiled. "You know me. I'm up for the hunt in my wolf coat—always."

Peter told the other searchers what they were going to do, and in the meantime, Darien, his brothers, and Nate stripped off their clothes and shifted.

Then the wolves raced out the door and the other men followed them and began to systematically search for scents in the woods, no need for flashlights as *lupus garous*. They all moved quietly, not noisily like the humans they were hunting would, especially traveling through unfamiliar woods at night. No one in the search party spoke a word.

They were also all listening for sounds—talking, stepping on underbrush, or snapping branches and twigs. And they were watching for any sign of movement—flashlights or cell phone lights or the lighting of a cigarette. They especially smelled for scents. From what Nate had smelled of them already, the housebreakers were sweaty, aggravated, and frustrated that their prey had given them the slip.

Nate and the other wolves didn't plan to show

themselves to the people when they found them. They didn't want to get shot, and Nate was certain the men would carry guns. When they found the people had split up, Nate split off from the other wolves. After walking about a quarter of a mile, he heard someone say, "Shit!" A snap and a thud followed, sounding like someone had tripped over something and fallen—the hazard of traveling in the dark woods at night.

He saw a faint light off in the distance and headed for it, still hidden in the darkness himself, safe unless he ran into someone else closer to him who he had missed. Then he saw Randy and Ann together, both holding cell phone lights up to search the darkness.

"This is so stupid. They could be hiding anywhere, and we wouldn't find them. None of us have high-beam flashlights that could really penetrate the darkness," Ann said.

"Shut up, Ann," Randy said.

"You know we're bound to get lost, and then what? We've been walking around forever, and we're not going to find anyone—"

"You're in on this as much as everyone else. If they get away and call the law on us, we're all going to get caught."

She shut up then, but at least now Nate knew Ann was as much involved in whatever had gone down. He just wished they'd say what. The murder of Durham

Manning? Most likely because they had seen the news report where he and Kayla found the body. Why would they care about the murdered victim and who found him otherwise? Committing the heists? Maybe. If Manning was responsible for the thefts and that tied them into why he had to die. Making Phil disappear? Probably. Since they were the last ones to see him and there were such mixed messages among the friends. Gerald's inference that he might be implicated in a crime still stuck in Nate's thoughts. Ann denying seeing the fight in the bar. Everest's disinterest in speaking about Phil's disappearance and not being worried about his friend vanishing. But neither Ann nor Randy was discussing anything.

"Ow, damn it." Ann paused. Randy kept going. "Wait for me!"

"What's wrong now?" Randy sounded like he could kill her because he was so angry about Nate and Kayla getting away.

"My hair is tangled on a branch."

Randy came back and broke the branch off, and Ann cried out. "That hurt!"

"Keep moving or walk back to the cabin by yourself."

"What if they returned there?" she asked.

"We got their phones. They slashed my damn truck tires and their own, so they can't leave except by foot any more than we can until Gerald gets his ass out here with some replacement tires. If they're back at the cabin, just hide in the woods until we return. The PI and his girlfriend can't notify anyone they're in trouble. That's why we have to find them before they reach anyone to call for help."

"What if I don't find my way back by myself? Not that you will be able to either." Then Ann mumbled, "Nobody was supposed to get hurt."

"Shut up, Ann."

Chapter 20

NATE HOWLED TO LET THE REST OF THE TEAM know he'd found a couple of the people they were searching for, since Randy and Ann weren't revealing any secrets that they needed to know.

"Wolves," Ann squeaked. Then she ran away from where Nate had howled. But she wasn't headed in the direction of the cabin. She was running toward the river.

Randy tore after her. "Hey, wait up! Are you sure this is the way back to the cabin?"

"Who cares? If the wolf is in the other direction, we have to get away from it. If the cabin is that way, we can't go that way anyway!" she bit out, her breath short while running. "Ah!" She fell and lost her cell phone. "Damn it!"

Randy was there, and then he reached her and helped her up. "Come on, damn it!"

"Wait, I lost my cell phone."

Nate was following them, hunting them, keeping them in sight.

Randy and Ann were searching for her phone and finally saw it half-buried in leaves where she'd dropped it, the light partially hidden. Randy grabbed it from the ground and handed it to her. "Put it in your damn pocket or something. And don't drop it again."

She put it in her jeans pocket and didn't move. "I don't know which way to go now. I don't know which way the wolves are."

Nate was amused she called them wolves when he was the only one who had howled. Then he heard a couple of people moving in his direction. Bad guys or Nate's friends?

If they were his wolf friends, they could smell that he and Randy and Ann had gone this way. So he didn't need to howl. Unless the ones headed in his direction weren't any of his friends. He figured for good measure he'd howl. If any of them were Nate's friends, they'd let him know. He lifted his chin and howled.

That sent Randy and Ann into a panic. "Shit, he's almost on top of us. He's chasing us," Ann said as she began to run and stumble and cry.

"Keep calm. Wait! Stop! Let's climb a tree until it goes away," Randy said.

"Do you see any trees we can climb? Wait, oh, we're in a clearing. The river. Can wolves swim across the river?" Ann asked.

"Hell, *we* can't swim across the river! Not in the dark. Can you even swim?"

"Of course I can swim."

"I mean, can you swim across a river? It's not

the same as swimming in your rich daddy's heated swimming pool."

Nate didn't want them to drown in the river, damn it. Then he heard someone running behind him, and he saw that it was Peter and CJ.

"Hold up! I'm Sheriff Jorgenson. The two of you stop! You're both under arrest for breaking and entering a cabin near here." Peter had his gun out because he knew the two of them could be armed.

Though Nate didn't believe that Ann was armed, he was certain Randy would be. If Randy had found them, he wouldn't have been able to force Nate and Kayla to go with them if he didn't have a gun on him.

That's when Ann did the unthinkable. She raced into the water to escape but got caught up in the river's current. Nate couldn't believe it! He bolted out of the woods and ran into the water after her. He was quickly caught up in the current. He began paddling for her, desperately trying to reach her.

"Holy shit! Shoot the wolf! Shoot the wolf before it kills her," Randy shouted at Peter, though he didn't make any move to go after her to protect her himself.

Then Peter and CJ were cuffing him, and Peter read him his rights.

"I'll sue you for not protecting her from the wolf! I'll have you all up on charges!"

"Yeah, yeah, save it for the judge," Peter said.

Nate was busy trying to catch up to Ann, who was sputtering and coughing in the river. Her head went under, and he feared the worst, but then she came up for air again. He heard Tom howl to let his friends know where he was. Good. He had found another one of the housebreakers. And then some distance from there, he heard Darien and Jake howling. Hopefully, they would have the rest of them rounded up soon. Nate had to pull Ann from the water before she drowned herself.

Then he thankfully caught up to the woman, bit into her shirtsleeve, and pulled her into shore. She was screaming and trying to attack him. Luckily, the shirtsleeve hadn't torn off in his mouth while he pulled her to safety. Immediately, he backed off so she would know he wasn't going to hurt her and howled to let someone know she was here and needed to be picked up.

She sat on the beach shivering, and he stayed near the water, hoping to stop her if she decided to go swimming again. But the thing was she probably believed he was calling for other wolves to come and get her. He couldn't help it. He had to alert the others he had found her. It seemed to take forever before Peter and CJ discovered them, wrapped her in an emergency blanket, took her into custody, and walked her back to the cabin.

"Some of the guys took the man in who had been

with her," Peter said to Nate, though the woman would believe he was talking to CJ.

Nate had moved into the woods so she wouldn't see him.

"That was a wolf. Why didn't you shoot it?" Ann asked, irate.

"Did he save you?"

"He was dragging me to shore to eat me. He was howling for his pack mates to get here."

The howling part was true.

"He saved your scrawny ass," CJ said. "And for your information, he wasn't a wolf. He was a dog that looked like a wolf."

"He howled! Wolves howl."

"Some dogs do too," CJ said.

Then they heard the other wolves howling to say they'd caught everyone and to head back in. That was one nice thing about being wolves and part of a wolf pack; they could all call out to each other that way. It meant Nate's job was almost done and he could return to the cabin too.

He raced ahead out of Ann's sight and hurried to reach the cabin. He was ready to return for Kayla. So much for getting a good night's sleep with his mate!

Once he reached the cabin, he saw Everest and Sarah being loaded into one of the police cars. Nate slipped in through the wolf door without anyone seeing him. As soon as he shifted and began getting dressed in his own clothes, Jake barged in through the door, shifted, and started pulling on his clothes.

Darien and Tom came into the house afterward, turned into their human forms, and began dressing.

"We got everyone, I take it." Nate wanted to close this chapter of their vacation. "I got Randy and his girlfriend Ann."

"I called out that I'd found one of the men," Tom said.

"That was Everest," Nate said.

"Jake and I found the woman," Darien said. "Did you take a swim, Nate?"

"Uh, yeah. I scared Ann, and she jumped into the river to escape me, and then I had to rescue her."

Smiling, Darien shook his head. "She'll never want to return to these woods again. Not when wolves are all over the place out here."

"Yeah, I was just glad I didn't accidentally bite her when I grabbed her shirtsleeve with my teeth to pull her to shore."

"I'll say. We certainly don't need a lawbreaker to be one of us. Who knows what crimes she has already committed," Darien said.

"We have another issue. Their friend Gerald was supposed to be bringing replacement tires for Randy's truck," Nate said.

"We'll leave a couple of men here, though if this Gerald sees Randy's truck is gone, he might just hightail it out of here, believing Randy had made other arrangements," Peter said. "He wasn't involved in the break-in, so we won't have him up on charges for that. However, if we see him, we'll bring him in for questioning. The men we leave here can return as soon as we learn Gerald is in custody."

Then they left the cabin, and Nate was glad to see that his van tires had all been replaced. His pack was the greatest. Peter handed Nate his and Kayla's phones, and Nate was glad to have them back.

Randy's truck was gone too. Everyone but the two men who were going to sit tight if Gerald showed up got into their vehicles, then headed back to town. It wasn't Nate's place to question the people they'd arrested, though he sure would love to know if they had anything to do with Durham Manning's death and Phil's disappearance. He knew Peter would tell him when they knew something, but maybe not right away because Nate was supposed to be enjoying this time with Kayla.

When Nate arrived at Darien's house, he found Kayla and Lelandi talking to each other, and then they said good night for what was left of the evening.

"We'll let you know what we learn," Darien said. "We'll let Nicole know if we find out what happened to Phil through any of these people too."

"Okay, thanks," Nate said. He gathered Kayla in his arms, and she practically purred to be with him again. "Let's go home."

"To the cabin," she said, making sure they were on the same page.

"Yes. Absolutely." Then he drove her back there. He hoped she would be able to relax and not worry about the housebreakers and being chased in the woods.

On the way to the cabin, they got a call from Peter. "Hey, when you reach your cabin, you won't find anyone there. We caught up with Gerald and have him at the station for questioning. These people should never have come to Silver Town to cause trouble."

"Hit them hard with charges and break them to learn what's going on with all this business," Nate said.

"We're sure trying our damnedest. And just for your information, the men were both armed with 45-caliber pistols," Peter said. "Gerald had a 9mm on him. You were right to run as wolves and come to us to stop them."

"Yeah, that's what we figured."

"Okay, well, we'll leave the two of you to get on with your own business, but if you sense anything's not right, let us know right away."

"We sure will, Peter. Thanks." Nate ended the call and glanced at Kayla in his van. She looked like she was half-asleep, her head pressed against the window. He smiled at her. They were sleeping in late.

They finally reached the cabin, and he parked. "Do you want me to carry you into the cabin?"

She smiled, yawned, stretching her arms over her head. "Nope. But I'm sure ready to go back to sleep. We have a lot of fun stuff to do after we wake."

"That's for sure. Only fun stuff."

They got out of the van, and he locked it up, then took her to the front door, unlocked it, and they headed inside, then locked up.

This time she didn't race him to the bedroom. She was moving way too slowly.

He scooped her up in his arms, and she wrapped her arms around his neck as he carried her into the bedroom.

She kissed his chest. "Was I moving too slowly?"

He chuckled. "I wanted to get you into bed as quickly as I could."

"That sounds awfully good to me."

He set her down on the bed and began to undress her, except she kicked off her borrowed flip-flops first. He removed her shirt. No bra? He ran his hands over her breasts. She began pulling his shirt off. "Sleep first," she said, sounding so sleepy, like she could just fall back on the bed, close her eyes, and pass out.

He smiled and kissed her lips and pulled off her shorts. No undies.

"I didn't want to borrow a bra and panties, knowing this is where we'd be headed when we returned to the cabin. Taking off our clothes. Sliding naked under the covers. Snuggling together."

He yanked off his shorts and boxer briefs. "Yeah, for sure."

Then they were both under the covers cuddling each other—just like they'd been before they'd been so rudely awakened and fled for their lives. "I love you, Kayla."

"Hmm," she said. "Love you too."

The next thing he knew, it was midmorning, pouring rain, thunderstorms right overhead. He couldn't believe they had slept through some of it, but they'd been exhausted.

"Hmm," Kayla said when they woke, running her hand over Nate's bare stomach. "We slept in a bit. I never can sleep in no matter how late I go to bed. Unless I'm sick."

"I must be a good influence."

She laughed. "Are you ready for breakfast?"

"Yeah, I sure am. All that exercise we had gave me an appetite."

"Me too. Do ham, hash browns, and eggs sound good?"

"Yeah, they sure do. I'll prepare the potatoes if you want to make the eggs."

"I got the easy part of the deal." Then she pulled on her underwear and he did the same, and they left the bedroom to make breakfast.

He began peeling the potatoes. "I guess you slept all right."

"Yeah, I was bushed. I'm sure I dreamed about something, but no telling what."

"I was dreaming about chasing and playing with you as a wolf before we were so rudely awakened by the guys breaking into the cabin." He washed off the peeled potatoes and then started shredding them.

"Aww." She started the eggs and ham.

"Yeah, it was a really great dream. Like you, I was so tired that I have no idea if I dreamed the next time we went to sleep or not." He began putting the shredded potatoes in a pan and cooking them, adding some lemon and pepper seasoning.

"Well, hopefully we'll have a good night tonight and you can dream about us having fun again." She served up the eggs and ham.

"I want to do it for real, but only if the weather lets up. It's supposed to stop raining in a couple of hours." He dished out the hash browns.

She was enjoying the rain and staying here with Nate for a while after all the wild excitement yesterday, but she didn't want him to know how she felt—not when he wanted to enjoy running all over and doing things with her. He was an Army Ranger after all. He wouldn't want to sit around the cabin all day. Though if she couldn't control her shifting, he probably would prefer to stay with her here.

"We can play some card games or board games

until then. And go swimming after the rain stops?" she suggested.

"Yeah, that sounds good. We can take another hike too. Maybe like we planned before but then woke up so late. We can run tonight as wolves too."

"Yeah, sure." She had to remind herself she was going to have trouble with the shifting soon. The storm had arrived earlier than they had expected. But at least they weren't having any hail. With Nate's van sitting out, they sure didn't want hail to damage it.

Nate poured himself some coffee while Kayla made her tea, and then they sat down to eat. "You know if you just want to stay at the cabin for the day, we can do that."

She sighed. "Well, you know I could have problems with shifting tonight, so we might have to stay in then. It wouldn't do for me to shift during the day if we're out and about."

"Yeah, sure. Anything you want to do."

Chapter 21

BECAUSE OF THE RAIN, NATE AND KAYLA HAD never gone swimming or hiking or running as wolves. They ended up just playing board games the whole day, except for taking a break to make love to each other and taking a much-deserved nap.

After making love to Nate that night, Kayla had been sleeping soundly with him before she began getting the urge to shift. Now she was awake again and she'd been fighting the need to shift for a while. Before long, she figured she would be a wolf curled up next to him. Not wanting him to know it, she hoped she could avoid waking him. Who wanted to go to sleep with their loved one and then have a wolf wake them up in the middle of the night?

She thought she'd slip out of bed and sleep on the floor if she could do so without waking him. Though she knew Nate wouldn't be bothered by it. Gabrielle and Nicole didn't mind that Kayla's brothers had the same shifting issues. It was just something that bothered Kayla. Up until now, she'd avoided staying overnight with Nate during the full moon when she knew she'd have trouble with the urge to shift.

She'd loved how he hadn't made a big deal of her not staying with him then. Even though they hadn't discussed it, she was certain he knew just why she conveniently couldn't sleep over at his place on full-moon days.

For now, she was glad she was naked. This way, she wouldn't disturb Nate with taking her clothes off. Even so, she tried to move away from him, but in a sleepy state, he wrapped his arms around her and pulled her closer.

She scoffed. She couldn't pull away from him, and she couldn't stop the shift. The full moon was definitely in play.

Then she felt the shift take over—her muscles stretching, heat filling her body like a comforting warm blanket, and then in the blink of an eye, she was one furry wolf. At least her back was to Nate so she wasn't digging all her paws into him.

"Hmm, my wolf lover," Nate said softly and hugged her.

She growled low.

He chuckled and just snuggled with her like he didn't mind that she'd shifted one bit. She relaxed. Okay, maybe he was fine being with her as a wolf in bed when she couldn't control her shifting.

"If you want me to shift, I will, but I love holding you like this," he said, as if he could read her mind.

She leaned her head down and licked his arm wrapped around her chest, telling him she was fine with this arrangement, since he was. It was nice, the closeness, his body tight against hers even if she was a bit furry. She was glad he was snuggling with her like this. She felt well loved, and she closed her eyes and fell asleep, dreaming of running as a wolf with her mate.

But when she woke in the middle of the night, she discovered he was a wolf too, his head resting on her neck in a possessively loving way. She loved him for doing everything to make her feel secure and perfectly comfortable with being who she was. She felt her body warming and muscles stretching. She was turning, and instantly she was in her human form.

Then she rested her arm over his chest, her face nuzzled below his chin, hugging him, human to wolf, and she enjoyed it just as much as when he had been in his human form and was hugging her when she was a wolf. Yeah, he was definitely the right one for her.

Late the next morning, Nate and Kayla were having waffles for breakfast, and she was thinking about the guy who had come for the keys at the lodge and then escaped the FBI agents.

As if her thoughts had triggered the call, Nicole called Nate.

"Hey, what's up?" Nate asked. "Putting on speaker."

"I just wanted to let you know that everyone's still watching for the guy who came for the keys at the lodge. The picture of him has been circulated to everyone in our area just in case he comes back."

"We thought he wouldn't return. Not when he's got the keys that he'd come for," Nate said.

"Two different wolves have said they saw him in your area. Since he broke out of custody and he seemed to be tied in with the dead armed bank robber, Darien said he didn't want anyone to try to apprehend him. Just to report any possible sightings."

"Okay, thanks, we just got up and haven't really checked our messages," Nate said.

"I figured that might be the situation. I didn't want to disturb the two of you, but I just wanted to warn you in case this guy heads out that way because you'd found Manning's body. The jewelry from the Green Valley store and the others hasn't been recovered yet. It doesn't mean any of the heisted jewelry is out there. But just in case, you should keep a look out while you're running around in the woods as wolves and on hikes and such. The insurance companies are offering high-dollar rewards for each of the robberies, and you'll get the reward for them if you find any of it. Also, Everest and his buddies all lawyered up, so Peter isn't getting anything out of them. And that guy Gerald had the tires for Randy's truck, but the police can't charge him with anything because he hadn't done anything criminal and he wouldn't admit to his friends doing anything wrong."

"Thanks, Nicole. That's great news—on the

reward—not that the other jewelry hasn't been recovered yet or that Everest and his friends have lawyered up, but I expected it. How are the other cases coming along?"

"I'm good. I haven't needed anyone's help. Still no success at finding Phil though."

"I'll help you with it when I get back."

"Thanks. Otherwise, have fun and enjoy yourselves."

"We will," Kayla said.

"We are," Nate said. "Call us if you hear anything further."

"I will."

Then they ended the call.

"I was just thinking about that guy with the keys. I wondered what could have happened to him."

"I figured he would be long gone by now," Nate said, then took another sip of his coffee.

"Unless he learned the safe deposit boxes didn't hold anything in them. Or at least not what he was looking for. And so he's in this area, trying to learn what he can."

"So then if the two witnesses weren't mistaken, he came back here to search for the jewelry? If that's so, he must have been involved in the robberies." Nate finished eating his waffles.

Kayla sighed. "Then we might be having company."

"Peter will have additional patrols out here just

in case the guy surfaces. The reports still might be a false alarm. The man was wearing a billed cap and mirrored sunglasses, and it was hard to make out his features on the video they had of him. But it's better to be safe than sorry."

"I agree."

"So what's our schedule for today?"

"We spent the whole day in yesterday. I shifted late last night, so I'm good for not shifting." She thought Nate was so sweet to always ask her what she wanted to do first. "Do you want to choose?"

"I've enjoyed everything that you've scheduled for us so far. You're great at planning. Nicole was always the one who was planning our trips and excursions when it was just the two of us going places."

"All right, well, if you ever want to choose something to do, just let me know."

"I will. So where are we going?"

She smiled. "Okay, let's make this our four-mile trip up to Hidden Lake. It's not supposed to rain until much later, so we'll be back before then. It'll be cold up there, snowy even, but I want to do it, don't you?"

"Absolutely. I was hoping you would want to. Since you were sleeping as a wolf for a good amount of time, you most likely won't have the urge to shift. But if you do, I'll carry your pack, and we'll head back."

"That's what I was thinking too. We could play

chicken-foot dominoes when we get back. Okay, let's get ready before the day gets away from us."

With hiking packs on their backs, they were soon on their way to the lake. She was excited about it. She'd never taken the time to go there, and she'd seen pictures of the aqua-blue water that reminded her of the Caribbean waters. In winter, Hidden Lake would be frozen, but even now in summer, the water would be cold.

"I'm so glad we're doing this together. I've always wanted to, but I have been so busy. And...well, truthfully, I really wanted to do this with you. That makes it really special," she said.

He took her hand and kissed her cheek. "I'm so glad you waited. I haven't been to Hidden Lake either. I can't wait to see it. With you. Even just making the hike up there will be beautiful."

On the hike, they walked past silver and gold mines and abandoned equipment that had been left there when the mines had closed. She looked over the valley. Alpine wildflowers filled it—pink mountain heather, subalpine heather, glacier lily, purple lupine. It looked like a fairyland. Off in the distance they could see the swinging bridge they wanted to go to that crossed a river.

It was a great hike—steep, and they'd get a wonderful workout.

"Do you want to go swimming when we get back?" she asked.

"Yeah. Sure, that would be great. By the time we return, we'll be hot and ready for a swim."

They took a break to get some water, and she took pictures of the valley filled with flowers. "This is just beautiful. I've seen some of the photos Jake has taken while up here, but it's even more vibrant, more real in person."

"I agree. Seeing it from this vantage point is beautiful. When we were walking on the trail through the valley, it was spectacular, but way up above like this, it's really amazing." He took a picture of both of them with the valley of flowers as a backdrop.

Then they continued on their way up the mountain. She was beginning to think if she was running as a wolf, she could manage this so much easier. She wasn't in as great of shape as she thought.

When she slowed down, he took her hand. "Are you getting tired?"

She laughed. "Yeah, you?"

"It's a long, steep hike."

"Well, that makes it all the more worthwhile." She wasn't quitting for anything. Even if it started raining. Well, maybe if it did, they'd be forced to return. At this height, there was no shelter if lightning started, and they'd stand out too much. But no storms were due in for the time being.

"It does. And being with you up here makes it doubly special," he said.

"I guess you don't want to carry me if I get too tired."

He chuckled. "You know I would do anything for you."

"I'd turn wolf first."

"That would work if you need to. I can carry your backpack."

But she didn't want to do that to him. She was making the climb all the way to the top. When they finally reached the lake, she sighed. "Now this was well worth the hike. We should have brought a tent and stayed overnight. It would be gorgeous to see the sunset on the lake tonight." She set her backpack on the rocks and then pulled out her jacket and put it on. "That is, if it didn't storm."

"Next time. We can hike a little later in the afternoon." He pulled out his jacket too and slipped it on.

"Yeah, that sounds great."

It would take too long for the sun to set otherwise. They could make their way back to the cabin without any trouble with their wolf sight at night. But they couldn't swim in the ice-cold water, and there wasn't anything else to do up here except enjoy the vista. Which was truly amazing.

They took pictures of themselves at the lake and of the vista. Then they ate tuna fish in easy-to-carry packages and apples before they began the hike back down. They saw a couple of red-tailed hawks soaring way up above, and Kayla shivered. "It's chilly up here after that long, hot hike."

"Yeah, but as soon as we head down, we'll be stripping off our jackets."

Then they saw six hikers headed up the mountain on the path they had taken.

"Looks like we're going to have company," she said.

"It'll take them awhile. We can take the other path down. It meanders a bit more, but then we'll have more privacy."

"Yeah, sure. I'm all for it."

They lifted their backpacks on their shoulders and headed across the ridge to the other trail. Then they started the descent. At least up here, they didn't have any trouble with bad guys. This was way too rigorous a hike for someone who might have hidden the other bags of jewelry from his cohorts, and no one would be foolhardy enough to look for any, way up here. So all Kayla and Nate would find were other hikers like them.

They had made it a good way down the mountain when, both of them getting too hot, they paused to peel off their jackets and stuffed them into their backpacks.

They finally made it to the base of the mountain, and she wanted to run for the cabin and get into her swimsuit. "Let's run," she said, getting a burst of energy.

"Yeah, do you want me to take your backpack?"

"Don't tempt me."

He reached for her arm and pulled her to a stop. "I'm an Army Ranger, remember? We carried way more than this on a run. I've got yours." He relieved her of her pack and then carried hers too.

Then they were running again. "You should have mentioned it before we made that climb," she teased.

He laughed. "I should have just carried everything in my pack. But if we had gotten separated at any point—"

"No way that is going to happen. We are sticking together through thick and thin." But she was running much faster now without her backpack. She finally reached the cabin door and unlocked it, then went inside.

Nate was right behind her, and he dropped their packs on the floor and locked up. She had already dashed for the bedroom. "Not shifting, are you?" he asked.

"Nope. Getting into my swimsuit and we're going swimming. Then we can return to the cabin, shower, make love, have dinner, play dominoes, and watch the sunset."

"You see why I let you make all the plans? They're perfect," he said, joining her in the bedroom. He hurried to yank his shirt over his head.

She already had hers off and was removing her

hiking boots. "So about dinner tonight. Do steaks sound good? Baked potatoes? Spinach?"

"Yeah, that sounds great. I'll grill the steaks and make my special herb butter." He removed his hiking boots and socks.

"Hmm, now you're talking." She slipped off her socks, but he unhooked her bra and kissed her shoulders.

"You are so delicious," he said, licking her skin. "Delectable." He slid his shorts off his hips and kicked them aside.

"You too." She licked his earlobe and nibbled on it, and then he was pulling off her panties.

She removed his boxer briefs, but then she pushed him onto the bed, deciding she wanted to ravish him first before they went swimming. He seemed just as eager to make love to her as he pulled her on top of him and wrapped his arms around her, pinning her on top of his body. He was already so hard, his arousal poking at her, and she loved it. Loved how masculine he was. How sexy.

No way could she put off making love to him before going swimming. That fun activity would have to come after this one.

Savoring every inch of his body pressed against hers, she kissed his mouth with fervor, and his own kisses grew hotter, pressuring, deep, enthusiastic. She loved him so much. She rubbed her hardened nipples against his chest, and they ached even more.

Long, drugging kisses made her head swirl, and she groaned against his mouth. He slipped her onto her back and moved her legs apart. His warm tongue slid over her rigid nipple, tantalizing her as he licked it. Then he closed his mouth around it and sucked. That nearly made her come unglued, enraptured by the feelings welling up inside of her.

He massaged her other breast with his free hand. She felt glorious. He moved his hand down her stomach in a sweet caress and then between her legs where she was wet and eager for his touch.

He slid his finger over her feminine bud, but then he passed it up; she wanted to moan loudly when he stopped, until he slipped his finger deep into her chasm and she groaned. She hadn't expected that of him, but she loved him for doing the unexpected.

She lifted her pelvis, increasing the deepness and the erotic feel of him stroking her inside. Oh, this was so incredible. But then he pulled his finger out and stroked her bud, making her soar. He was heating her blood so hot, her heart pumping wildly and so was his. They turned each other on with kisses and touching and loving. They had started a slow burn and stoked it into a raging inferno.

She could barely breathe, anticipating the climax, the end, the beginning. She so wanted him thrusting inside her again, but this—this was for her too, and she longed to feel that shattering moment all because of his intimately sensual touch.

He stroked her harder now, kissing her mouth with whispered caresses and then switching to fierce and passionate kisses, as if he couldn't hold himself back any longer. He tongued her, making her feel hot and loved and sexy, every bit as much as he was hot and loved and sexy to her.

Then she was coming, pleasure bursting through her, the climax deep and satisfying.

In one fluid motion, he pressed his erection into her, deeper, until he could go no farther. He held himself still, gave her a cocky smile that she loved, and then began to thrust.

———

Nate was glad Kayla wanted to make love before they went swimming because every time he saw her naked, this was just where he wanted to be with her, bringing each other to orgasm, loving every bit of each other in a carnal way. He'd waited so long for this, and he would never get enough of her.

She bit his lip gently, then licked his lips and thrust her tongue into his mouth, making him nearly come, he was so close to the precipice. Damn, she was hot.

She moved her hips in conjunction with his thrusts, making him penetrate her even deeper, and he moved her legs over his shoulders and dove in even more.

"Oh, yes!" she cried out.

He smiled, their hearts pounding like crazy, in sync, their blood pulsing like fire through their veins. He was glad they had waited until they'd been sure about each other, but he was even more glad they'd finally come to this—mated bliss.

Her sheath was still contracting and clamped down on him in an erotic way, then releasing. He loved it, loved her, and the way she made him feel like someone so special in her life, just like she was in his.

He was holding himself still, holding on to the moment, and then he began to pump into her again until he could hold back no longer and spilled his seed deep inside her. He continued to thrust until he was done. Then she slipped her legs off his shoulders. He settled between her legs, just hugging her close, just loving on her, kissing her.

"Better than a swim?" she asked, kissing him back.

"I was so glad you wanted to do this first."

"You might have been too worn out after the hike and then a swim."

He smiled at her and nipped her chin gently with his teeth. "I would never be too worn out for this, no matter what other activities we pursue."

"Okay, good. That's just what I wanted to hear."

For a long time, they just lay together like that, him not wanting to let her go, her hugging him and seeming to feel the same way. He didn't want to squish her for too long and finally kissed her cheek. "Are you ready for a swim?"

"Yeah, before we end up taking a nap instead. I want to enjoy the great out-of-doors while we can before I have to shift again."

"A swim it is then." He rolled off her and then pulled her up from the bed and into his arms to hug her again. "And then more of this."

She laughed. "Good. I'm glad we think so much alike."

They hurried to throw on their bathing suits and raced each other out the back door, running until they reached the water and dove in. This time they swam across part of it and then just played in the water after that.

"I'm so glad you scheduled this for now when we can swim in the lake. If we'd come out here much earlier in the year, it would have been too cold. Much later, and it would have been the same thing. Right now it's perfect," she said.

"That's exactly what I was thinking. I wanted us to be able to do as much as we could out here—the hiking, swimming, running as wolves, just watching the sunset—all of it." The water was warm and silky, but even better with Kayla in his arms as they treaded water and felt the warm breeze sweeping over them and the hot sun beating down on them.

They would have their steaks for dinner, drinks

while watching the sun set, play some dominoes, and then they were off for a run as wolves in the woods.

———

That night after having such a beautiful day, Nate and Kayla had gone to bed and were cuddling, not drifting off to sleep just yet when they both thought they heard something moving around the cabin. Though it could have been just the rain, thunder, and the blowing wind.

She kissed his chest. "Should we check it out?" She was torn between looking for whatever had made the noise and staying here and just enjoying snuggling with Nate in bed. She knew Everest had bonded out of jail and the others might have too, but they hadn't heard a vehicle pull up. She suspected they wouldn't come here again that soon after their last mistake in doing so.

"Only as wolves. Our wolf coats will protect us from the rain, and we can move lower to the ground. But only if you think you can stay in your wolf coat while we're checking things out."

She sighed. "I can. I think." She wanted to go with him, to watch his back like she knew he'd watch hers. She didn't want to be some helpless woman sitting in the cabin worrying about him.

"Okay, let's go check it out."

She loved him for knowing she could handle herself when she was a wolf and that he was only concerned that she might shift unexpectedly into her human form. But that wouldn't be for a while, she thought. She got out of bed, and he joined her, pulling her into his arms and kissing her. "It's going to be wet out there."

"Hmm, yeah, but you know if we don't check it out, neither of us is going to be able to sleep."

"Yeah, that's just what I was thinking." They shifted, and then as wolves, they headed out of the cabin through the wolf door and found just what had disturbed them.

A big, male cinnamon bear.

It was the same bear they'd smelled before on a hike.

They began chasing it off, growling and barking, and the bear loped off. They followed him for about three miles in the pouring rain before Nate bumped into her and indicated with his head that he wanted her to return with him to the cabin.

She was ready, hoping that they'd chased the bear off for good. She hoped she could make it back to the cabin all right without shifting. She hadn't planned to run for that long, but it felt good to run as a wolf and stretch her legs, especially when she was on a mission—protecting themselves and the cabin. But she hadn't meant to go quite that far.

They were loping toward the cabin, and she

suspected they still had another mile and a half to go when she felt the urge to shift. *No, no, no!* She didn't want to shift right now. Not with that far to go through the woods. Not with it being this cold out at night.

She hesitated, and Nate had to turn around. He stopped and looked at her, a question in his expression. He raised his brows and appeared to suddenly realize what the problem was. But she finally got the urge to shift under control. Sometimes now she could use mind over matter, and it worked.

She dashed off again, but this time he followed her so he would notice if she needed to shift; he didn't want to accidentally leave her behind. She appreciated his concern for what she was going through.

For a while, she was able to put off shifting, but then she felt the urge strongly again. Heat poured through her muscles, but she kept running, trying to reach the cabin or at least get as close to it as she could. Running through the woods naked was going to be cold and wet!

She let out her wolf breath. She still wouldn't have let Nate go by himself to check out what had been moving around outside the cabin. And she was glad they had found the bear and chased him off a long way from the cabin. Of course, ideally, she wouldn't be shifting out in the woods.

Then she stopped, figuring they were about a

mile from the cabin. She shifted and started to walk as fast as she could, but she had to watch where she was stepping so she didn't injure herself. At times like this, she really appreciated when she was in her wolf form. Before she could look around and see where her wolf mate was, he was human and naked, sweeping her up in his arms and carrying her.

"Ohmigosh, Nate. You don't have to carry me."

"Are you kidding? You have to keep me warm."

She laughed and wrapped her arms around his neck. "You were perfectly warm in your wolf coat."

"Yeah, but this is just too nice."

"Ha!" They were both dripping wet, but she had to admit it really was a much nicer way to go than her walking the rest of the way. "But hey, if you get tired and need me—"

"To carry me?" Nate asked.

She smiled and snuggled tighter against him. "I was going to say 'to walk.' You could get into your wolf coat, run home, and bring my clothes with you."

"I won't leave you alone in the woods, naked, without a lick of protection."

She sighed. "All right. But if you get tired, let me know. I don't want you to be all macho and—"

"Wear myself out?" He chuckled. "Not happening. I could walk a million miles carrying you in my arms. It's my pleasure."

"How far do we need to walk? I'm sorry. I was thinking about a mile now. We should never have chased that bear so far away while I was having shifting issues."

"We were having the time of our lives. I only indicated that I believed we should return to the cabin when I thought we had chased him far enough that he might stay away."

"And you figured I might need to shift."

"Yeah, but we were having fun, and that's important too. And truly? This is fun too. But I agree with you, honey. I think we have about a mile to go," he said.

The rain was still pouring down on them, the lightning flashing all around them, the thunder rumbling overhead.

"That's the same bear we smelled earlier," she said.

"Yeah, it sure was."

"Good. I'm glad we don't have a whole slew of them to worry about."

"Me too."

They finally reached the cabin, and he set her down on the porch, shifted, and ran through the wolf door. He quickly unlocked the back door for her. She came in, and he locked up. Then they hurried to take a hot shower. She figured they'd just warm up, clean up, and return to bed to sleep, but showering with him was never conducive to sleep, and after washing up, they began making love in bed instead. Now that was the perfect way to get back to sleep on a wild and exciting bear-chasing night.

Chapter 22

THE NEXT MORNING, KAYLA AND NATE GOT UP late again, loving these lazy mornings after such wild days and nights. They decided to take a walk through an area they hadn't checked out before and spied something unusual. When they partially unearthed it, they realized it was an illegal old moonshine still with rusting copper barrels and tubing near a stream.

They laughed about that and continued on their way. About a mile from the cabin, Kayla saw an unusual purple plant and was going to take a picture of it but then realized it was the peeling from some unusual fruit instead. Purple with long spikes. She didn't know what it was. Neither did Nate.

He got on his phone and Googled it and found it was a kiwano, horned melon. He laughed. "I thought it was something alien growing out here."

"Me too."

They continued to hike until they reached a boulder the size of a house split in two, the path going between the two halves. "This is really cool." She took pictures of them standing in between the two boulders. "Glacial age, betcha."

"Yeah, for sure."

They finally returned to the cabin and went swimming first. They showered and made grilled ham-and-cheese sandwiches for lunch, made love to each other, and then napped. When they woke, it was another trip to the lake for swimming. For dinner, Nate was grilling chicken wings, and she made mashed potatoes, gravy, and green beans.

This had been another perfectly fulfilling day.

"You know, I might have planned our activities for the most part while here, but you did an outstanding job on planning meals," she said.

"Thanks, I just thought of what we both liked and what would be easy for me to grill."

"Well, everything has been delicious." They really did complement each other. "Hey, did you want to just take a walk tonight? Not as wolves? Hopefully the weather will hold out." She ate another chicken wing. She felt she could eat a couple dozen at a sitting all by herself, they were so good.

"What about your shifting?"

"I should be good. So I figured we'll take a much shorter excursion than we did when we were chasing the bear."

"Okay, let's do it."

They cleaned up the dishes after they finished eating, and before it got dark, she and Nate went hiking on one of the trails near the river—a short hike this time because of her shifting issues and also because the weather was so iffy. Storms were coming in after a while, or they'd stay out longer, but they wanted to see the sunset at the lake too. When they returned home, they wouldn't have the view they had here.

They were headed in a different direction than they'd gone on any of the other hikes, hand in hand, nuzzling, periodically kissing—a nice, leisurely walk, not like on the earlier ones where they were trying to get somewhere to see something in particular. She was so glad they were having such a great time despite all the interruptions in their vacation earlier.

As much as she knew she shouldn't be thinking about anything but just her time here with Nate, the news they'd heard about the housebreakers kept bugging her. "It's so disappointing that those guys all lawyered up and won't say anything incriminating about themselves. Which means they have to be guilty about more than just breaking into the cabin—and of course coming after us, though they denied they had done anything more than taking a walk after breaking into our place."

"Yeah, like any of us believe that when they were in full search mode. Not to mention they were armed and pissed off that we bit the tires on their truck and they couldn't leave. At least when Everest's father insisted that we were charged with cutting the tires, Peter proved that a wild animal had bitten the tires and ours too."

"True. Though I can't imagine how breaking into our cabin, armed to the teeth, could be twisted around into us doing some criminal act against them."

"I know, right? That's what Everest's dad and his team of lawyers are all about."

"The guns they were carrying were all registered to their owners, so they couldn't be charged on that, but one of the guns might have been used in the killing of Manning. The police wouldn't know for sure because Peter and his men couldn't find any bullets or spent casings. We thought a weaker link would come clean about all that had gone on, but Everest's lawyers sure made certain they all kept their mouths shut." That had really frustrated Kayla. "Money could probably get them all off any charges—even murder, if they were responsible for it."

"I agree, as much as I hate to think they'd get away with it."

"You'd think if they're worth a lot of money, they wouldn't be involved in an armed robbery," Kayla said, then realizing right after she said it that it was silly. "Strike that. Rich people can be just as involved in criminal enterprises because they can never have enough money."

"Exactly."

She took a deep breath of the fragrance of pine and of the rain coming, centering herself in the woods, wiping these vile people from her thoughts.

But the incident still came back to haunt her. She started thinking back to the black pickup that had nearly run into them as they were coming home from the Great Gatsby restaurant. "The black pickup—the one that forced us off the road and might have been involved in the jewelry store robbery in Green Valley—"

"Yeah, Randy's truck wasn't the same one that forced us into the curb. His truck is blue. And Nicole and I checked to see what vehicles Phil's friends were driving, but none were the same one as that one."

"What if Randy painted his pickup?" she asked.

"It's still not the right model."

"Oh, okay. The armed robber's pickup maybe?"

Nate nodded. "Hmm. Yeah, maybe. If we could just find it. Who knows though? It might have been a stolen truck and not even the armed robber's."

"That's true." She glanced down at her hiking boots caked in mud. All the rain had turned everything muddy. She had splatters of mud on her legs too. They would have to really wash up when they arrived back at the cabin. "Are you worried Everest and his friends might return to the cabin?"

"Or send someone else. A couple of Peter's men are watching the road that runs past our place just in case though."

"I'm so glad we stayed here to enjoy ourselves."

"Absolutely. We could have gone somewhere else for the rest of our vacation, but—"

"We wouldn't have been free to hike like this in case I had to shift. And running as wolves might not have been as safe in places that weren't part of our pack territory." Though they'd had quite a few trespassers who had caused trouble during their stay. "Did Peter and his men look for the jewelry around the area where Manning died in the event he'd had it with him? Or the waterfall?"

"Yeah. They scoured the whole area. They figure he didn't have it on him when he swam across the river unless he did and lost it in the river. They searched the river too but couldn't find anything. Though the current could have swept the jewelry away. And nothing else was in the stream above the waterfall."

She sighed. "That means his cohorts could still come back to search for the jewelry."

"Correct. Which is why we have more patrols out watching for trespassers. I'm sure people, other than the ones who were involved in the jewelry heists, will also be looking for the jewelry, though it's stolen property so anyone caught with it could be in a legal bind if they try to pawn it. However, with the business of the insurance companies offering a reward for the return of the stolen jewelry, that can also be an incentive to come and search for it." They kept walking, and he leaned down and kissed her cheek. "Hey, how are you feeling?"

"Like it's going to rain." But she figured he sensed it too.

"No, I mean about the shifting issue."

"I'm good so far."

"Okay, so we keep going then?"

"Yeah, let's do it." She was having fun, and she didn't want to end this too quickly. "Another half mile?"

"Sure."

She loved how he was always so accommodating. They kept hiking, her boots squishing in the mud. She did think if it started raining, they'd be washed off a bit. If she did shift into her wolf, poor Nate would have to carry her muddy things back to the cabin. But when they reached what she thought would be another half-mile point, she turned. "It's time to head on back."

"Are you feeling hot?"

"Oh, yeah, baby."

He chuckled. "I mean, like you're going to shift."

"Nah. I just figured we'd hiked far enough, and when we return, we can watch the sun set off the lake, have some wine, and just enjoy the evening and what follows."

"That sounds great." He put his arm around her shoulders, and they walked like that for a while. "But showers first."

She laughed. "You think?"

The clouds began to roll in and cover the sun.

But the sunlight was still shining through the trees as the sun went down, and she figured they'd have a spectacular sunset if the clouds didn't overtake the sun all the way before they settled down to watch it.

That's when Kayla saw something shimmering in the mud near a boulder, and she headed off the trail to check it out. With all the rain they'd been having, it appeared something had been half-buried or lost or tossed there and the rain had unburied it. Could be a pop-top from an old soda can. Or some other piece of shiny metal trash. The wolves never left trash behind in the woods, but human trespassers would.

When she and Nate got close to it, she dug it out of the mud and wiped it off with her free hand. "Ohmigod, it's a diamond necklace. Or one of those fake silicon-carbide diamonds that look so much like the real thing. I suspect it's from one of the robbery heists."

"Yeah, I agree." Nate crouched down where she had pulled up the necklace and eyed the mud.

"Do you think there's anything else there?" Her heart already beating faster at the prospect they might have found some of the stolen jewelry, Kayla pocketed the necklace and started poking around at the mud.

"We were just talking about the jewelry heist, and you found what appears to be a high-dollar necklace. We should make sure there isn't anything else here in the event the jewelry was actually buried here, unlike the necklace that had been found in the stream above the falls." That's when Nate found something else shining in the mud. "Whoa, I think we might have hit the jackpot."

He handed it to her, and she rubbed off some mud. "Amethyst-and-diamond ring. Beautiful cocktail ring. Real gems or not, it's gorgeous." She frowned. "Did anyone notify Manning's parents about his death? They must have been devastated."

"Unfortunately, his dad and brother are in prison for their own cases of armed robbery, which might have been the reason Manning was also committing them. His mother had taken off with another man after Manning's father was convicted of armed robbery and sentenced to sixty years in prison."

"Oh, okay, so I guess no one really missed him. That's sad," she said.

"I agree. So Durham Manning could have buried the jewelry here, traveled upriver to get some distance between him and the jewelry, and then run into one of his cohorts, who tried to learn where he put it. If Manning was involved in the armed robberies, he wouldn't talk, and whoever was trying to get him to reveal the location shot him. Possibly Manning was trying to get away from him in the river. In any event, he ended up in the river, swam to the other side, and died," Nate said.

Thunder rumbled off in the distance.

"Okay, well, if there is more jewelry, we've got to find it, take it to the cabin, secure it in the safe, and call Peter," she said.

They were both digging through the mud as quickly as they could to see what else they could uncover. She felt plastic and realized it was a black garbage bag, partially shredded. Nate and she began slowly drawing the bag out of the slick mud so as not to tear it any further or lose any jewelry. She found some pairs of earrings. They were on display cards, or they could have been lost forever—pearl earrings, diamond earrings, ruby and sapphire ones.

"Rings, watches, necklaces, bracelets. Several pieces of the jewelry had fallen out of the bag." Kayla couldn't believe they'd uncovered jewelry from one of the jewelry store robberies. Unless it wasn't from that, but then why else would a sack of jewelry be buried out here?

"I can't think of another reason why it would be here. Manning's body was so far away from here that if the shooter had been looking for the jewelry in his direction, he would never have found it," Nate said. "Which is a good thing for us. We've got to make sure we get every last piece of jewelry. If we didn't have issues with your shifting and the storm coming, we could stay here until Peter arrived with his men, but we need to head back."

"Yeah. It's a good thing this is in our pack territory or someone might think we stole some of the jewelry from the find if any pieces are missing in the mud. As if wolves even wear jewelry."

"It's also good that we can move the jewelry from the crime scene without getting into trouble with the sheriff's department since we're all wolves and handle things differently in Silver Town," Nate said.

———————

Nate stopped digging in the mud, pulled out his phone, and called the sheriff while Kayla continued to find more of the jewelry that had slipped out of the flimsy plastic bag the robber had used. "Hey, Peter, it looks like we might have found a cache of stolen jewelry in the woods." He gave him their coordinates. "Don't let anyone other than our own people know about it for now. We don't want this to get on the news for the bad guys to learn of it and come after it while we're armed with only water bottles and first aid kits. Or someone else who just wants to get their hands on the jewelry who had nothing to do with a jewelry heist—even to get the reward money."

"Yeah, you know it. You're sure it's from one of the robberies?" Peter asked.

"As many pieces of expensive-looking jewelry as we found, I'd say so."

"We're on our way. We'll have to touch base with the police handling the jewelry store theft in

Green Valley and at the other locations to see who can identify the stolen jewelry if it's theirs, but only after we have the jewelry secured." Nate heard vehicle doors slam and vehicles roar off over the phone. "Then we'll let everyone know it has been found and secured so no one will be looking for it out there—or anyplace else."

"As long as we're not missing any pieces and more sacks of jewelry aren't hidden out here from some of the other heists. We'd stay here, but the storm is coming, and Kayla could shift at any time."

"Uh, okay. How did you find it, by the way?" Peter asked.

"The rains washed some of the leaves and earth away, and Kayla actually saw a diamond sparkling in the sun. The robber had put it all in a black trash bag, but he must have gotten one of the cheaper brands, and some of it was ripped away."

"Bear claw marks are all over the sack over here." Kayla showed him the claw marks.

"Scratch that. Kayla found evidence that a bear"—Nate took a deep breath and smelled the scent of the bear they'd encountered here before— "uh, the one we chased off earlier, must have been rooting around for something to eat and tore up the bag a bit."

"A bear? Did you tell Darien about it?" Peter sounded concerned for them.

"No, we chased him off."

Kayla stopped what she was doing and quickly joined Nate, whispering, "Someone's coming."

"Someone's coming," Nate said to Peter.

"None of us are there yet. Don't worry about the jewelry. Get yourself to safety."

Nate tucked his phone into his pocket, leaving it on so if they ended up in trouble, Peter would know about it. "Come on, Kayla," Nate said.

But she handed him the sack of jewelry. "Take it," she whispered. "I've got to shift."

"No." *Not now!*

"Yes, damn it. I can't help it." She sounded so frustrated he realized he'd made the mistake of thinking she was going to shift to protect them as a wolf.

She quickly stripped out of her clothes and shifted, and he bundled her clothes up around the torn sack of jewelry.

She ran off in the direction that she had heard the noise. He wanted to tell her to stay with him, but this could work out better. Whoever or whatever it was wouldn't see her as well while the sun was going down, but he swore it was descending lower in the sky more slowly than usual. They needed the cover of darkness *now* to give them the advantage! But in the light, they wouldn't be together, and he would be more of a target, which was just what he wanted.

He was running for the cabin, which would be

the only real protection he had until whoever was out there couldn't see him. Under normal circumstances, Kayla and Nate shouldn't have disturbed the crime scene, but if someone was looking for the jewelry, he might have found it and taken it away from there. Then all the evidence would be gone anyway.

Nate just hoped Kayla was okay and didn't get herself hurt. He had to hurry to secure the jewelry and come for her. Panting, he finally reached the cabin, sweating up a storm and worried about his mate. He unlocked the door, then locked it shut. After racing to the safe, he opened it, then slid the jewelry into it. He shut the safe door, locking it. Wanting to get back to Kayla pronto, he yanked off his clothes and shifted into his wolf and ran for the wolf door, then barged outside.

Kayla would probably stay in her wolf form for the duration, but he didn't want to risk it if she turned into her human form. He didn't want to take a chance leaving her out there if the man who had murdered Manning was searching for the jewelry.

He howled for her.

Way off in the distance, she howled back, and his heart skipped for joy to know she was still okay. But for how long?

Chapter 23

KAYLA HAD FOUND THE MAN WHO HAD BEEN coming for them, and he was someone her loving mate had been looking for—presumed dead but very much alive. Phil Peterson. She couldn't believe it. But he looked just like the picture Nate had shared with everyone in the pack in case they found him.

Phil was wearing camo gear, making him blend in better with the woods, but his blond hair and white skin were perfectly visible.

Had Phil's friends known he was alive? Had they been covering for him? Or had they thought he was dead all this time—that Manning had killed him and run off too? What if Phil had killed Manning and that's why he had gone "missing," but he really had gone into hiding? She wondered how Phil's parents would take the news!

She heard her wolf calling for her, and she howled back. She knew Nate had to have secured the jewelry in the safe and was returning to protect her. But she wasn't leaving just yet. She needed him to know she'd found Phil, and they needed to let Peter know it too. At least that mystery was solved.

She was glad Phil was alive, and he might actually help to unravel the business of the armed robberies.

The sun had already set, and Phil was using a high-beam flashlight, swinging the light in her direction. She moved away from that area so he wouldn't see and shoot her if he was afraid of her. She didn't want to spook him into running away. They needed to catch him and prove he was not missing at all.

She wondered if the sheriff and his men would be at the cabin soon. If they were there, they would have heard their howls. The rest of the wolf pack must have been off doing other business or someone would have come to learn what the trouble was this time.

Nate howled again. He was getting closer. She suspected he was howling to let any of their wolves who could hear him know they had trouble out here. Yet again.

But this time, they weren't running from the bad guys. Kayla and Nate were in charge.

"Hey, Phil, where the hell are you, man?" a man said from deeper in the woods, and she realized Phil wasn't the only one out here looking for the jewelry—as she had suspected.

Great. That changed the game plan. That could mean lots more guns, more flashlights, just more trouble for Nate and her. So much for the wolves being in charge this time.

She heard the other guy stumbling through the brush. And then someone else was following him.

"Crap, Everest," another man said. "I can't believe we're out here again in the dark. You know if we get caught trespassing out here again—"

"My dad will bail you out like the last time, Randy. We got to find the damn jewelry. We can't leave it out here for someone else to stumble across. Not now that they've announced a damn reward for it for whoever finds it on top of everything else."

"Like we can find it in the damn dark. Whose idea was it to come out here when the sun set again? I can't see shit. And that one wolf was nearby."

"So? You got a gun. If it attacks, shoot it."

"That's if I can see him. I mean, hell, we can't locate the jewelry in the dark, and we can't even find Phil now. What if Phil knows where the jewelry is and he's heading right for the spot? Then he's going to take off with it and leave us with nothing?" Randy asked.

"If he'd known that before, he would have already come out here and taken off with it and not told us where to meet him out here to search for the jewelry. He said he got into the safe deposit boxes Manning had and the jewelry wasn't in them. Use your head," Everest said.

"Well, Phil was the idiot who lost his head and killed Manning before learning where he hid the jewelry." Randy scoffed. "I told you we shouldn't have used Manning."

"He was the only one of us who had committed armed robberies and gotten away with it before," Everest said. "We knew he could do it."

"Except for his time in the slammer," Randy said.

"Yeah, but we got away with it for several heists. Besides, we grew up with Manning, and we knew him and trusted him. Everything was going fine until he kept the jewelry during the last of the heists and hid the take from us," Everest said.

"That's because he and Phil had a beef over the cut. And, damn it, I still think those people at the cabin found the jewelry. They found Manning. Who would have ever thought it? So what if on their hikes they found the jewelry?" Randy asked. "Or they found it on him?"

"It wouldn't have been sitting on top of the ground in full view for them to see."

"Yeah, but do you think Manning had a shovel with him when he buried it?" Randy asked.

Everest stopped. "No. I'm sure the police would have found the shovel on him or somewhere near the river where he swam across."

"Right. So he would have just buried the jewelry under leaves and tree branches or maybe dug a little into the earth with his bare hands. But in the woods, it would be hard to do—you know, because of all the tree roots."

"A log then? He could have scooped some earth out and hid it under a log."

"Yeah, that's possible. But there could be hundreds of fallen trees in the woods. You know, even though Phil killed him out here and everyone's thinking Manning had the jewelry on him, what if he hadn't? What if he had buried it or hid it somewhere else?" Randy kicked at the ground with the toe of his boot, looking frustrated. "We should never have trusted him to keep the jewelry to pawn it and turn it into cash."

"He's done it before and knew what he was doing. And he had a guy who was converting the stuff for him, and he wouldn't tell us who it was. He just changed the rule when it came to everyone's cuts was all—because he was the one who was doing most of the workload and we were mostly along for the ride," Everest said.

Kayla had also wondered if Manning had buried it somewhere else. She wished she could have been recording all of their conversation. Then she heard someone approaching, and she smelled another man's scent. She frowned. Where did she know that scent from? She realized it was the man who had come for Manning's keys at the lodge. Phil hadn't been that man. So whoever the shaved-headed guy was, he had to have given the keys to Phil to go to the bank and use them on Manning's safe deposit boxes.

She moved farther away from his approach.

"Hey, wait up for me."

"Gerald, why do you always have to be so damned late to the party?" Everest asked. "Phil said next time he'd take care of you too."

He didn't look at all like the shaved-headed, bare-faced man in a baseball cap who had come to the hotel for the keys. Now he had a red fuzzy head and was growing out a beard and mustache.

They all used flashlights to peer around at the woods.

"Where's Phil?" Gerald asked. "I thought we were supposed to meet him. That he figured out where the jewelry was."

She recognized his voice now—low and deep, annoyed, just like the shaved-headed man's voice had been when he came for Manning's keys at the lodge. She hadn't heard Phil's voice yet. That would cinch that she'd heard him speaking in the woods with Manning when she and Roxie had been running as wolves.

"Phil is out here somewhere. But you know it's private property and yelling for him isn't a good idea," Everest said.

"Besides, there are wolves out here," Randy said. "They chased us before, and we heard them howling again."

"Wolves?" Gerald's voice was dark with worry.

"Yeah, so don't run or they'll chase you and eat you," Everest said. "Come on. I think I hear him this way."

She wondered where Phil had disappeared to too. He had been there, but then the arrival of the other men had taken her attention, and suddenly he was gone—like a ghost vanishing in thin air. If he had wanted to meet up with them, why was he hiding from them now?

Then Nate howled. He was getting closer to her location, but she didn't want to howl and alert the men she was really close by them. She was afraid they'd all turn and shoot a bunch of times at the woods, and she might get hit. Nate would be able to follow her scent and would know that she was close to the men or she would have howled back.

Maybe he was howling to let others of the wolf pack know they were out there again, giving their location. And probably to scare the men off so they would leave and she wouldn't be hurt. But she wanted them here so Peter could catch them out here again.

"Shit, we got to get out of here," Randy said.

"You go, but if Phil's got the jewelry, we're not sharing it with you," Everest said.

"You didn't have wolves chasing you the last time. So where the hell is Phil then?" Randy and the others moved off, and Kayla heard something heading in her direction.

When she saw Nate moving toward her in the underbrush, quiet as a mouse, she smiled. It was her loving wolf. He brushed up against her, licked her face, and nipped her ear. She suspected he wished she had gone to the cabin with him, but she wanted to make sure their people found these men and took them into custody.

But then she realized she had a problem. She was feeling the urge to shift. *No, no, no!*

She wanted to hurry back to the cabin now! She needed to make sure she didn't run into Phil or any of his friends when she shifted, though they might not be able to see her in the dark. Not unless they moved their flashlights in her direction.

She licked Nate's face and then began to lope for the cabin, listening to the sounds of anyone moving about in the woods. Nate was running with her, sticking close to her to protect her.

Phil was the unknown quantity, as far as where he was located right now. Though Randy and Everest's girlfriends might be out here too. But Kayla didn't figure they would be out here on their own. They would most likely have come with the guys.

The urge to shift hit Kayla again, and this time she couldn't stop it. She felt the heat filling her, and she wanted to hold off so badly, but she couldn't. The next thing she knew, she was a naked human, trying to get to the cabin as fast as she could.

"Don't you dare shift," she whispered in warning to Nate. If she ran into someone and she was naked, wandering through the brush, she wanted Nate to be a wolf and he could protect her.

He woofed at her. She loved how he was so agreeable when she wanted to do this her way.

She still wanted to tell Nate right away that Phil was in on all of this and the whole gang of his friends were armed robbers and that Phil had killed Manning. But for now, she just had to get back to the cabin without running into any of these men.

She was running as fast as she could without hurting herself and trying to watch out for the men when they grew quiet. She didn't like the silence. Except for the cicadas making their noisy tune, frogs riveting, and crickets singing that filled the night with song—those were welcome sounds. The ones the humans who were a danger to her were making? Those were eerily silent.

Nate ran ahead of her and to the sides, circling her, making sure no one was getting close to her. She so loved her wolf. She heard a twig snap, and she whipped around, saw a flashlight, and ducked down behind a fallen tree.

Nate quickly joined her and nuzzled against her, her hero, keeping her warm, telling her he would keep her safe. But the person moved toward her as if he knew she was there and he would soon see her. He was getting too close. She moved down lower. But Nate stood up, and she knew that when the flashlight hit his eyes, they would be fluorescent, a glow that could be scary to a human. But she also worried the man would most likely be armed.

She couldn't look. She was leaning down on her hands and knees, her head down, hiding behind the tree trunk. She didn't know if it was Phil or one of the other men. The wind was blowing in the wrong direction to share his scent with her.

Then Nate growled softly. *No, no, no!* She knew he was going to attack the man. She didn't want him getting shot. But Nate leapt over the tree, and she looked. She had to. She had to rescue her mate if the man shot Nate.

Nate ran so fast the man didn't have time to get a shot off. Nate lunged at him, knocking him down, and the shot went wild, hitting a tree nearby. Then Nate grabbed the gun in his teeth and raced to rejoin Kayla, but she was naked, for heaven's sake, and she knew he wanted her to run with him back to the cabin. But the guy would see her!

Then she looked more closely at the figure, and he wasn't moving. Either playing dead, just knocked out, or really dead?

She made her move to run to the cabin with her wolf, so proud of him. But the gunshot had made the others head in that direction, and she was afraid they'd run into them.

She had hoped everyone would take off the other way. That's normally what she would do, but of course as a wolf, gunfire wasn't something she took lightly. She wished she was a wolf with all her being so she could run faster, lower to the ground, unseen in the dark.

She couldn't let them find her. She just couldn't. She didn't want Nate to be put in the position of rescuing her against all the others. She didn't think he'd win. Together, if they were both wolves, the two of them could take care of the robbers, though they didn't want to kill anyone. But if they were given no choice...

The cabin was finally in sight, and she heard the men calling out, "Damn, it's Phil! Over here, Randy! He's been knocked out." Their voices traveled through the woods because they were talking so loudly, and her enhanced wolf hearing certainly helped her hear them.

"Where's his gun?" Everest asked.

"He doesn't have one, but the other guy sure did. Hell, if I had known someone else was out here shooting, I would have gone the other way," Gerald said.

"Hell, you always run the other way. I don't know why you're even part of this," Everest said.

"Because we've always been friends. Damn it. And I'm the best getaway driver there is. Besides, I'm the one who actually got Durham Manning to agree to go along with this after Phil tried to convince him because Manning liked my uncle and me. He didn't trust all of you. Now I can see why. Well, I mean—" Gerald stopped speaking, as if he realized he had said too much. That maybe Phil would want to get rid of him next. He changed the subject. "Whoever it was really knocked Phil out cold."

Good news on Phil being knocked out though. Maybe it would give the sheriff enough time to reach them before the men got out of there. Unfortunately, Phil and his friends weren't too far from the cabin— which meant they might end up there again.

Someone groaned, and she suspected Phil was coming to. Too bad. At least no one was coming after her and Nate, who was sticking close to her, keeping her safe in case anyone else tried to shoot at her.

"Hey, Phil, who shot at you?" Randy asked.

"What? Hell, I shot at a wolf. It attacked me. Oh, God, my head hurts." Then Phil didn't say anything for a moment. "Where's my gun?" He sounded panicked, like he could be all tough when he was carrying a gun, but without it? He was a coward. But the bad news was that he was probably alert enough to leave the area now.

"We didn't find any," Randy said. "Don't tell me it's the one you used on Manning."

"Look for it, damn it. It's got to be around here somewhere." Phil didn't deny he'd killed their friend with it.

Kayla realized then that when Peter had checked Everest's and the other friends' guns out, they hadn't been the ones used to kill Manning. She thought about the glass windows being shot out at the jewelry stores. Bullets and shell casings would have been left at the scenes. So the guns must not have been used at those crime scenes or ballistics would have proven they had been.

"I don't understand. Did the wolf bite you? Why did it run off?" Everest asked.

"No, damn it. I mean, yeah, it knocked me down and ran off. It didn't bite me."

"Good thing for you," Randy said. "Those wolves are big and scary-looking."

"Don't you think I know that? Its eyes glowed in the dark. Scared me shitless. Where's my gun?" Phil asked again.

"We looked, Phil. We thought you were carrying, but you didn't have a gun on you. Do you know where the goods are?" Everest asked.

"No. I thought we'd find them, but you got here too late to help me look for them."

"Yeah, like it's all our damn fault. You're the one who killed Manning. And, damn it, he hid the damn jewelry," Everest said.

"It was a case of self-defense. I told you that already. Manning was going to kill me, and I killed him first. So deal with it. Stop whining about it. We just need to get the jewelry and go. But we'll have to come back before sunrise. Somebody help me up, damn it. We gotta find my gun."

Kayla finally reached the cabin, but before she could crawl through the wolf door as a human, Nate ran though the wolf door, shifted, and unlocked the door for her. She ran into the cabin, rubbing her arms because she was so cold.

Nate quickly locked the door and pulled her into his arms. "I'm so sorry, honey."

"Oh, you have nothing to be sorry for. I shouldn't have stayed out so long, but I had to learn what I could about this, and now we know Phil killed Manning for sure. We've got to call Peter with all the news."

"Yeah. I'm right on it."

"Good. I'm taking a shower to wash off the mud and warm up."

"Be there in a couple of minutes." Then Nate called Peter, and once he finished the call, he joined Kayla in the bathroom to shower too. "You know they'll deny everything that was said tonight in the woods."

She was so muddy, brown water mixed with the soapsuds as they ran down the drain. "I know. But we both were witnesses to it. We'll have to testify. Come join me in the shower."

"Without real evidence, just our witness statements won't put them behind bars, I'm afraid."

"Unless Phil's gun was the same one used to kill Manning," she said.

Nate joined her in the shower, and she soaped him up too while he pulled her into a slippery hug and kissed her thoroughly. "I sure as hell hope it is. I'm ready to testify against them."

"Everest's dad will have a high-powered lawyer to defend Everest and maybe the others involved in this so that none of them turn on each other, don't you think?" She rubbed her soapy body against Nate's, so glad he hadn't been shot, so glad they'd made it safely back to the cabin.

"Right." He ran her hands over her slippery breasts. "We should be going to bed and making love."

"We're going to have to talk to Peter about all this tonight, won't we?"

"Yeah. But it shouldn't take long."

"God, I was so scared Phil might have shot you."

"I was so afraid he'd see you and kill you. He was too rattled when I ran at him to make his mark."

"Yeah, but you didn't know that he would be so shaken and not be able to aim and hit you."

Nate smiled at her and kissed her nose. "I had to take the risk. If he had moved much closer to the tree trunk where you were hiding, he would have seen you. I couldn't chance him targeting you."

Then they heard a knock at the cabin's front door.

"I figured the police would try to find Phil and his friends first, and we'd have a little longer at"— he smiled and kissed her—"this. I'll go get the door. Peter will need to gather up the jewelry and take it with him." Nate quickly rinsed off and left the shower, while Kayla continued rinsing the soap from her hair.

Chapter 24

NATE WANTED TO KILL PHIL AND ALL HIS FRIENDS who were involved in the robbery. They owed him a tire. Hell, they owed him his van tires too. And Phil sure as hell needed to pay for shooting at Kayla and him. He'd about had a heart attack when Phil had fired at him.

Nate threw on some clothes and hurried to the front door, wondering why Peter didn't just come in since he had a key to the place.

Looking through the security peephole, Nate made sure it was Peter and not Phil or any of his accomplices. When he saw it was the sheriff and Jake, Nate unlocked the door and let them in, glad it was just them.

"Hey," Peter said, shaking his head.

"Yeah, we're so sorry we had to come here like this," Jake said, locking the door behind him.

"Bothering you again. A dozen men are out searching for them. Have you got the jewelry?" Peter asked.

"Yes," Kayla said, dressed in shorts and a T-shirt, bringing the bag of jewelry out to him. "Take it with our deepest gratitude. We might have missed some.

A ring had fallen out of the bag, which helped us to find the rest of it."

"Kayla found it," Nate said, wrapping his arms around her shoulders. Then they took their seats in the living room.

Peter got a call and said, "Okay, thanks." He ended the call. "That was CJ calling; they were too late in coming and weren't able to catch them. They didn't find any vehicles in the area, so they assumed they'd gotten away," Peter said. "Nate wasn't able to say a whole lot to us about what had happened before we got here, except Phil had killed Manning and you'd found the jewelry. But I understand there's more to the story than that."

They both told him what they had heard while Peter recorded their testimony. Then he had them write up witness statements so that could be used to help build the case against the men.

"But it's only our word against theirs," Kayla said.

"Right, but we can try to lift prints off the jewelry and the bag," Peter said.

"The problem with that is that they were probably wearing gloves when they committed the robbery," Kayla said, getting everyone some water to drink.

"True. But you never know. We'll attempt to lift fingerprints, just in case one of them did finger the jewelry afterward, figuring they'd never get caught," Peter said. "Oh, and in other news—we searched

Phil's parents' property and discovered a black pickup truck, the same model and make as the one the two of you identified that had run you off the road in Green Valley. Manning's luggage, cell phone, wallet, and ID were all in the back seat. The tires were gone, windshield and sides of vehicle bashed up good, the license plates removed, probably trying to make it look like it had been there forever. All kinds of old rusted farm equipment was out there and an old truck and car rusting away. A strand of trees hid the area from the farmhouses and the road."

"So maybe Phil drove it there after he killed Manning," Kayla said.

"I'd say so. A forensics team is going over it now, looking for fingerprints," Peter said.

"What other evidence do we have against them?" Kayla asked, sounding disheartened that they hadn't found any of the men in the area. At least they could have gotten them for trespassing again and then taken them in for questioning. "Anything?"

Nate smiled and slapped his thigh, remembering the gun. "Phil's gun." He motioned to the floor where he'd dropped it when he'd rushed through the wolf door so he could open the back door for Kayla. "Phil fired a shot using that gun. From what they said in the woods, it was the same gun Phil used to kill Manning. It will have a little wolf saliva on it though."

Peter smiled. "Now *that* is just the evidence we need to put Phil away. The gun, of course. Not the wolf saliva." He retrieved the gun and put it in an evidence bag. "Any other surprises?"

Nate laughed. "No, sorry. I had forgotten about it. I was just trying to get Kayla safely in the house, and then we needed to call you and wash off all the mud we'd been in."

"No problem. As a sheriff, I love those kinds of surprises. Since Phil was shooting in the woods, we should be able to find a shell casing and a bullet."

Their sense of smell was so sensitive that they could smell for the scent of gunfire and they should be able to locate the casing and bullet.

"Yeah, we sure will. And we'll help you look for it in the morning," Kayla said. "I shouldn't have an issue with shifting, and I want to help."

"Sounds good to me," Nate said.

"The other thing was Phil said he was the one who solicited Manning to do the job with him and the rest of their friends. I'm sure Phil is the guy Roxie and I saw in the woods talking to Manning about a job while trespassing on our land. We were running as wolves at the time. One of them said they were doing it for Gerald's uncle, so if Gerald only came for Manning's keys at the lodge, his uncle is overall responsible. The man who came for the keys had a shaved head and face, but Gerald has red fuzzy hair now and he's growing a beard. I recognized his voice though from when he was at the lodge," Kayla said. "And I smelled his scent."

"He shaved off his beard and hair before he went to the lodge," Peter said, nodding. "And that can make someone look really different."

"Gerald's hair was long, tied back in a ponytail, and he had a mustache and beard when Nicole and I spoke with him at his apartment about Phil going missing," Nate said. "When I questioned him about what had happened to Phil, he was afraid he would be considered an accomplice. I thought it meant with respect to Phil's disappearance. But now it seems he meant regarding soliciting Manning to do the heist with them when Phil's attempt had failed."

"If Gerald is on social media, you can probably see pictures of him with the old hairstyle and beard," Kayla said.

Jake was already on his phone.

"They said they wondered if the jewelry had been hidden somewhere else," Kayla said.

"The police have found some of it that the robbers sold at a pawn shop in one of the towns north of Green Valley," Peter said. "That jewelry belonged to one of the shops at a town south of Green Valley. The police haven't uncovered any of the rest of it, and we'll need to identify which store these pieces are from. Then you'll get your reward." He smiled. "After all you've been through on your vacation, I'd say that you're past due for it."

"Yeah, you can always use it to take a vacation away from here," Jake said.

"We'll put it toward our new house," Kayla said, and Nate was proud of her for sounding so eager to get started on the project.

He knew it would be stressful. It would be for anyone taking on the venture, but he wanted to be there with her every step of the way, fully invested in the process of building a home for them.

Jake showed them some pictures on Instagram. "Before the haircut and beard was shaved off, shorter hair and only a mustache here, then no hair or facial hair."

Everyone looked at the pictures. "Yeah, that's Gerald," Kayla said.

"Okay, good. We can share these with the FBI agents. We'll leave you in peace then for the rest of the night," Peter said. "But we'll certainly learn who Gerald's uncle is."

"That's great," Nate said.

"I brought a gun for you to use for your own protection, should you need it. I should have brought one to you before this," Jake said. "We're posting some of our armed men in the vicinity too. The couple of men who were patrolling the area were in a whole different region up north near the falls and nearer to where Manning had died because they'd heard voices, but it turned out that it was just campers in the national forest and their voices had carried. The men wanted to apologize for not being nearby to help protect you."

"They can't have been everywhere at all times, and who knew but they might have caught the right guys in their area," Kayla said. "No need for them to apologize. As to the gun, that sounds like a winning idea. I know how to use one, but I'll let Nate handle it since he's an Army Ranger and one of your reserve deputy sheriffs."

"Yeah, thanks," Nate said. "That's a great idea."

Jake gave him the fully loaded 9mm and wished them a good night.

Then Jake and Peter drove off with the jewelry, and Kayla and Nate went to bed. But this time he had a gun on his bedside table just in case they had any more unwelcome visitors.

Of course, now that they were prepared and had around-the-clock protection, in addition to the reports that went out saying the jewelry had been located by a couple of hikers who had turned it in to the sheriff's department in Silver Town, Nate and Kayla didn't have any more trouble. Peter did tell them that the necklace found in the stream above the cliffs had belonged to a jewelry heist in one of the towns other than Green Valley.

With no more issues with trespassers because of all the patrols going on in the area and all the suspects in the armed robberies having done a disappearing act, Nate and Kayla had been enjoying their hikes, running as wolves, making love, and working on house plans. He'd also contacted Phil's parents to let them know he was alive and well, except for the bump on his head that Nate had given him, but he'd left that part out. It was soon in the news that Phil and his friends were wanted by the police and FBI.

Peter called up with news about Gerald's uncle too. "I was in Green Valley checking with the police detective in charge of the armed robbery case and told him what we learned. It turns out Gerald's uncle owns the jewelry store that was robbed."

"That was the uncle Manning had referred to when he said they'd been hired to do a job for someone's uncle. So Gerard's uncle hired his nephew and the others to rob his own store?" Kayla asked, surprised.

"Yeah. The uncle's jewelry store had been robbed two years ago, and that gave him the idea. He and his wife were divorcing, and she had cleaned him out, but he got the jewelry store. He wanted to get the insurance money for the jewelry, sell the shop, and start over somewhere else.

"I sat in on Gerard's uncle's interrogation earlier today. I told him that one of the men he had hired, all friends of his nephew, had murdered another of the men he had hired. Then he immediately began to spill his guts. I think he believed he wouldn't get any prison time because he'd flipped on the others and hadn't been involved in Manning's murder," Peter said.

"But it doesn't work that way," Nate said. "He hired the men to do the job, and in doing so, he's largely responsible."

"Exactly." Peter had located the spent shell casing and CJ had found the bullet Phil had fired at Nate that morning.

———

At the end of Kayla and Nate's vacation, it was time to return to the real world. Nate planned to do everything he could to ensure Kayla wasn't too stressed out about the construction of their new home.

For now, she wanted to stay with Nate at his apartment. He wondered about her affinity with Princess Buttercup and Rosco, but the first night home from work, he got his answer. She came home with Princess Buttercup in a carrier, and he brought in Buttercup's litter box, food, and bed from Kayla's car.

"Rosco needs the acreage to take walks on, so Roxie will keep him at the house. I see him at the lodge and take him for afternoon walks, so he's happy to be with me like that. Well, he goes crazy when I arrive at the lodge too, but he does that with all of us. The problem is that Buttercup might be upset and unable to sleep without Rosco tonight. In that case, I'll have to take her back to Roxie's house after work tomorrow. When we live in our own home, we can take both of them, if you don't mind, on a week-to-week basis. As long as Rosco and Buttercup are happy with the arrangement."

"Yeah, sure, whatever you'd like to do. You know I love them both."

"That's why I love you too."

That night, Buttercup cried and ended up in bed with them, inconsolable because she wanted to sleep with her canine pal. Thankfully, Nate was good-natured about the whole thing, even though Buttercup's favorite place to sleep was right in between them. Nate was just the right man for Kayla because all he did was laugh about it and never groused.

At breakfast time, Nate was smiling as he and Kayla made waffles and sausages together.

"Okay, so that didn't work out," Kayla admitted, chuckling.

"Do you want me to take all of Buttercup's things to your house?" Nate asked.

"Nah. You can help me load them up in the car, and then when I get there, I can manage them. Buttercup will be over the moon to see Rosco and vice versa."

The Fourth of July celebration was less than a week away, and every day was a new adventure for Kayla and Nate. Juggling work, getting in nightly wolf runs, checking on the progress on the house building, and making love every chance that they could get. They hadn't expected it, but the house construction had been checked on daily, not only by all their family but also by the Silver family and several others.

The pack members were fun. Being the promoter that Kayla was, she was already planning a big open-house celebration with family and friends for when their home was completed. Roxie kept telling Kayla that if she got too stressed out, she could take the new house and Kayla and Nate could have hers. But Kayla loved the plans for the new house, and she felt building it with Nate was a work of love. She couldn't wait to move the beautiful hope chest Nate had built for her into their new home.

Every day they headed over as wolves to the site of their new home to check out the progress of the house and run afterward. The groundbreaking, excavation, and footings were done. Next week, the foundation would be poured. They couldn't wait.

Kayla had thought that building a home, moving even, was going to be so stressful. But she was excited, thrilled to do this, and nothing was stopping her. Nate was so good about everything, making sure she was fine with everything they'd done so far. He was such a dream come true in a mate.

Tonight, they were going to have a big Fourth of July party for all the pack members in the three ballrooms before going to the pack fireworks on the pack leaders' property. Even Gabrielle's friends—the two jaguar sisters—had come to town from Daytona Beach, Florida, to celebrate with them. Both were JAG agents who took down corrupt jaguar shifters and now even wolf shifters. The wolves were going to run with the jaguars tonight after the fireworks.

This morning after making love, Kayla and Nate had taken a wolf run and now were back at his apartment, where she had fixed extra-special lemon berry napoleon pastries topped with strawberries and blueberries as a patriotic touch for breakfast. If Nate hadn't asked her to mate him at the cabin retreat already, this was how she had planned to ask him to mate her. She'd scheduled herself off for the day in anticipation of mating Nate, even though things had changed. But her siblings wouldn't think of having her at work today. Not after all she had done in planning the Fourth of July celebration party and when she'd had plans to spend this day with Nate.

"Hey, this is a real treat," Nate said, pulling her into his arms and kissing her, and she kissed him back soundly.

Then they sat down to eat at the dining room table.

"After our wolf run this morning, we needed this." Which was their morning routine. She felt bad that she wasn't running with Roxie in the mornings, but when they moved into their home, she and Nate would run with her since they would be so close by. "You know, I had planned to ask you to mate me today if you hadn't at the cabin. I mean, I didn't even know about the cabin trip when I had scheduled the day off and planned to do this with you."

"Aww, honey, I should have asked you a long time ago."

"I know. I should have asked you. I should have known you were planning to propose to me once you bought that van." She took a bite of her sweet breakfast treat.

"Yeah." He chuckled. "I couldn't get anything past my parents or my sister. They knew for sure I was getting it for us and for when we have our own kids."

She smiled and reached over and squeezed his hand. "I love being mated to you."

"I feel the same way about you. You're alright staying here, aren't you?"

"Yeah. When we live in our home, you'll have the daily commute. And the trip to the lodge isn't that far away. So for me, this isn't any big deal. It'll be so late after the fireworks tonight and then running with the wolves and jaguars on Gabrielle and Landon's acreage that I thought you and I could see the progress on the house and run as wolves or take a hike through the woods before we go to the party. We'll be nearer to the lodge that way."

"That works for me."

They spent the day playing video games with each other and watching movies, and then for lunch, Nate grilled ribs and corn on the cob while Kayla made a cherry cobbler for them. Then they sat down to eat. "This is delicious," she said, and took another bite of the meat on a rib.

"Yeah, I can't believe how wonderful it is being here with you like this, celebrating our first Fourth of July together, the first of many. Not only that, but after a busy day, I just enjoy being with you, sharing what I'm doing and hearing about the crazy and fun stuff you have to take care of at the lodge."

"I feel the same way as you."

Once they finished lunch and ate her cherry cobbler that he raved about, which she totally appreciated, they grabbed their clothes for the party and packed them in a bag, then drove to Roxie's house. Since a lot of Kayla's things were still there, they were using the house whenever they needed to until their permanent home was built.

There, they left their bag in her bedroom and then stripped off their clothes, trying not to get distracted, and knowing after the run with the wolves and jaguars they'd be back at it tonight—making love—they shifted. Unlike when she ran with her sister and raced her down the stairs, she knew Nate would be a gentleman and let her go first. Then they were out the wolf door and racing through their yard, then Blake and Nicole's yard, past the construction work on their home, and finally they were out in the woods.

They were running, playing, but then she was drawn to that place where Phil and Manning had been talking about doing a job together the day that Roxie and Kayla had been running in the woods as wolves. Nate followed her, but then he woofed at her, and she turned around to look at him, wondering what was wrong.

He pawed at the ground, and she ran back to him. That's when she saw a little black plastic sticking out of the dirt. Oh, wow, it couldn't be…and yet, she'd just wondered if maybe Manning had come here with some of the treasure and hidden it. Not all of it by where he had died, but some of it here too.

She began digging with her paws, thinking the two of them were going to be dirty after this and have to shower before they dressed for the party. But wouldn't the find of some more jewelry add to the excitement of the Fourth of July party?

If they got another reward, that would be so nice too, and they'd use it toward the house expenses. She was so excited, digging away next to her mate, like two wolves digging for a precious bone.

Then they looked around, and seeing no one,

they shifted and began to gently pull the black plastic sack out of the earth. It was rotting in parts, and they didn't have any clothes to wrap it in. Sure enough, diamond rings, necklaces, watches could be seen through the tears and holes. One of them would have to return to the house and bring back a canvas bag for all of it.

That's when they heard someone moving in the woods. Two people, she thought.

Kayla and Nate shifted into wolves. She had a really bad feeling about this. She hoped it was family or friends, anybody but who she worried it was.

Nate barked at her to go—to get help. She couldn't leave him alone. She lifted her chin and howled. She howled for her siblings, for any wolf within hearing distance that could come and aid them now. And Nate nuzzled her, appearing proud of her, and howled his heart out. They were in trouble. They needed help. They were protecting the jewelry and each other.

Howls rent the air from far away. Not close enough.

But then she heard Blake shouting, "We're coming!"

Oh, God, yes! He'd be armed with a gun, but she was afraid someone could start shooting back at him.

A wolf howled, closer to them.

Landon shouted, "On my way!"

Kayla howled again, but whoever was walking through the woods wasn't moving now.

"Yeah, they're in trouble again. I swear it follows them everywhere," Blake said on his phone, his breath short as he was running through the woods.

Hopefully, he was talking to Peter, and the sheriff was getting the troops together.

In the meantime, she and Nate were protecting the jewelry, even though she knew Nate wanted to check out who had been in the woods. Even if it hadn't been anyone with evil intentions, she and Nate had to get the jewelry into the sheriff's hands.

They twisted their ears this way and that, hearing movement all through the woods, and they were watching, looking for whoever was making the noise. Then she saw Roxie running toward them as a wolf. No! Kayla didn't want her out here!

Finally, Blake and Landon raced to reach them. "We'll take it from here," Landon told Nate and Kayla.

That's when four men came through the woods, guns raised, pointing at them. Everest, Gerald, Randy, and Phil. "You can hand that over now," Everest said. "Thanks for finding that for us."

"You really don't want to do this," Landon said.

"Yeah, we do," Everest said.

"No one's going to let you get away with it. Not this time," Peter said, coming from behind Everest and his friends. "Drop the guns, now!"

Kayla was barely breathing, worried the men would whip around and shoot Peter and the other men with him.

"You're outgunned!" another man said, and Kayla realized Darien was here himself.

Their pack leader. She loved him.

"Drop them now!" Jake said.

Then she saw at least a dozen men surrounding the robbers. All the Silver brothers and cousins— Darien, Jake, Tom, Brett, CJ, and Eric. She realized they'd come for the Fourth of July party. Everyone was here—even all the deputized wolves and a half-dozen former military special forces soldiers who had retired from the armed forces and were now living here and part of the pack. They had this covered.

Everest finally dropped his gun, and the others dropped theirs. Peter and his deputies quickly handcuffed the men.

Everest shrugged. "My dad will get me off. He always does."

"How did you know the jewelry was here? Why didn't you come for it before this?" Peter asked.

"We're not saying anything," Everest said.

"That's all right. We'll learn the truth before long." Peter had them searched for weapons and drugs, and CJ smiled and waved a piece of paper at them.

"Looks like a map," CJ said. "A treasure map. Written by Manning? And a key ring with a skull on it that looks suspiciously like Manning's. Phil had both on him."

"We'll have handwriting experts determine the truth and verify those are Manning's keys," Peter said. "We'll take care of these men, and then we'll see you at the party."

"Thanks," Landon said.

"Yeah," Blake said. "Looks like our sister and brother-in-law are getting another reward."

Nate licked Kayla's face, and she nuzzled him, and then they did the same with Roxie. The three of them raced off, Roxie hurrying to stay up with Kayla. Sure enough, as soon as they reached the front door of their home, the two of them wriggled in at the same time. Some things would never change.

At the party, Peter toasted Kayla and Nate for being supersleuths and uncovering another bag of stolen jewelry. "Gerald's uncle and the rest of them are being questioned as we speak. Though from what I learned, Everest's dad has told him to turn on his friends so *he'll* get a lighter sentence. The two women were also questioned, and it turns out their role in this was to provide alibis for the men. They weren't involved in the robberies or murder, but just the cover-ups. Also, the insurance company will be paying the reward to you and Kayla for the stolen jewelry."

"Oh great. Perfect for paying on the new house." Kayla had been so eager to work on the house plans that Nate was glad she hadn't seemed at all worried about it.

"If I lose anything in the woods, I'm coming to the two of you to help me find it," Darien said. Lelandi, his mate, agreed.

"I guess the reward money will make up for them ruining my tires," Nate said.

"And them being charged for the crimes will make up for them chasing us through the woods," Kayla said.

"We'll keep you informed as to when the court date will be so that you can testify against them, but until then, it's time to celebrate." Peter raised his glass of punch in another toast.

The siblings and their mates joined Kayla and Nate and smiled at them. "Only the two of you could take a vacation and turn it into a wild adventure," Landon said. "And then come home from your vacation and continue the adventure."

The jaguar sisters joined them then. Both were blue-eyed, but Odette was the taller of the twin sisters and the older. "I was going to offer our JAG services to make sure these men were put behind bars, but the two of you did all right on your own," she said.

"Yeah. When our good friend Gabrielle mated Blake, we thought this was a perfectly safe place for her to be," Zelda said, her dark hair sun-lightened to lighter than her sister's.

Gabrielle smiled. "It is. Everyone has everyone else's back."

Dance music began to play, and several people started to dance.

"They're playing our tune," Kayla said, taking Nate to the dance floor and slow dancing nice and close to him.

"Oh, yeah?" He kissed her cheek. "I didn't know we had a tune."

"Yep. Any that is nice and slow like this? That's our dance. You see, I'd planned to ask you to mate me today, so the celebration was supposed to be part of the seduction."

He laughed. "So you were in charge of the playlist."

"You better believe it. Wolves love to cuddle with wolves, so no one will object to my choice of dance music."

He smiled and held her close. "Me, least of all."

After feasting and dancing, they all headed over to the pack leaders' home to set off an extravaganza of fireworks that would continue when Nate and Kayla returned home to their own special fireworks that said just how much the two wolves loved each other.

Tomorrow wouldn't be just another workday, not now that they had each other to share their dreams with. Every day would be an adventure, and good or bad, they were ready to tackle it together.

"What did Phil's parents say when you told them Phil was alive and well?" Kayla asked on the way home.

Nate shook his head. "They wished they hadn't hired me."

"Because you learned the truth about what Phil had been up to." Kayla smiled at Nate as they got out of the van at the apartment. "Tonight is the final stage of our Fourth of July seduction. At least for a little while. Tomorrow? It starts all over again."

"I was just going to say this is just the beginning." Nate swept her up in his arms and carried her into their apartment.

This wasn't exactly what she'd planned, but it had sure worked out well for her too. That was the thing about their relationship. They both added so much to it—planned or otherwise—to make it super special.

Epilogue

THREE MONTHS LATER, THE MEN INVOLVED IN the robberies and Manning's murder were all going to trial, and Kayla and Nate were ready to testify, hoping all of the men would be put behind bars for a very long time. At least Sarah and Ann took a deal to testify against the whole lot of them.

Kayla and Nate had their wedding and were staying at the same cabin for their honeymoon. They'd had a wild adventure last time, but they figured it would be quiet this time. And they'd made reservations for the cabin in between the new moon and the full moon so Kayla could shift at will. She loved that, though Nate was all for taking her someplace else for their honeymoon, far away so they could really be away from everything here. But she loved being here with the pack close by.

Here, they could still run as wolves when they wanted to. It was fall, perfect for warm fireplace fires and roasting hot dogs outside on the firepit. S'mores too. And cups of hot chocolate at night. The aspens leaves were bright yellow, fluttering about in the chilly breeze that night, bold orange to red maples, green pines, just beautiful. The temperature was sixty-six during the day, nearly freezing at night, but it was fine for running and swimming as wolves.

The fall was also great for snuggling during the day or the night! And it would be the last time that they could get away like this before their siblings' twin babies were born.

Their first order of business was making love; then they ran as wolves and decided to make their way up to the waterfalls to watch the sun set. But as soon as they reached the top of the cliffs, they saw three men wading in the stream, trying to reach the edge of the Greater Silver Waterfall.

Not déjà vu. She glanced at Nate. He let out his wolf breath in frustration, his warmed breath a frosty mist. They should just let these people deal with the consequences of their actions. But if they got into trouble, Kayla and Nate didn't want to have these men's deaths on their conscience.

They couldn't rescue them as wolves though. They'd probably scare them into trying to cross to the other side of the stream. That was even more dangerous. There was no way to get down from there.

But there wasn't any way Kayla and Nate could make it all the way back to the cabin in the time it would take them to run here, even as wolves, so they had no choice but to cross the stream and herd the men back to the safe shore. Kayla and Nate headed away from the stream so the men wouldn't see them, then along the stream so they could go further up and cross, then come around the men and force them back to shore.

They had to hurry though. The wolves could see at night. These men couldn't, and if Kayla and Nate panicked them, the foolhardy men might end up walking or running off the cliff.

When she thought they were far enough from the men to cross, she began to make her way across the slippery stones, her larger wolf feet spreading and the fur between her toes helping keep her from slipping. Nate had moved in beside her, closer to the waterfall, and she knew he meant to rescue her if she lost her footing and was carried downstream. But she was keeping her footing, and so was he. Much easier as wolves with their lower center of gravity.

They reached the other shore and started to hurry toward the cliff edge. The men were snapping selfies.

She and Nate headed into the water and started to move toward them. At first, the men were looking away from them, then one of the men saw them. "Holy hell, are those wolves?"

"Crap. Get moving. Now!" one of the men said.

"Not too fast or we could slip and fall and be carried over the waterfall."

Which was why they shouldn't have put

themselves in that position in the first place! Kayla wondered just how many people had risked their necks like this and survived who they'd never known about.

"And the wolves will chase us!" one of the men said.

But Kayla and Nate stayed still, standing in the water, waiting for the men to make their way across the stream the rest of the way safely. They finally reached the bank and glanced back to see the wolves just waiting.

"Keep moving," the one man said. "I told *you* others reported wolves out here, and you wanted to see them!"

"Hey, I didn't believe the others who said they had seen wolves out in the woods here. I figured they were dogs and the people were mistaken."

"Well, now we know they weren't." The men headed down the rocky cliff, and when they were out of sight, Kayla and Nate crossed the stream.

Once they reached the shore, Kayla and Nate peered down at the men, still making their way down the cliff. Then she and Nate sat next to each other and watched the sun set, just like they'd planned to as wolves. She licked his cheek, and he licked hers back. Then he nuzzled her face, and she sighed, loving it up here. Loving the cold weather, the hot wolf, the sun setting. And being mated to the wolf she loved.

Nate adored Kayla, enjoying this time with her, glad they had saved the men who had put themselves in peril and the end result had been good. He couldn't imagine trying to rescue the men if he'd had to shift and cross the stream naked in that icy-cold water. He was glad that Kayla had come up with the perfect plan when he'd only been still trying to figure out how to get the men to safety without spooking them.

He sighed. This is where he wanted to be. With her as wolves, enjoying the sunset as wolves liked they'd planned to do—albeit after a minor rescue mission.

He licked her face as the last rays of the sun disappeared behind the mountain, the men's voices fading as they laughed and talked about the wolves, but then they headed off in a different direction, away from the private pack territory, for which he was glad. He certainly didn't want to have to call Peter about any trespassers this time.

Then Kayla nuzzled Nate and rose to her feet. The sun was gone. Time to make their way down the cliff.

As soon as they reached the bottom of the cliff, they glanced back at the beauty of the waterfall, the moonlight shimmering on the surface of the water and the river below.

Nate was eager to race Kayla back to the cabin—not only to enjoy mated bliss but wedded bliss now too—until Kayla and he spied something shimmering in the water. Fool's gold was what he first thought, but when they ran to inspect it, they found a diamond ring.

She sniffed around the site, woofed, and he and she began to dig, much faster than as humans could with their bare hands, and discovered a black bag of jewelry. This one wasn't torn, but the bag hadn't been cinched closed, and the ring had fallen out.

Nate shifted, put the ring into the bag, tied it closed, shifted back into his wolf, and with the bag clamped in his jaws, they raced back to the cabin. He hoped they wouldn't run into anyone looking for the jewelry. Okay, so they had one more thing to do before he made love to his lovely wolf mate—call Peter and have him pick up the last bag of jewelry.

When they reached the cabin, they ran into the cabin through the wolf door, shifted, and set the bag of jewelry on the dining room table.

Nate had his phone out and was calling Peter.

Kayla spread out the jewelry on the table and smiled at Nate, then headed for the bathroom.

"Yeah, Peter, we found the last of the bags of missing jewelry from the store robberies. Have someone come and get them. We have other plans for tonight."

Peter laughed. "You know, you'll get another hefty reward for it."

"My reward is waiting for me to join her."

"Okay, well, you enjoy your time with her. We'll be there soon and let ourselves in and try not to disturb you."

"Sounds good to me." Thankfully, several people in the pack had keys to the cabins in case of emergencies. Then Nate joined Kayla in the shower, and after washing each other, they hurried into the bedroom. Then he was making love to her.

And after that, they were snuggling together, getting ready to fall asleep when they heard Peter and a couple of other men enter the cabin, talking softly, but at least Nate and Kayla knew it was just them and not someone else who had broken into the cabin.

"Hey, Peter, Tom, CJ," Nate said, meeting them in the dining room wearing his boxer briefs. He had thought of staying in bed with Kayla, but he'd like to see the men off himself and lock up.

They were looking over the jewelry.

"Quite the haul these guys made," CJ said, fingering the jewelry. "You two sure have all the luck."

"We owe it all to Kayla. She has an eagle eye."

"Remind me to take her with us on treasure hunts from now on. We'll take it from here," Peter said. "And get out of your hair."

"Thanks for coming as soon as you could."

"Yeah, we wanted to get it off your hands so you could enjoy your stay here in peace."

CJ and Tom said good night too.

Then Nate locked the door and returned to bed to join Kayla, pulling off his boxer briefs.

Kayla cuddled against him. "Another bounty, eh?"

"Yeah, but all I care about is getting back to this." He began kissing her, and she wrapped her arms around his neck and began really getting into the kiss too, her body rubbing against his in a sexual frenzy.

"That's just what I wanted to hear."

They hadn't needed to go anywhere to enjoy each other to the fullest. They were home right here with their pack, their territory, their family, happy to be a mated and wedded pair with a brand-new home situated next to Blake and Nicole's and wolf runs with Roxie and them whenever they felt the urge.

As to Rosco and Buttercup? They loved living at one house or the other on a weekly basis.

Now all that was needed was for Roxie to find that special wolf that made her heart sing.

Acknowledgments

Thanks so much to Darla Taylor and Donna Fournier for all their help with the story, always eager to read the next one, which is a joy to me. And to Deb Werksman, who I've worked with for over a decade on all these fun-loving shifter stories. Also I want to thank the cover artists who make such beautiful covers for each and every book.

About the Author

USA Today bestselling author Terry Spear has written over a hundred paranormal and medieval Highland romances. One of her bestselling titles, *Heart of the Wolf*, was named a *Publishers Weekly* Best Book of the Year. She is an award-winning author with two Paranormal Excellence Awards for Romantic Literature. A retired officer of the U.S. Army Reserves, Terry also creates award-winning teddy bears that have found homes all over the world, helps out with her grandchildren, and enjoys her two Havanese dogs. She lives in Spring, Texas.

Also by Terry Spear

LOVING THE WOLF

Love and danger from *New York Times* bestselling author Paige Tyler's SWAT: Special Wolf Alpha Team.

SWAT werewolf Trevor McCall is sure Jenna Malone is "The One" for him. The problem? Jenna is a fellow pack mate's sister and her brother doesn't want her dating Trevor. But Jenna is already falling for Trevor big time.

The stakes are raised when their plan to spend quality time together in Jenna's hometown of Los Angeles turns into a search for her sister who disappeared a decade ago—and for the terrifying supernatural creature who kidnapped her.

"Unputdownable... Whiplash pacing, breathless action, and scintillating romance."
—K.J. Howe, international bestselling author, for *Wolf Under Fire*

SEVEN RANGE SHIFTERS

Cowboys by day, wolf shifters by night
Kait Ballenger

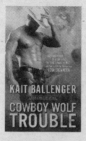

Cowboy Wolf Trouble

Bad-boy rancher Wes Calhoun, former leader of a renegade pack, has given up his violent ways and sworn loyalty to the Grey Wolves. But with the supernatural world on the verge of war, Wes's dark past is catching up with him, and human rancher Naomi Evans is caught in the middle.

Cowboy in Wolf's Clothing

Commander Colt Cavanaugh has spent his life defending his pack—until he meets Belle Beaumont, known enemy of the Grey Wolves. When rivalry turns into passion, Colt will fight to the death to protect the only woman who can heal his battle-worn heart.

Wicked Cowboy Wolf

Years ago, Grey Wolf Jared Black was cast from the pack for a crime he didn't commit. But when a vampire threat endangers their entire species, Jared must confront his former packmates again, even if that means betraying the only woman he's ever loved.

Fierce Cowboy Wolf

For Sierra Cavanaugh, becoming the first female elite warrior in Grey Wolf history comes with a condition: she must find a mate, and her rival Packmaster Maverick Grey, is the only wolf who's offering. The only thing more dangerous than the enemy at their backs is the war of seduction building between them.

Wild Cowboy Wolf

One intimate spark turns to wildfire between Grey Wolf warrior Dakota Nguyen and her best friend, security expert Blaze Carter. But as a hidden enemy threatens to destroy the pack, there could be deadly consequences to acting on their desires.

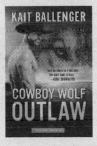

Cowboy Wolf Outlaw

With the pack facing their most challenging battle yet, Grey Wolf assassin Malcolm Grey's mission is simple: locate their enemies and destroy them. And when sassy, southern belle Trixie Beauregard makes a proposal he can't resist, Malcolm has all he needs to take them down.

WOLF IN THE SHADOWS

The legend continues in Maria Vale's wild and
strikingly original series: The Legend of All Wolves

Julia Martel was once a spoiled young shifter surrounded by powerful males who shielded her from reality. Now she is a prisoner of the Great North Pack, trusted by no one and relegated to the care of the pack's Omega, Arthur Graysson. But being the least wolf has its advantages; when the pack is threatened, Julia and Arthur form the strongest bond of all, ready to stand and to fight for the wolves they love the most.

"Prepare to be rendered speechless."
—*Kirkus Reviews*, Starred Review, for *Forever Wolf*

For more info about Sourcebooks's books and authors, visit:
sourcebooks.com